PLAYLIST

"Ocean Eyes" by Billie Eilish
"What A Time" by Julia Michaels, Niall Horan
"In The Kitchen" by Reneé App
"The Wisp Sings" by Winter Aid
"Killer + The Sound" by Phoebe Bridgers, Abby Gundersen, Noah Gundersen
"Only" by RY X
"Obstacle 1" by Interpol
"Bored" by Billie Eilish
"Butterflies" by Tom Odell, AURORA
"Ode to a Conversation Stuck in Your Throat" by Del Water Gap
"A Sight to Behold" by Devendra Barnhart
"Vampire" by Olivia Rodrigo
"Saturn" by Sleeping At Last
"Fine Line" by Harry Styles
"The Way I Do" by Bishop Briggs
"Where is my Mind?" by Pixies

MOONLIT TEMPTATION

ROSEWOOD
BOOK 1

PENELOPE BLACK

for erica
and for every book bestie who ate up those single dad/nanny romances and begged for more

PROLOGUE

EVANGELINE

"KISS ME."

The quiet plea floats in the limited space separating our mouths. I wait, my nerves dancing like the sparklers we wrote our names with in the night sky.

It seems impossible that it was mere hours ago. My head feels light with lust, my fingertips weightless as they flutter against my bare thigh, right below the hem of my flared skirt. Anticipation hums in my veins, buzzing like fizzy candy as I wait.

And wait.

And wait.

The moment stretches on until I feel like a rubber band stretched too tight. Hesitation hangs around his neck like a thick scarf, holding his body so, so still in front of me.

I hover in front of him, his knees bracketing me as I kneel between them. The breeze picks up the ends of my long hair, my big barrel curls long fallen in the hot night air. Grains of sand dig into my skin, but I barely feel it. My attention solely on the enigmatic man in front of me.

Waiting to see if he'll take the gift I'm offering him.

Or if he's going to brush me off under the guise of some misplaced honor.

I'm not an idiot. I know what I'm offering—and from the way his eyes darken as his gaze roams my face, I'd be willing to bet he knows too.

Nana Jo always told me that I would just *know* when I was ready.

And even though it sounds cliche as hell, I'm on the beach with a guy I met six hours ago, and *I just know.*

I swipe my tongue across my bottom lip, catching remnants of the fruity wine cooler and the s'mores he made for us over the bonfire. He grunts, his hands curling in the sand next to his hips, like he has to physically ground himself.

And then I understand. It's not hesitation. It's *restraint.*

There, the twitch in the corner of his mouth, the way his hazel eyes have darkened into endless pools of deep desire. "You sure, baby girl? I might develop a taste, and then you'd never be clear of me."

I nod, my gaze zeroing in on his mouth and ignoring his half-hearted warning. If it was that at all. Him developing a taste for *me* isn't the deterrent he thinks it is.

He swipes his tongue along his plush bottom lip, and I have to hold myself back from leaning forward and copying his movement.

He tilts his head, looking at me from underneath his impossibly long lashes. "Need your words."

I trail my fingertips up his arm, round his shoulder, and sink them into the hair at the back of his neck. I lean into him, making sure I fill his vision completely.

"If you don't kiss me right now," I murmur, my top lip brushing against his bottom one. "I just might die—"

His eyes flare with heat, and before I can finish my dramatic plea, his lips crash into mine. He pulls me flush against him, the sides of my skirt riding higher on my thighs between his legs.

And I can't find it in me to care. I kiss him back with equal fervor, gripping his hair between my fingers to keep our bodies close.

The sound of the waves gently lapping the shore, the scent of the bonfire smoke, the low hum of chatter from people down the beach, it all fades into the background as we lose ourselves in each other.

I had no way of knowing that my whispered words, drenched in lust and maybe even propelled by the looming end of summer vacation, would seal my fate years from now.

That one day I might just die *because* he kissed me.

1

EVANGELINE

"YOU'RE FIRED."

I blink, a prolonged sweep of my lashes until the image of my boss clears in front of me.

"I'm sorry, Evangeline. Truly, I am. But I didn't want you to have to rush back from your grandmother's funeral—"

"Reading of the will," I interrupt.

Her head tilts back a little, to the left. "Pardon?"

I clear my throat and look at the Executive Project Manager for Residential Interior Design, Tasha Powers. Mid-thirties with a killer wardrobe. Classic and preppy, like most of the firm. And my boss.

Ex-boss now, I guess.

"My grandmother passed away a year ago." She had already planned all the details for her celebration of life. She said funerals were dreadful affairs that bummed everyone out. So she requested an event with live music, sparkling champagne, and fancy hors d'oeuvres," I answer, almost absently.

"Okay," Tasha says slowly, her brows crinkling in confusion.

I clear my throat quickly. "But the reading of Nana Jo's will was set for exactly a year after her death. Which is this weekend."

It had been a point of contention in my family since last year. Nana Jo's passing wasn't sudden, and she never shied away from the conversation of what would happen *after*. No matter how many times I tried to change the subject.

In some ways, it was an absolute blessing to have more time with her. I wouldn't change those days and memories for anything. But in other ways, I feel like we've all been in limbo for years, existing on borrowed time. Nana Jo's time ran out last year.

And we're all still stuck in the quicksand of limbo.

Until tomorrow.

My mom had been fighting hard for a more traditional Catholic funeral, despite what my grandma wanted. Kept demanding Nana Jo's will be executed sooner. Thankfully, my aunt was upholding Nana Jo's wishes valiantly. My mother is an obstacle on the easiest days and a downright terror when she doesn't get her way. Everyone chalks it up to her profession.

She made her career getting what she wants. She's a political animal and has never backed down from a fight. Ever.

Tasha spreads her hands open from their clasped position in front of her and offers me a grimaced smile. "Right, well. I don't want to keep you from that. So please accept my apology for the timing, but the partners have decided to terminate your contract early."

I wet my lips, tasting the butterscotch gloss I coated over the top of Pillow Talk lipstick. Nana Jo gave it to me a month before she passed away. I've worn it so much since then, it's become my signature color. It's not the first lipstick she gave me, but it will always be the *last* one.

An unfamiliar emotion settles around my breastbone, sinking tiny tendrils of shame into my bones. I've never been fired before, not that I've had that many jobs in my life. But out of the generous handful, this is the first time I'm leaving on their terms.

My mouth is open, the question leaving my lips before I've thought it through.

"Is this about the Rothschild account? Because I informed Mrs. Rothschild that I'd be—"

Tasha holds up her hand, palm facing me to halt the word vomit I was about to unleash. She lowered her hand back to the desk between us, and her shoulders lost some of their tension. "No. It's not about that. The partners have decided that your unique eye doesn't quite . . . fit in with this *particular* firm. But we wish you the best of luck in all your endeavors."

She pauses the recycled phrases and overused speech and looks at me, pity tugging down the corners of her eyes making her expression soft. I hate that look.

It's the same one my teachers wore every time my parents bailed on an event in high school. It's the same one my grandma had when she found out my sister and mom went to Mexico during my birthday. Without me.

I straighten my shoulders and hold my head up high, just like I've done my whole life. I nod once, a swift dip of my chin and lean forward, sticking my hand out for a handshake.

"Thank you, Tasha. It's been a pleasure working with you these last six months."

She slips her hand in mine, and just like that, I'm out of a job.

I leave Tasha's office, stopping by my cubicle to gather my things. Someone conveniently placed a banker box on top of my desk, which I'm choosing to take as kindness at this point. The office is quiet, which isn't uncommon since we're often in and out meeting clients.

But I can feel their eyes on me through the back of my dress. It's the color of faded, fuzzy peaches with a gorgeous embroidered white floral pattern and chiffon puffy sleeves.

It's not the kind of dress you get fired in. It's the kind you're wearing when you meet your soulmate.

The dress that sparks the great love affair of your life.

I sigh and heft the box up, resting it against my hip. It's not terribly heavy, since I don't keep too many personal things at my desk. A pie of the day tear-off calendar, backup chargers for my phone and laptop, some mints in a fancy tin, and a few envelopes addressed to me. Most likely little notecards from clients.

If this is the grand total of the last half-year, then I guess I get it. Maybe I wasn't as invested in this job as I wanted to be. If I'm being honest, Tasha's not wrong. My expertise doesn't exactly jive with their aesthetic.

So maybe this is a good thing, I think.

I hear Nana Jo's voice in my ear, reminding me to always leave things better than you found them.

Internally, I nod my agreement with her. The Pine Valley Design firm taught me a lot of things about myself and my skill. But also about interior design and how to figure out what someone needs when they can't articulate it themselves.

And for that, I'm grateful.

With my head held high, I turn around and cross the office toward the elevator bank. I bid everyone farewell and offer pleasantries and generic well wishes. Some people offer to grab coffee or lunch, but they're empty plans. Ones I wouldn't cash in on anyway, so I just nod and smile with as much grace as I can muster.

The elevator door closes at the same time my phone rings. I juggle the box for a second as I dig my phone out of my pocket—the best part of this dress outside of the romantic sleeves, if you ask me—and see the name of someone who always brings a smile to my face.

I answer it on the third ring. "Hello, my favorite cousin."

"Hey," Coraline says. "Just calling to make sure you're on the road okay. You should've let Graham drop me off last night. Then you wouldn't have to drive home alone."

I smirk at the word home. "You mean the flat you share with three roommates?"

She tsks, the sound sharp in my ear. "I meant *Rosewood*, Eve."

She says Rosewood like *duh*, and I chuckle.

"And besides, it's not so bad. And my flat is definitely better than Beau and Graham's place and their endless parade of half-naked women. I love my brothers, but there are things a sister should never have to see. *Or hear*."

I can hear the heavy exhale down the line, followed by a sharp tsk. My cousin's words hang in the air like a lingering scent, and I couldn't help but gain some comfort from them. Even if they were laced with disgust. Her melodramatic commentary never fails to amuse me, and the corners of my lips turn up for the second time during the phone call.

"It's only a few hours, and you know I don't mind driving. I like to take the scenic route to Rosewood. It's . . . I don't know, peaceful. Having full control over the music, windows down and wind in my hair. Singing show tunes and Taylor Swift as loud as I want."

"God, you and those goddamn musicals," she says on a groan. "I love you, but I don't know if I can sit through three hours of the same ten *Hamilton* songs over and over again."

A loud chuckle bursts from my lips at her mock disapproval. "Oh, puh-lease. Don't act like you weren't belting out the chorus with me!"

She clicks her tongue, but it's all teasing. "I know, but it's more fun if I can give you shit about it. I'm just excited to have you here for the weekend." She chokes on a breath. "God, that sounds terrible, all things considered. But I miss you, and I'm glad you'll be here, with me . . ."

Her voice fades to the background when the elevator pings

and the doors open to the parking garage. A faint smile tugs up the corners of my mouth as I have a literal lightbulb moment of clarity.

I found a silver lining.

"Yeah, about that," I interrupt her spiral. "I think I'm going to need something a little more permanent in Rosewood."

"What? Why? Did they give you extended bereavement leave or something?"

I shake my head and spot my car down the row. "No, I got fired."

She inhales sharply. "Oh my god," she grits through clenched teeth. "I'm going to kill those pretentious—"

I sigh. "It's fine, really."

Her immediate indignation is balm to the bruise on my ego. My boss wasn't wrong. Pine Valley Design is coveted for their coastal influence. And while I'd like to think I can deliver any style a customer wants, coastal is definitely not my sweet spot.

"No, it's definitely not fine. Who the hell fires someone on their way to their grandma's will reading?" Her voice gets louder and louder as she goes, her pitch just shy of shrill by the end.

"Pine Valley Design," I deadpan.

There's a beat of quiet before both of us chuckle, a resigned sort of amusement.

"Bunch of assholes," she grumbles. I can picture her planting her palm on her hip and delivering the full weight of her narrow-eyed stare. That look bends a lot of people for my cousin. It's a bit of a signature move by this point.

"Ready for the silver lining?" I inject some enthusiasm into my voice. It's not too much of a hardship. I *am* excited about my new idea.

"You and your silver linings," she says with a huff. "One of these days, I want to hear you just wallow. Talk shit about something. Sit on the couch and binge-watch *The Vampire Diaries* and sulk about that shitty ending."

"Hey, I think they did the best they could after Elena left. I mean, should they have ended the show then? Probably. But then we wouldn't have really gotten the Caroline and Stephan experience."

"Ugh, it should've been Klaus and Caroline, and that's a hill I'll die on, Eve."

I laugh as I open my trunk and settle the box inside. This isn't the first time we've had this conversation, and I doubt it'll be the last. "You know I agree. Who doesn't want to be wooed by a man who will burn the world down to save you? It's the ultimate woo."

Her laughter is infectious as I close my trunk. The resounding thunk echoes a bit in the parking garage.

"You and your woo. You're the only person I know who uses that word like that. Like it's a necessary stop in a relationship."

My amusement slides off like raindrops on a duck's back. "Yeah, I guess I'm the only one left." It was one of the many things Nana Jo taught me.

"You know what we need?" she asks, her voice quiet.

"Uncle Harry's," we answer at the same time.

"I'll meet you there in a few hours."

"See you then, Eve. Drive safe. Love you," she sing-songs the last few words.

"See you soon, Cora. Love you."

I end the call and slide into my car, already running through the mental checklist of what else I need to pack. We got side-tracked by the Salvatores, and I didn't even get a chance to tell her my silver lining.

But it's fine. Because nothing pairs better with ice cream than good news. And I'm about to tell my cousin that I'm moving to Rosewood for the summer.

WELCOME TO ROSEWOOD

IT'S YOUR FAVORITE NEIGHBOR, ***and I'm back with the juiciest gossip in town. The only thing hotter than the summers here are the St. James men, and I'm not just talking about their motorcycles.***

The president of the reformed bad boys was spotted downtown getting ice cream with his adorable little boy last Tuesday afternoon. Does Silas St. James need a nanny? We happen to know plenty of willing tributes.

But that's not all, my dear readers. Bane and Nova St. James have been awfully quiet this last week. Did they sneak away on vacation without Silas? Is there trouble in the St. James family?

Summer's almost here, and you know what that means? The annual Reapers car wash, where things get steamy, and I'm not just talking about the weather.

Until next time,
—Rose

2

EVANGELINE

"WELCOME TO ROSEWOOD," I murmur.

The sun is just starting to set as I pass the familiar Welcome to Rosewood sign. It's the color of red bricks left in the sun too long, with white block lettering and scrolling gold accents. A few rose blooms adorn the corners, framing the whole sign for the town's namesake.

Nana Jo helped touch up the paint on that sign every summer. The sun shines so often here that these older style wooden signs need more attention than the newer ones. It's always been a point of pride for residents.

Nostalgia squeezes my heart as I cruise into the city limits of Rosewood. I rest my left elbow on the windowsill, dancing my fingertips in the wind to the quiet beat of my favorite indie radio station. Contrary to what Cora said, I *didn't* listen to Hamilton for three hours.

Just one, I think with a smirk.

The wind is warm as it snakes through the car, twirling my hair away from my neck before fluttering the pages of a book on my front seat.

I take a deep breath and trap the familiar scent of juniper and marigold in my lungs. The ache of familiarity sits heavy in my heart.

Being in Rosewood has always been like that for me—bittersweet. I've always loved my time here, but in the back of my mind, there was always a clock. A timer slowly counting down the minutes, hours, days until I had to leave.

But this time will be different.

I take the familiar curves of the roads, passing reminders of my youth. Passing Nana Jo's street, childhood friends' neighborhoods, the drive-in theater tucked off the road and closer to the woods.

The soft notes of a teenage love lost provide the soundtrack. Memories seem to pop on each corner and building, like fireworks frozen in time. The last time I was here, *really here*, I had taken Nana Jo thrifting a few towns over, followed by Uncle Harry's, of course.

Life's more fun with ice cream, she'd say.

Downtown Rosewood greets me the same way she always does: like a movie set for a quirky rom-com.

Lights twinkle from storefront window displays, couples stroll hand-in-hand down the sidewalks, little kids chase one another down the hill of the nearby park.

Everywhere you look, there are touches of whimsy. From the annual summer sidewalk art contest to the crisscrossed strings of fairy lights and Edison bulbs, Rosewood's charm is irresistible.

The brick buildings haven't aged in all the years I've been here, standing strong and silent against the backdrop of the rolling hills above them. Pink wild rose bushes stand tall in barrel planters outside each building, these bright explosions of color. The only other place I've ever seen this particular type of rose is in the pacific northwest. Nana Jo used to tell us stories about Rosewood, its origin and how the quirks became traditions. I never could tell if she took creative licensing with her version of history.

I pull into an open parking spot on the street and check my phone. Cora texted me when she left, so she should be here soon. Which gives me enough time to check out the weekly flavors.

Uncle Harry's has the best custard I've ever tasted. *Ever.*

And I've had the pleasure of tasting some of the freshest custard the dairy state has to offer a few years ago.

I roll up my windows and lock my car more out of habit than necessity. There isn't much crime here, but that's more from the Rosewood Reapers than the idyllic rom-com movie set.

A group of allegedly reformed bad boys who ride motorcycles, fix cars, keep the town safe, and throw some of the best parties in town.

They've also raised an alarming amount of money for various charities every single year, including Cora's personal favorite fundraiser: the annual Reapers car wash.

The way she hypes it up, it sounds like a literal fantasy. Another perk to spending the summer in Rosewood.

I marvel at the quiet hum of activity as I walk down the block to Uncle Harry's. You'd think I'd be used to it by now, the steady stream of people always out and about. But it's different here than back in the city where I live.

Where I *used* to live.

I packed up everything of importance and tossed it in my trunk. I'm not sure if I should be happy or depressed about my considerable lack of must-have material possessions.

There's a part of me that recognizes that Pine Valley never really felt like home to me, but it was the place I was *supposed* to be.

There, the hustle and bustle is no-nonsense. Quick steps, rigid shoulders, and straight faces. Unapproachable.

In Rosewood, it's all smiles, ten-minute hellos to your neighbors you saw yesterday, and people meandering around downtown with lattes and ice cream cones.

It's nice. Really nice. For the first time since I got the devastating phone call about Nana Jo, I feel like I can take a breath.

I stand in line behind a trio of teenage girls, who chat and toss around ideas on what to order. I glance at the menu board overhead and try not to eavesdrop, but their giggles and lively banter make it difficult to ignore.

The blonde girl in the middle scrolls intently through her phone while the line moves forward in stuttered increments. "Oh my god," she breathes out, her head bent over her phone. "Did you see what Rose wrote yesterday?"

The tall brunette on her right snorts and flips her hair over her shoulder. "Duh, Kelsey. Why do you think we're here?"

The blonde, Kelsey, jerks her head up. I catch the glare she sends her friend. "I know that, *Anna*," she says, an edge of annoyance in her voice. "I meant about the nanny thing. Do you think we should apply?"

The other brunette on Kelsey's left shakes her head immediately. "No way Silas pays a bunch of sixteen-year-olds to watch his kid when he's got all of those women around the club offering for free."

Anna makes a noise in the back of her throat as the line moves forward a little. "My mom says that's not all they offer for free."

Kelsey snorts. "Don't you guys remember what happened a couple years ago at that bonfire on the beach?"

"Oh my god, yes. Asher is so hot. I'd let him—"

Engines roar down the block, drowning out whatever she was going to say. I was strangely riveted to a conversation about people I don't even know. Nana Jo used to say that Rosewood could run on gossip if the nearby power plant ever went down.

The closer they got, the louder the engines grew, echoing off the pavement and building like thunderclaps. I twist to the left, searching for the source and expecting to see a fleet of motorcycles in a flying V like those hockey players from that kids movie.

My breath catches at the sight of four bikes cruising down the street, a sea of gleaming chrome and polished black.

The Rosewood Reapers.

3

EVANGELINE

IT'S like I conjured them with my thoughts about a car wash. They slow considerably as they get closer, and my heart skips a beat as the two motorcycles in the front swing my way.

Dark jeans, white tees, leather kuttes. They look like they were ripped off the pages of a romance novel.

Jesus, Cora wasn't kidding. All too easily, my mind conjures up images of the men in front of me shirtless, wet, and using those muscles stretching out the cotton in their tees for something entirely different.

The girls in line next to me let out a collective sigh and one of them whispers, "Oh my god."

Same, sis, same.

My gaze scans the men in front of me, greedily gobbling up every detail to relay to Cora when she gets here. I'm half-tempted to look for her, to make sure I'm not imagining this whole thing in some grief-induced fever-dream.

But then they pause in front of me, dropping their boot-clad feet to the pavement. And I can't pull my gaze away even if I wanted to. It's like they're unlocking some sort of kink I didn't know I had. Something about the coordinated move with the same look.

It's giving me *sharing is caring* vibes.

I sink my teeth into my bottom lip and try my best to not let my cheeks heat at the dirty thoughts now crowding my brain.

In a move so exact I'm convinced it's practiced, they slowly walk their bikes backward until they're backed into a parking spot across the street. Right in front of The Wild Boar.

"Holy shit, I think they're staring at us," one of the girls whisper-shouts.

"What if they come over here? I would absolutely die," Kelsey says.

I let my gaze ping-pong between the two men in the center, waiting to see what they'll do next.

I watch in fascination as the one on the left with tousled dark blond hair says something to the dark-haired guy next to him. They're too far away to hear the exchange, but the brunet shakes his head a few times. The blond guy just smiles at him as he swings his leg over his bike and starts crossing the street.

It's hard to tell behind the black sunglasses, but it feels like his gaze is on me. Or someone very close to me. A quick glance over my shoulder reveals a bored-looking guy in his early twenties, head bent low over his phone and thumbs flying across his screen.

"Oh my god, he's walking over here! I'm going to have a heart attack. You guys better delete my kindle history when I die, okay?" Anna mutters, straightening her dress next to me.

I remember being a bit boy-crazy at their age, so I find their dramatics sort of endearing. I breathe out a quiet chuckle, surprised to realize that I'm curious. It's been a long time since my true curiosity was piqued.

He looks like a man on a mission as he crosses the street without bothering to look both ways. He walks with an air of confidence that borders on cocky. I kind of hate that it works for me. I don't know what it says about me, but I've always been attracted to a man who knows what he wants.

And multiply that attraction by ten if he isn't afraid to go after it.

I try to ignore the heat pooling in my lower belly at the image of him striding toward me with the sun sinking into the horizon behind him. It's nearly impossible, the vision of him is tripping nearly all of my internal wires.

I blink, and it's another face walking toward me like some fucked-up déjà vu, determination etched in every footstep. Shock squeezes my heart for a single, agonizing beat. I've done everything I could to forget that face—forget that *man*—for the last eight years.

I curl my fingers into a fist, the sharp bite of my nails grounding me. I blink again, and his face is gone. His memory slinks back into the carefully locked box I keep buried inside my chest with his name on it.

He stops within a foot of me, staying in the street, on the other side of the wrought-iron fence. He flashes what Nana Jo called a *good ol' boy* grin. All charm and artfully curated bad boy vibes.

His aura would be a true red. The fiery color of the sky when the sun says its final farewell before it sinks into the horizon. A field of bright red poppies swaying in the breeze.

The girls next to me are talking in hushed whisper-shouts, but all my attention is on the man in front of me.

He slides his sunglasses off and hooks them in the vee of his T-shirt. His bright, mossy-colored gaze flicks all over my face, pausing on my lips before springing up to my eyes.

His lips quirk into a smirk as he looks at me, and I'm annoyed by how charmingly effective it is. He leans forward a little, like he's letting me in on a secret. "So, can I get your number?"

I blink a few times and stare at him. I hate that a tiny balloon of expectation started to inflate when he walked over. Because his seriously shitty pickup line popped it faster than my sister's famous stiletto style nails.

"Seriously? After all that show"—I twirl a circle in the air with my index finger—"I was expecting something more than *can I get your number.*" I drop my tone deep in a poor imitation of his voice.

One corner of his plush lips pulls up higher on the right. "Is that so?"

I drop my hand from the air and slip it into the pocket of my cutoff jean shorts. I'm thankful I changed clothes after work, unwilling to risk one of my favorite dresses getting ruined from hauling boxes and suitcases. "Yep. You kind of had this whole motorcycle bad boy thing going, and I gotta say, I'm disappointed. You had such potential." I twist my lips to the side to stop the smirk from spreading wide.

A surprised chuckle spills from his mouth, and I swear to god, his eyes freaking sparkle before he tips his head back in genuine laughter.

I'm blaming it on the angle of the sun.

"Damn, sweetheart," he says, running his hand down his short beard. Mirth lightens his face. "You don't pull any punches, yeah?"

I lift a shoulder in a half-hearted shrug.

"I can respect that." He curls his hands around the top of the fence and flashes me a boyish sort of grin. And goddamnit, it's just as charming as his smirk. He leans toward me, the muscles in his arms bunching and flexing. "So, I'm going to level with you . . ." he trails off, clearly fishing for my name.

But Nana Jo didn't raise me to give in to every pretty face I met. *Make them work for it, Eve.* I hear her voice in the back of my head as clearly as if she's standing next to me.

I shake my head a little ruefully. "You're going to have to work harder than that, playboy."

"Nova," he says instantly.

"Like Supernova?"

"Oi, your time's up, Casanova! The first round is on you," a guy from across the street yells.

I glance over *Casanova*'s shoulder to see the guy yelling drop his hands from around his mouth to flash me a goofy sort of grin. In our brief conversation, more people have pulled up outside The Wild Boar. Smoking, talking, and doing that man handshake sort of hug thing.

I bring my gaze back to the man in front of me. I arch a brow. "Casanova, hm?" I guess my playboy assessment was spot-on.

"Well, shit," he drawls, dragging his palm over the back of his neck. He looks at me from underneath his long, dark lashes. He looks both contrite and cocky—and I almost roll my eyes at how effortlessly he pulls it off. "This isn't looking good for me, is it?"

I give in and roll my eyes, a little scoff slipping free.

"Next," a deep voice yells from behind me.

Surprise dances along my shoulders when I realize that I was so wrapped up in our . . . whatever that was, I completely missed how the line moved on behind me. I didn't even notice the lack of the whisper-shouting from the girls.

"Shoot, I'm sorry," I tell the guy behind me. He just bobs his head, never pulling his focus from his phone.

I walk backward a few steps, toward the ordering window, keeping my gaze on *Casanova* in front of me. Is that his first name? Last? Or some nickname because he runs through girls like water.

Ugh.

I hate that the last possibility doesn't deter me as much as it should.

I bite the inside corner of my mouth, my brows furrowing together as I appraise him. Clever and good-looking.

Whatever. It's fine. Totally fine. Maybe some fun is exactly what I need. No-strings fun. I keep that thought tucked close to my chest as I smirk at him.

"Try harder next time, playboy."

He lifts his chin, a wide smile on his too-handsome face. "So, you're saying I got a chance."

Silence is my only reply, turning to face the window with a hair flip worthy of an Oscar.

"I like those odds, sweetheart," he says with a chuckle.

It takes everything inside of me to block out the way his gaze feels on my back as I order my butter pecan hot fudge sundae and Cora's strawberry landslide float.

4

NOVA

MY HEART BEATS FASTER with each step backward, my eyes glued to the dark-haired goddess. She stood with her back to me, hair sliding across her face every few seconds from the warm breeze. Her faux dismissal is clear. It's a shame it doesn't deter me like I bet she thought it would.

Nah, the fact that such a gorgeous face delivered sass with the charm and ease of an aging southern debutante only piques my interest more. She practically rang the dinner bell with her feigned disinterest.

There are only three things I'm good at in this life: being a fucking amazing uncle, drawing shit on motorcycles, and recognizing when a woman's interested.

And that temptress wearing the hell outta those jean shorts is *definitely* interested.

But she doesn't want to give it away too early. Or she caught on to the little bet that sent me over here in the first place. And luckily for the both of us, I can work with either of those scenarios.

I run my hand across my jaw, the stubble scraping against the calluses on my fingers. I remember when I naively thought that choosing art would keep me out of a garage like my old man. It's not that I didn't love working on bikes and cars, but I can admit that I was deep in the trenches of teenage angst for a while. And if my old man wanted me to do it, I'd run headfirst in the opposite way out of sheer spite.

I took my first painting class because I was pissed at my dad for something I can't even remember now. Went to the beach to fuck around and kill time, and ended up watching Mrs. Carter teach a bunch of old ladies how to paint landscapes. Impressionism has never been my favorite style, but I can appreciate it.

Thanks to Mrs. Carter.

I still remember when she told me a talent as good as mine *shouldn't be wasted on some punk determined to kill his future.*

A small chuckle slips free as fondness settles around my shoulders like a familiar blanket.

"Damn, Nova. She shut you down hard, man." Gunnar claps my shoulder with a laugh. "Guess you're buying, huh?"

I lift my shoulder to dislodge his hand. "Yeah, yeah, laugh it up, asshole."

Gunnar takes his happy-go-lucky ass into The Wild Boar, but I can't peel my eyes from her. From this angle, I have the perfect view of her sitting down at a picnic table on the right side of Uncle Harry's.

"Yo, Terry," I pitch my voice to the left, where I know the nosy asshole is just lingering.

"'Sup, Nova?" He strolls the ten feet separating us, his hands shoved into the pockets of his jeans.

I tip my chin toward my girl. "You ever see her before?"

Terry squints like he hasn't been watching the whole thing unfold like some fucking daytime tv show.

My brows cave in toward the middle, and I shake my head as I look at him. Just under six feet tall, messy dark brown hair with gray at his temples, and a strong weasel vibe. "Man, you're a fucking terrible actor, you know that?"

He laughs, the lines in the corner of his eyes deepening with mirth. "Nah, can't say I know her. Though she does look familiar somehow. Maybe she's one of Helen's girls?"

"Yeah, maybe." I know she's not though. Helen's girls reek of desperation most of the time.

Or maybe I'm fucking jaded and free pussy has lost its shine after so many years. Helen is the like the den mother to the club bunnies. They're nice girls for the most part, but too many of them believe that a quick fuck in the clubhouse is a gateway to claiming a seat on the back of someone's bike.

And nothing about my girl screams desperate.

"Yo, Bane! Our boy's losing it today. He's been staring at some chick who turned him down hard. Any longer, and she's gonna think he's a stalker or some shit."

Ace's booming voice jolts me out of memory lane. I have to blink a few times to get my vision to clear. I glare at my friend, but there's no heat and he's not even paying attention to me anyway. Too busy greeting my cousin, Bane, and a couple guys who came with him.

I lift my chin in acknowledgment as Bane saunters toward me with his hands tucked casually into the pockets of his jeans. He's always fucking meandering like he never has a care in the world.

"You crash and burn, Nova?" Bane asks, eyebrow arched with a smirk.

"Please, I wasn't even trying."

Bane arches a dark brow, the fucking signature St. James look that says you're full of shit. Fortunately for me, I'm fucking immune to it.

"Don't let him fool you, man. He's got the first round for everyone tonight," Gunnar yells from inside the bar's doorway.

Bane rolls the toothpick from one side of his mouth to the

other with a grin. "I thought I taught you to only bet on shit you can win."

"What can I say? I love a good underdog." I roll my shoulders back, a one-liner on the tip of my tongue when I spot someone greet my temptress with open arms.

Coraline fucking Carter.

"Fuck." The harsh curse leaves my mouth in a heated murmur, my brows crashing low over my eyes.

Bane whistles, somehow packing judgment and disbelief in the high-pitched sound. "Jagger know you're making a play on Coraline?"

I scoff. "Fucking please, I like my balls where they're at, thanks."

Coraline's a fucking preying mantis, gobbling men up after she's had her fill. At least that's the way Jagger tells it. From the sounds of it, It's a miracle he survived her relatively unscathed. She's been vocally anti-Reaper ever since their thing blew up.

Which might be problematic for me, considering I'm a legacy Reaper. Locked in for life.

Bane claps a hand on my shoulder, digging his fingertips into the soft spot by my collarbone. "Good luck getting through Coraline to her friend, man."

I grunt in response. Then a lightbulb flashes in my mind, bright white and startling in its clarity.

They have the same hair color. Like the *exact* same shade. Looks black from a distance, but up close it's a deep, rich brown with reflective auburn tones.

My ma would always say you could pick out a Carter girl from the crowd just by their hair. A genetic gift passed down through generations on their maternal side.

My little temptress is a Carter.

5

EVANGELINE

THE LOW BASS of motorcycles approached from a distance, growing louder until it seemed to fill the air. Cora and I pull apart just as three motorcycles come into view. Gleaming chrome glinted in the sinking sunlight, casting long shadows on the street and sidewalk. They don't stop at The Wild Boar like I anticipated, instead cruise down Main Street.

I feel her stare burning into the side of my face but I keep her in my peripheral vision for another moment.

"Ugh, no, babe," she says, shaking her head. "I love you but no."

My gaze snaps from the grim reaper patch on the back of their kuttes to her. I let my face fall into something neutral, relaxing my expression. "What?"

"Ugh, don't even bother," she replies, rolling her eyes. "They're not worth the heartache. Lying, cheating, big-dicked assholes who fuck around just because they can."

My brows arch toward my hairline. I don't even know why I'm surprised. Cora never minces her words, and she's unapologetically authentic.

But she usually doesn't lay it all out there five feet away from some kids eating rapidly-melting ice cream cones with their parents.

My lips twist to the side to smother the smirk I feel. "Why don't you tell me how you really feel?"

She huffs out an exhale and sends me a pointed look. "Whatever. My point stands. You're wife material, babe, and they're whatever is less casual than casual."

"I thought you wanted super casual with that guy." I press my tongue along the back of my teeth for a second and tease her with a single arched brow. "In fact, I seem to recall you were the one who pushed for casual because you had a thing for his brother too."

She tips her chin up, narrowing her gaze as she looks down her proud nose at me. "First of all, it was barely his friend. More like an acquaintance. And secondly, just because I wanted to *be* shared didn't mean that I wanted *to* share. And lastly, I now remember how easily it is for you to call me on my shit. So that's going to take some getting used to."

"Babe," I deadpan.

"Yeah, yeah. I know it's a ridiculous double standard, but that's how I feel," she says, lifting her shoulders.

I tilt my head to the side, feeling my brows crowd my eyes. "Feel? As in present tense?"

Cora rears back like I flicked her in the nose. "What? No. No, absolutely not. I meant felt. *Felt.* Past tense. Not current anything." She's practically tripping over her words.

I nod slowly a few times. "Okay."

"Ugh. We're not talking about me and my momentary lapse in judgment. We're talking about you not staring at those *men* with moon eyes."

I slip my fingers into the front pocket of my jean shorts and rock back on my heels. Amusement flutters over my skin like a fine mist. "I don't know, Cora, you kind of roped me in with that whole big-dicked comment."

The apples of her cheeks turn pink for a second as she does her best fish out of water impression, her mouth opening and closing a couple of times.

I laugh at her expression and let her off the hook. "I'm just kidding."

Kind of.

I mean, I was a little interested but I'm not about to tell her that. Not right now at least.

She snaps her mouth closed and stares at me for a beat. "You forget I've known you my whole life. Plus, you wear your emotions on your face, babe. I can see your interest written all over it."

I roll my lips inward, tucking my amusement away. "I'm just . . . curious."

"Mm-hmm." Her gaze flutters across my face. "They'll eat you up and spit you back out, Eve. The Reapers don't play by the same rules as we do."

I tilt my head to the side and sit down at the picnic table I snagged for us. "I thought you told me they're less Sons of Anarchy and more . . . I don't know. Whatever show is more wholesome but with hot guys who ride motorcycles."

She arches a brow. "*Hot guys?*"

My cheeks get warm at her teasing. "You're the one who's been telling me about the infamous shirtless car wash." I don't bring up the photos she used to send me back when she was hanging out with them.

Or the fact that I was one artfully executed pick-up line away from grabbing a drink with one of the hottest men I've ever laid eyes on.

Cora tucks into her ice cream and shakes her head. "Enough

about them. Let's talk about you. Tell me who I need to hunt down for firing you."

I let out a soft chuckle. "No finding necessary. I liked my job, but I didn't love it, ya know?"

Cora's lips press into a thin line, her eyes sparkling with fierce loyalty. "Ugh, they didn't deserve you or your talents, those unimaginative dicks."

A surprising laugh slips past my lips. Warmth sinks into my limbs at her protectiveness. "It all turned out though, because now I can spend the summer here, in Rosewood."

"Oh my god, yes!" she shouts, pumping her fist in the air once. "Just like when we were kids! We're going to have so much fun. Wait until I tell everyone. Abby comes home a couple times a month, and Beau and Graham's place is nearby too. Not that we'll spend much time there because—ugh." She does a full-body shudder, and I laugh again.

Sometimes I envy the relationship Cora has with her brothers and sister. When I spent my summers here as a kid, I used to pretend that they were my brothers and sisters too.

Sure, they still get into it with one another well into adulthood, but at the end of every day, they still have one another's back.

Unequivocally.

What would it be like to walk around life knowing that you have such a special bond with someone, knowing they'd come running if you called for help.

I don't have that. I never have, not even with my actual sister.

But I have Cora. And she's the ultimate best friend, cousin, and *sister* I could ever ask for.

My amusement settles into something more. A bone-deep appreciation for our friendship. "It's really good to see you, Cora." My voice comes out quiet, emotion stealing my volume.

"I'm so happy you're here." Cora reaches across the picnic

table and squeezes my free hand. As if she didn't already wrap me in a rib-crushing hug for five minutes.

Guilt settles heavily around my neck, sinking my shoulders. I should've come back sooner.

"I'm sorry. Work was crazy for a while." And Rosewood reminded me too much of Nana Jo. It's an excuse, a flimsy one at that.

Cora's eyes soften and she bobs her head just the barest inch like she can read my mind. Knowing her, she probably can.

Coraline Carter has been my best friend for my entire life. Literally. She's two years older, but if you ever asked her, she'd claim I'm the more mature one.

"I didn't mean it like that. Just that it's good to see you. Video chatting is great, but sharing ice cream is better," she says.

"I'm glad I'm here too," I murmur, enjoying the way that saltiness of the pecans cuts through the super sweet caramel drizzle.

"And besides, the amount of times your mom and sister have been in Rosewood this last year is nuts. I don't blame you for steering clear. They've been buzzing around like a pair of vultures. I swear Lizzy has been at Roberts Law more than Auntie Ginny."

My mouth parts, and she points a spoonful of strawberry ice cream. "Don't you dare, Evangeline Bailey."

I arch a brow and work to keep the smile from my face. "Ooh, you're middle-naming me now?"

She emphasizes her spoon once. "Hell yes I did. I can see excuses written all over your face. You're too forgiving and generous, and I already told you, we're done making excuses for Lizzy and her shitty behavior."

I lift a shoulder and let it fall back down just as slowly. The simple action the best representation of my muddled thoughts and opinion on my sister. "My feelings about her are complicated. She's had a hard life."

Cora scoffs, the noise loud even in the middle of a full courtyard of people. "Please. That girl was born with a shitty attitude. She's always been entitled, but she's only gotten worse as she's gone on tour with that guy, what's-his-name. She's a fucking know-it-all, Eve, and she makes you feel small every time she opens her mouth. I don't know why you take her shit, babe. I really don't." She shakes her head and looks down at her melted sundae.

My heart beats a steady, slow beat of quiet acceptance. "She's my sister." It's my only response, and somehow, it means nothing and everything.

Cora looks up at me through her thick fringe of black lashes. "We make our own family, Eve."

The Carter family motto floats between us, ballooning to fill the space around our picnic table. A smile hooks up the corner of my mouth as I take another bite.

The comfortable silence stretches between us.

"Do you think it'll ever get easier? Missing her?"

The question feels out of left field, and yet, I know exactly what she's really asking. Who she's asking about.

I nod slowly, letting my gaze drift over her shoulder and look without focus. "I think I'll always miss her. But lately, I don't know, it feels like she's still here too. In the juniper and marigold breeze. In the sun as it sets and creates vibrant pink and orange streaks across the sky. In her murals and paintings around the town."

Heartache steals my breath for a moment, the sharp pain as sudden as it is intense.

"Grief doesn't change, Cora. It's always going to be there, this ache behind your ribs. But over time, I think we just learn how to live with it. Until one day, we realize that it doesn't hurt anymore."

"Damnit, Eve." Cora sniffs, wiping underneath her bottom lashes with the little white rectangular napkins from the black holder in the middle of the table.

"You know, I thought it might be hard, being here."

She sniffs, crumpling up the napkin in her fist. "And is it?"

"No," I tell her, my voice soft. "It's nice. Welcoming."

It's the best I can offer her. My heart aches, still coming to terms with the fact that the only feeling of home I've ever had is no longer here.

6

EVANGELINE

I TAKE A DEEP BREATH, and I can almost taste the scent of honeysuckle in the air. The sun wraps around me like a warm embrace, reminding me of summer days spent running around town, mostly with Cora. Ice cream sundaes, bags full of candy from the Sweet Shoppe, lazy days on the beach. Boy crazy, endless laughter, and the feeling that we had all the time in the world.

But things have changed since then. As they should. It's been eight years since I spent the summer here, not since the summer before I left for college.

My parents were still my parents, but when I was here, it was like all of that faded away. So many incredible memories were made here.

The faint sound of waves lapping at the shoreline down the street makes my chest ache in the best way. I close my eyes, letting myself sink into the sweet nostalgia of the summer I turned eighteen in Rosewood.

The wind whispers through my hair, tugging at the strands ever so gently. My nose itches, and I blindly reach up to swipe them away. A low groan rumbles underneath my ear, and my hand halts in the middle of the air. My eyes spring open in shock, as I realize that wasn't my sound machine set to the ocean setting, and I'm not in my bed.

I slowly turn my head, and my breath catches in my throat at what I see.

No, I'm not in a bed at all.

I'm at the beach. Sleeping on a man.

I blink a few times, but with each sweep of my lashes, his image becomes clearer and little snippets of last night sear themselves on the inside of my eyelids.

Dark, messy hair I tugged on when I kissed him.

Broad, tattooed shoulders I clutched as he laid me down on the blanket.

A strong, chiseled jawline I ran my fingers along while we talked until the early hours of the morning.

Everything about him oozed sex appeal, from the way his muscles rippled beneath his skin to the way his lips curved into a lazy smile when he caught me looking at him.

Even when he's sleeping, he's still so goddamn good-looking it should be a crime. I didn't know men could have this many muscles. I'm pretty sure I said something to that effect last night as I traced his abs with my fingers.

The sun is flirting with the horizon, and it casts the most ethereal glow over him. He's the kind of gorgeous that would make me do something stupid, like blow up my plans and stay another two weeks in Rosewood.

I can feel my cheeks heating up at the realization of what happened last night. It's not like me to be so impulsive, to let go of all my inhibitions and give in to my desires.

But I can't deny how good it felt. Not only all the amazing, toe-curling things we did together, but shedding the tight restraints of my parents' expectations and just living.

Plus, he really is hot as hell. Cora's going to lose her mind when I tell her I hooked up with a stranger last night. She's going to be so mad that she skipped the bonfire. I roll my lips inward to stifle my amusement. I can just picture the look on her face.

He stirs beneath me, and I freeze, trapped like a deer in headlights. My heart beats against my ribs, and for the first time, I realize that I'm wearing his oversized tee.

And that's it.

"Ready?" Cora's voice breaks the spell.

I open my eyes, my stomach fluttering a little like it always does whenever I think of that night spent with him.

"You okay, Eve?" she asks from next to me, her voice quiet in the early morning cadence of Rosewood.

"Yeah, just tired." I feel like I barely slept last night, worry eating me from the inside out as I tossed and turned. Not even my current read, an epic fantasy romance with one girl and her many men could ease the burden.

But letting myself remember *that night* in such vivid detail helps settle me a little bit. Most girls recall their first times with eye rolls and exasperation. But not me.

At the risk of sounding like some cliche Hallmark movie, it was . . . magical. I left for college the next day, but I found myself casually looking for him every time I came back to visit, not that I was here too often.

Birds sing to one another nearby, the unmistakable warble and coo of mourning doves. Soft wistfulness blankets my anxiety at the haunting melody.

"Do you hear that?" I murmur, as if the volume of my voice would scare them into silence.

"Yeah," she says softly, a slow smile pulling the corners of her lips upward.

Nana Jo used to have generations of mourning doves nesting around her yard. It was a point of pride for her. She loved hearing them sing, convinced herself one solo male was Grandpa. She figured since mourning doves mate for life, and he was likely too impatient to wait for her, he'd come back as a mourning dove until they could be reunited again. I'm still unclear about her leaps of logic, but it made her feel good to hear them sing all the same.

She tips her head toward the square-shaped brick building in front of us. "You ever been inside before?"

Four stories tall and wrapped in faded red brick with lots of long, skinny six-paned windows to let the natural light in. The Law Offices of Robert have been here for generation upon generation. If you wanted to be a lawyer and work in Rosewood, then you joined their firm.

Three men all named Robert roomed together in law school, became best friends, and moved to Rosewood to open a law practice. Or so the story goes. I honestly don't even know their last names.

I shake my head slowly, trying to breathe through the anxiety clawing up my throat. "No."

"Yeah," Cora says with a sigh. "Me neither. Part of me is glad that they're following her requests to the letter, ya know? I wouldn't put it past some people to conveniently forget to carry out Nana Jo's last wishes."

I roll my lips inward and hum a noncommittal noise. I don't need to voice my opinion, we're both thinking of the same people.

An iced latte blocks the view of the lawyers office. "Here, I got this for you. Figured you might need it this morning. And before you try to pay me, let me remind you that you wouldn't take my money for ice cream last night."

I look over my shoulder at my cousin, a smile already tipping my frown around. I accept the caffeinated gift. "Thank you. And you're right, I definitely need this today."

I've tried my best to not place any expectations on this meeting, and I think I've succeeded. Mostly. But the swirling anxiety buzzing in my gut begs to differ. The truth is I *am* nervous.

This feels like the farewell to Nana Jo. Like a *final* farewell. And I just . . . I don't know how to process that, I guess.

I let my gaze trace the edges of their sign, their practice name written in a simple serif font. I catch movement from the corner of my eye, and my muscles freeze on instinct. A bird flies from the tree on the corner, swooping low before soaring high. I let my shoulders fall with an exhale.

"Why do you think she wanted it read individually? Why not have them read it once to everyone?"

Cora sighs. "You know, I've been wondering that myself. Mom and Dad don't know either, but Mom said she'd call me when they're done." She pulls out her phone from the pocket of her black sundress and glances at the screen. "Which is in a couple of hours. She's after you, I think. So maybe we'll wait for her."

I bump my shoulder into hers as she slips her phone back into her pocket. "You don't need to wait for me, you know. I'll be fine. I can catch up with you for dinner or something later."

She scoffs, but it's a playful sound. "Like I'm going to waste a moment of our summer together? You're stuck with me, babe. Except for the days I have to work. But you can always keep me company in the bakery."

"Don't worry. I can keep myself busy easily enough. Though I have missed your blueberry scones." I smirk as I take a sip of my latte. I never miss a chance to tease her about her well-loved blueberry scones. Mostly because it's actually my recipe.

"Oh my god," she says with a laugh, pivoting to face me and pointing her finger at my face. "I knew you cared!"

My smirk turns into a wide smile, a laugh slipping out. "No, I don't mind. I was just teasing you."

"You say that now, but one of these days, when I become one of those celebrity bakers, we're going to be right here again. Because you're going to sue my ass *for stealing your legendary recipe*."

I hide my smile behind my cup and glance at her over the lid. "I mean, I don't know if I would call it *legendary*." I pause for a second, mirth dancing in my veins. "But maybe award-winning. Blue ribbon decorated. Most coveted recipe in Rosewood."

"Don't forget: marriage proposal inducing." Cora barely gets the words out before she lets her giggles fly. "Oh my god. Do you remember when Billy Blackthorne proposed to you once he found out you made those scones at the Rosewood festival?"

Her words immediately conjure an image of him. Sweaty face, dark hair swept to the side with too much gel, down on one knee in the middle of the stage.

My shoulders shake with repressed laughter. "How could I forget? He stormed the stage and stole the microphone from the band and got down on one knee and everything. I was *mortified*."

"Oh, Eve," she says between a wheezing sort of laugh, bending forward a little. "I can still picture the look on his face."

"Is there something funny about my mother's death, Evangeline?"

7

EVANGELINE

THE SHARP ENUNCIATION of my name in my mother's cold voice sucks the air out of my lungs like a quickly deflating balloon. Every last ounce of amusement sinks to the ground beneath my feet, shriveling into itself until nothing remains. I turn toward my left and subconsciously smooth my hand down the silky fabric of my skirt. The need to be presentable drilled into me for so long that it's become almost a reflex when I see her.

"Auntie Ginny," Cora replies.

I rush out my own greeting, talking over Cora. "Hello, Mother."

My shoulders hitch toward my ear. My mother *hates* to be called by her adolescent nickname. It's probably why Aunt Hazel, Cora's mom, still uses it.

And Cora, apparently. Though I think she did it to get under my mom's skin more than any sort of childhood fondness like Aunt Hazel.

Virginia Carter is a commanding presence regardless of her stage. A boardroom, a black-tie party, a fundraising gala.

The cracked sidewalk of her hometown.

Semi-sheer white blouse with bishop sleeves, gathered on her right shoulder and draped across the front. A dark gray belt through the loops on her cream-colored pleated slacks.

And of course, her signature four-inch heels. Soft white with red soles.

With her hair smoothed back into a tight chignon, she looks like she's heading into stakeholders' meetings in a big city and not the only lawyer's office in town.

"Well?" She barks the word out quickly, tilting her head toward us. "Please, enlighten me on what could possibly bring such joy to you both on such a dreadful day. And for goodness' sake, stop fidgeting like a child." She cuts me a sharp look, somehow packing in enough derision to send me right back to those days of childhood.

I slide my hand into my pocket to resist the urge to do something really childish like flip her off. "Just reminiscing with Cora." I don't bother replying to her childish comment. Maybe it's just her nerves getting the best of her. I can't imagine it's been easy for her since we lost Nana Jo.

I force a smile to my face, but it feels all wrong and stiff. My mother stares at me for a long moment. And I swear I can feel the way her eyes scan me from head to toe behind her big black-framed sunglasses.

She exhales an impatient sigh. "Well, reminisce elsewhere, Evangeline. Your father is on an important call with a client, and I'm about to walk into my meeting with Robert."

I glance from her to the sleek black town car idling at the curb, the windows tinted too dark to see inside. Cohen, their longtime driver, stands stoically by the rear passenger, hands clasped together in front of him.

I often wondered what exactly Cohen's job entails, if he was more than just their driver. I wouldn't be surprised if he was really some sort of security detail too, a bodyguard of sorts.

As though on cue, Cohen steps forward and opens the rear passenger door, and my father steps out.

Edward Remington III doesn't look a day over forty. He murmurs his thanks to Cohen and ambles down the sidewalk, willfully oblivious to my mother's heated gaze.

Her arms are folded tight across her chest, her coral-painted lips pressed into a tight line of disapproval.

I track the tension quickly filling the air between them, sticky and thick like sap. And I grind out my knee-jerk inclination to fill the silence beneath my favorite pair of vintage peep-toe wedges. I'm well versed in the artful dance of avoidance when it comes to my parents and the way they communicate.

But that doesn't mean I'm immune to the anxiety that builds in my chest when I'm in the thick of it. It feels like a weighted vest wrapped around me, tick-tick-ticking higher and quicker with each moment.

My father pauses next to her, head bent low and attention pinned on his phone. "Ready, Virginia?"

When she doesn't respond, he finally clues in. He raises his head slowly, no doubt accustomed to her behavior after all these years. Not that he has a leg to stand on.

He turns to face us, pocketing his phone with a wide grin. "Oh, girls. What a pleasant surprise. What are you doing here?"

I do my best to hold in my wince, shifting my weight from one foot to the other. I avoid my mother's gaze, not that she's peeled it from my father. Anger radiates off of her like a cloud of icy fog. I already know I'll be the one to bear the brunt of Dad's brushoff later.

"Dad, hi." I offer him a little wave, not daring to cross the frosty valley of tension that separates us. My mother.

"We're here for our meetings about Nana Jo's will," Cora offers, not skipping a beat at the swelling awkwardness.

God, I love her. I make a mental note to buy her another sundae just for this.

"*Nana Jo.*" Mom sneers under her breath. "Why she ever allowed her beautiful name to be butchered like that is beyond me." She rests her fingertips against the hollow of her throat and gazes away from us.

"You girls enjoying your coffee?" he asks, tipping his head toward us.

Mom adjusts her crocodile-leather, apricot-colored handbag over her forearm. She tilts her head to the right, facing our direction without actually looking at us. "Haven't we been waiting long enough, Edward?"

The dig is clear. We've been waiting a year to hear the results of Nana Jo's will.

"Yes, well, Remingtons are prompt and punctual," my father says with a nod. He holds out his elbow, and my mom rests the tips of her fingers against his forearm. They head toward Robert's Law without a backward glance.

My father might not be as obvious about his general disdain for everyone and everything as my mother, but they're cut from the same cloth. They share philosophies on many, many things in life.

Including parenting.

I'm a fifth generation Carter girl, and proud of it. Growing up, I was embarrassed to not have the same last name as my dad. But now, I'm so grateful to always have a piece of Nana Jo and the generations of Carter women before me.

Nana Jo's grandmother, Ruby Faye Carter, decided she didn't want to take her husband Earl's last name and become Ruby Newby. Pretty revolutionary stuff for the time.

Mom pauses at the top of the steps, glancing at me over her

shoulder. "Oh, and Evangeline. Maybe think about a different outfit, hm? That hemline isn't flattering for a woman with your shape. Don't forget, you're a direct reflection of *me*."

Her words hit me right where she intended. They sink into my chest, their poisoned letters embedding themselves into my bloodstream. With each pump of my heart, shame licks at my skin and my cheeks warm.

"Jesus, Eve. She's the fucking *worst*," Cora says, emphasizing the last word. "How you survived that for eighteen years is nothing short of a miracle." She shakes her head as she takes a deep sip of her coffee.

"Yeah," I reply, my voice quiet. I keep my gaze on my parents until the door closes and cuts off my view. I inhale and exhale in calm, measured breaths.

It takes effort to shape my mouth into some semblance of a smile. My fingers twitch with the urge to smooth down the fabric of my favorite black skirt.

"Alright, let's go try to eavesdrop on your parents." She slides her arm around mine, hand curling around my bicep. Our shoulders bump together as we follow the same path as my parents. She leans in toward me like she's divulging a secret. "Is it bad if I hope she gets nothing?"

A laugh catches me by surprise. Not for the first time, gratitude fills my heart for Cora's steadying presence next to me.

I lean my head against her shoulder just for a moment. "Did anyone ever tell you that you're the best?"

"Yes, you. But probably not enough, so feel free to keep reminding me." I hear the smile in her voice.

"You're the best," I tell her, all cheek and sass. I reach out and grab the monogrammed door handle. One hefty tug, and the solid oak door swings open. Cool air conditioning pours over us, reminding me of the way a freezer froths over every time you open it when the house is hot.

"Perfect. Want to tell me tomorrow, over breakfast? At the diner?"

My stomach perks up at the mention of Honey Bee Cafe. They have some of the best Belgian waffles I've ever had. "Absolutely, but don't you have work?"

"I go in at four tomorrow, so let's meet at nine? Then I'll head back to the bakery and finish up afterward."

"Sounds good."

We both sit down at the navy blue plush loveseat in the waiting room to the right.

After a few moments, I break the silence. "You know, if Nana Jo didn't leave my mom anything, then I don't think they would even be here."

"True, but a girl can dream, right?" Cora flashes me a cheeky grin.

I raise a brow at her. "Should we try to listen? We don't even know what floor they're taking meetings today. And not that it matters much, but she's going to be so mad if she catches us eavesdropping."

"Then I guess we better not get caught." She laughs, tugging me up to stand.

Before we take more than two steps, an assistant appears in the doorway, crushing our silly adventure dreams. "Coraline Carter? You're next."

"See you after?" she asks me as she crosses the room to him.

"Yep. I'll meet you outside once the coast is clear and my parents are gone."

Do I sometimes feel weird about the lengths I go to avoid sharing space with my parents? Yes.

But my parents are like my own personal rainclouds, always overshadowing my sunshine. And today, I have an inkling that I'm going to bask in the sunshine.

8

EVANGELINE

"MISS EVANGELINE CARTER," the receptionist announces as she opens the door and ushers me into an office. Like I'm some kind of royalty that needs announcing.

A man behind a long oval-shaped table pushes to his feet. I'd put him in his mid-sixties with thick chestnut hair cropped short. His suit is dark and boxy, but his smile is bright and sincere. The gray hair at his temples matches the streaks in his neatly trimmed goatee.

He clasps his hands in front of him, inclining his head a little. "Miss Carter, thank you for coming today."

"Of course."

"Please take a seat." He sweeps his arm out in front of him, gesturing to the three chairs in a movement worthy of the infamous Vanna White.

I take a seat in the middle and cross my legs at the ankle, trying to maintain a calm exterior despite the nerves in my stomach. It feels like a bundle of porcupine needles rolling around in there.

I can't explain why I'm so nervous except that I am. I have a feeling the results of this meeting could change my life. Or maybe I'm projecting a bit, considering I'm currently jobless.

And staying at a motel. But that's my choice. Cora already offered her house multiple times.

"I'm Mr. Lee," he says, extending a hand for me to shake. I take it, noticing how firm his grip is without being crushing. "I've handled your late grandmother's affairs for many years now." He pauses, glancing toward the table with a slight smile. "We'd developed an unconventional sort of friendship over the years. Grab a cup of coffee at the diner and talk about those fake dating shows. My wife's obsessed with them, and I guess somewhere along the way, I started liking them too."

I nod, my own smile tugging up the corners of my mouth. "Sounds like her. She was the best. And she had lots of opinions on those shows."

I still remember during the weekends we'd spend together; she'd talk my ear off until I caved and watched an episode. And before I knew it, we'd be down four hours and an armful of snacks.

"My sincerest condolences, Miss Carter. Jo was a bright spot in our community here in Rosewood, and she is sorely missed," Mr. Lee says softly.

"She is," I agree, keeping my voice quiet.

He exhales quickly. "Well, let's get down to it, yeah? I bet you're eager to hear the news."

He leans forward, the creak of his chair almost echoing around the quiet room. His hands are steady as he slides a brown file folder across the table and flips the top open. "As you know, your grandmother led a remarkable life and left quite the legacy—not only in her community but also in her will."

Mr. Lee clears his throat and pulls out a stack of papers from the folder. "Her estate is being divided between her children and grandchildren."

I nod, already having pieced that much together. My mother has made it clear that she expected a generous share—if not all—of Nana Jo's assets. Despite the fact that Mom hasn't willingly come back to Rosewood in at least fifteen years.

Though come to think of it, I'm not sure if all of the grandchildren are even here today. It's hard to say with these private readings, but I feel like Cora would have mentioned it.

Mr. Lee grabs a pair of glasses from his breast pocket and perches them on the edge of his nose. "However, as you know, she left personal directives for everyone." He clears his throat before he reads from the paper in front of him. "And to my granddaughter, Evangeline Bailey Carter, I leave my house and property on Magnolia Lane, as well as all the contents inside. I also leave her one-quarter of my collection of vintage jewelry. It is my wish that Evangeline always have a place to call home in Rosewood, but should she choose to sell, she will retain the profit."

My eyes widen and my lips part in stunned silence, unable to fully process what I've just heard. Did Nana Jo really leave me her house?

A wave of emotion cascades over me and memories flash across my consciousness in an instant. Almost every happy moment in my childhood can be traced back to Magnolia Lane.

My heart thunders inside my chest. "Oh my god. That's . . . that's—did you say her *house*?" I whisper, my words failing me as shock holds me hostage.

He adjusts his glasses and sets the papers down on the file folder. He closes the folder with a flick of his wrist and pushes it across the table toward me. "Yes, Miss Carter. Your grandmother thought very fondly of you. Of her grandchildren."

My mind races, too fast to pin down any one thought. But one emotion dominates all the others: love.

Even from beyond this plane of existence, Nana Jo is still loving me, wrapping me up in warmth and genuine affection.

"Thank you," I manage to say, my voice still shaky with disbelief. "Thank you so much, Mr. Lee."

"Of course, Miss Carter. This folder is yours. You'll find all the details in here. The deed to the house has already been transferred to your name and filed with the bank. There is no mortgage as your grandmother had paid it off some twenty-odd years ago. And she had set up a trust with enough to cover property taxes on all three acres for at least the next twenty."

"I—I don't know what to say. I'm shocked, to say the least."

Mr. Lee smiles warmly at me. "I understand, Miss Carter. It's a lot to take in. But I have a feeling your grandmother would be very proud of you and whatever you'll do with the property and house. And now, if you'll excuse me, I have another appointment to attend to. Please don't hesitate to reach out if you have any questions or concerns."

I stand up, still in a daze, and reach across the table to shake Mr. Lee's outstretched hand. "Thank you again."

He inclines his head toward me and gestures toward the door parallel to the table. "If you don't mind, Janet will walk you out."

"Oh, of course."

Janet, the receptionist, opens the door as if she was magically summoned.

I pause at the threshold. "I do have one question if you don't mind."

He looks at me expectantly, a smile still firmly in place. "Yes?"

"Do you know why she made everyone wait a year to hear her will?"

He takes his glasses off, tucks the arms behind the lenses, and places them on the table in front of him. "It is my understanding that she wanted to give a grace period . . . for certain people to comply with her stipulations. And she wanted to ensure her wishes were carried out without any interference."

I nod slowly, processing all the things he isn't saying.

"Thank you, Mr. Lee."

I exit the room, still feeling like I'm walking on clouds. Nothing permanent under my feet and struggling to stay tethered to the ground. The weight of uncertainty has been lifted with just a handful of words on a piece of paper, and suddenly the future feels bright with endless possibilities.

A house.

I have a *house.*

And not just any house, but Nana Jo's house. The one that holds so, so many memories. I can picture myself sitting on the front porch swing, sipping lemonade out of old mason jars and reading a really good book.

Or dancing around her kitchen while baking my favorite pumpkin muffins.

My kitchen now, I guess.

I'm so lost in my thoughts that I walk right past the small waiting room off the hallway.

"Eve?"

I turn to see Cora jogging up to me. She's got that crazy sort of twinkle in her eye that always clues me into her excitement.

"Cora." I pull her into a quick hug on impulse. "How was it?"

She pulls back, keeping her hands on my biceps. She looks at me then, her gaze jumping all around my face. She's only a couple of inches taller than me, but she looks so similar, sometimes it's like looking at myself in an alternate reality.

"Holy fucking shit, Eve," she whisper-shouts, her fingers tightening their grip on my biceps.

"What? What happened?"

"Nana Jo left me a trust with fifty grand in it. Fifty. Thousand. Dollars," she crows the last few words, her voice rising with excitement and awe.

"Oh my god!" I yelp as she crushes me to her for another hug.

"And I have to use it for my bakery. Can you believe that?" Her voice is muffled as she jostles us around in her wonder and joy.

"That's—that's *amazing*," I breathe out the last word and join in on the weird hopping, swaying hug we're in the middle of. "How come you didn't tell me you wanted to start your own bakery?"

She pulls back and looks at me. Her cheeks are pink, but there's a brightness in her expression I haven't seen in years. "I don't know. It was just this pipe dream for as long as I could remember. Something I would casually dream about. I guess she was listening, huh?"

"She was always listening. She still is," I murmur.

Her eyes are glassy, like she's on the verge of tears. The sight trips my waterworks wire, and like a reflex, my eyes start to fill.

She runs her index fingers underneath her eyes and blinks a few times while looking toward the ceiling. "Shit, I'm sorry. Enough about me. Tell me how it went for you."

I waft my hand in the air, as if I can physically brush away her worries. We walk side by side down the hallway toward the rear exit. "No way, you're not getting off that easy. I wanna hear all about your new bakery soon."

She bumps her shoulder into mine. "Of course, but stop deflecting."

I exhale and chance a glance at her. "Her house."

Her hand flies out in front of me and she stops instantly. "What?"

"Yep." I scrunch my nose a little to keep the smile threatening in check. It feels weird to be this happy about Nana Jo's will. I'd rather have her.

"No shit," she whispers, all wide-eyed.

"She left me Magnolia Lane and everything inside. It's already in my name, I guess."

She tosses her arm across my shoulders and pushes open the door with a flourish.

I inhale the fresh air, letting the sun soak into my skin. It feels good, like the beginning of something exceptional.

"Welcome home, cousin."

9

SILAS

I SPIN my black baseball hat around from the back to the front, grimacing at the feel of the soggy material.

Shit. Now I needed a new air conditioner *and* a new hat. Probably.

"Tune, order whatever you have to and get that fucking air conditioner fixed, yeah?" The air conditioning stopped working six hours ago, and it's fucking hot as hell in here, even with all the bay doors open.

"On it, boss." Tune nods and goes into the office in the back of the garage, presumably to source parts or a whole unit. He's a good kid, shit at singing though. The guys dubbed him Tune, as in *can't hold one* before he even patched in.

"See you assholes Monday." I tap the top of the doorframe twice before I walk through it and head toward the clubhouse. I try not to keep the guys too late on a Saturday if I can help it. Thankfully, all the garages have been running smoothly. Which usually means shit is going to go south soon.

But not today, so for now, I'm out.

A small chorus is my farewell, a mixture of grunts and a

couple laters. If my old man were still here, he wouldn't let their grumbles slide. He never could remember that this was a brotherhood, not a fucking personal army to do his bidding.

He'd mistake their words as disrespect and not for what they are: a garage full of men who've been sweltering in the brick oven we call a garage.

Mutual respect isn't something my old man ever mastered before he met his maker. That motherfucker would pick a fight just because it was a Tuesday afternoon.

He unleashed his pent up rage on anyone who breathed wrong. And Raymond St. James had enough rage to fill six lifetimes.

He grew up in the *boys will be boys* generation. And if it weren't for my ma, my brother and I would've probably grown into replicas of him.

Angry, bitter, and quick to violence.

To the club, he was the President of the Rosewood Reapers. A title he took literally, reveling in delivering the ultimate price for those who wronged the club.

But to us, he was Pops. Some mutated version of what he thought a father should be around the house, and the Prez around the club.

The man made more than his fair share of mistakes, but there's a standout moment in our relationship. One single decision he made that was entirely selfless. Some of the old timers even called it self-sabotaging, second-guessing his right to lead the Reapers.

Five years ago, I asked him to end the war we'd been in for years after one thirty-second phone call. Not for the club or Ma or even me.

But for my son.

And that psychopathic motherfucker did. He ended the warring between clubs with the ultimate sacrifice.

My general annoyance rises with each step toward the clubhouse. Thinking about the complicated relationship I had with a complex man usually does that to me.

The sun beats down on my back as I clear the courtyard of RGRC, Rosewood Garage and Repair Company. It's what we call the collection of mechanically-inclined businesses on Reaper property.

The Vault is a garage on the left, dedicated to restoring classics. And Southern Steel is the studio building on the far right. All custom art goes through my brother inside Southern Steel. That asshole has more talent in his pinky finger than the lot of us combined.

And in the middle is the original RGRC garage that's been standing for generations, in desperate need of a new air conditioner.

Beads of sweat roll down my back, and I find myself longing for a cool shower to wash the day off. Normally, I'd march my ass up to my house at the back of the compound and do exactly that. But today is a Grandma Day for my boy. And the way he treats it, you'd think it was some national holiday, and not something that happens every week.

My brother, Nova, and our cousin, Bane, and I came up thick as thieves together, and they've been a godsend when it comes to pitching in to help with my independent five-year-old. But on days when the three of us are all needed in one of the garages? Then Ma hangs out with him.

She sent a text an hour ago that she's at the clubhouse. Something about the kitchen and Helen.

Helen is a bit like a den mother to the club bunnies, the girls that hang around the club. Most still hold out hope for some rags to riches love story with a brother.

A lot of shit has changed when I stepped up as president, including the way the bunnies are treated. And as long as they don't cause problems, I really don't give a fuck who's in which brother's bed.

Helen Whittiker and Ma have been friends since high school. She's turned down six offers for a permanent seat on the back of a brother's bike, allegedly content to live unattached, hopping from one bed to the next.

And as far as I know, she never fucked my old man. Not because he was a pious man either. That asshole stuck his dick in whatever he felt like *whenever* he felt like it. But there's no way she'd still be breathing if she did that to Ma.

Dixie St. James is a fucking menace to society if you cross her. And the only thing that gets her heated faster than blatant disrespect is if you threaten one of her boys.

My brother, my cousin, my son, and me.

I wrap my appreciation for her and all the shit she does for us around me like armor, preparing myself for the onslaught of people and questions as soon as I step foot inside the clubhouse.

You'd think these people didn't have access to me every single day by the way some of them trap me in forty-five minute conversations sometimes. Like they gotta cram every detail about some reality show I've never seen into one run-on sentence. It's fucking exhausting.

I love my club and my guys. But my brother is the mouthpiece of the Reapers for a reason, and it's not because he's better looking, no matter what that little shit says.

I sigh and pull open the back door, cool air washing over me in a blissful stream. I walk down the corridor toward the front, where the kitchen is.

Hopefully, Ma sorted the problem out. I'd hate to add another thing to my list of things that need replacing.

The president patch along my right pec feels like it pierces my flesh with its sharp, weighted corners.

Thankfully, it's a weight shared. My brother and cousin have stepped up to share the spotlight with me. And, of course, the other members of the club and the council.

The Reapers aren't a dictatorship. Even more of a democracy now than when my old man wore this patch. Every big decision comes down to a vote. From the trivial things like should we get the new game console in the shared living space to the big shit like should we continue to provide protection to the businesses on the other side of Rosewood's city limits.

I expel a sigh, shoving my crowded thoughts to the back of my mind. The unmistakable smell of chocolate chip cookies hits me in the chest, and my stomach rumbles right on cue.

I should've guessed he'd sweet-talk Ma into baking today. He's been obsessed with chocolate chip cookies ever since watching a cooking show with her two weeks ago.

I scan the open doorways as I pass them, looking for the familiar mop of messy dark brown hair.

My boy runs around this place often enough to know all the best places to hide, and I hope like hell he's not currently in the middle of one of those games. There are too many shadowed corners and small places for him to sneak away in a place this size, and my patience is running thin today.

Nothing a cool shower and a hot meal won't fix though. It's a mantra I find myself repeating often.

"Yo, Prez. We got a meeting tonight?" Gunnar asks from somewhere inside the room on my right.

"Nah, not today," I call over my shoulder and keep walking.

"Hey, Prez. Want some company tonight?" Lydia asks.

She's a regular bunny, been here for close to a decade now. Long enough to have her own room. And in all that time, she's never given up on hopping into my bed. I'm not sure why she thinks using that high pitch is attractive, but she's wrong.

Not that I go for bunnies anymore. Not since *her.*

"I'm good, Lydia." I give her my best tight-lipped glance.

Quincy jogs up behind me, hovering just behind my shoulder. "Hey, Prez, when you get a second, I—"

"Tomorrow, Quince. Just here to grab my boy, club business will have to wait, yeah? If it's an emergency, call Bane." I keep my strides long and tamp down my rising irritation. I'm not in the mood to mingle or fix problems or entertain requests.

Bane is my vice president, and arguably the most important brother the Reapers have. Without him, our shit wouldn't run nearly as smooth, if at all.

"You got it, Prez," Quincy says.

I follow the sound of voices, recognizing Hunter's familiar giggle. I slow down, walking carefully over the tile floor to keep my steps quiet. Paranoia has me pausing, cocking my head to the side, and listening in on the conversation just inside the big living room area.

It's two thousand square feet of converted showroom space. A bar along the opposite wall, several sets of couches, tables and chairs, a gaming corner with a pool table, foosball, and a giant screen with every gaming console in front of a plush U-shaped sectional couch.

When there are more than ten people in here, you can't hear shit. But when it's two bunnies and one little boy? It's like I'm standing right next to them, just in time to hear them seal their eviction.

"I'm going to be your new mommy, Hunter. Your daddy and me are about to be real serious, but don't worry, I'll treat you better than your momma ever did."

10

SILAS

A VEIL of red descends over my vision, my blood boiling faster than a frog in a dried up creek.

I take a single step into the room, letting my gaze sweep across them. I plant my feet and cross my arms over my chest. I know how intimidating I can be, and while most of the time, I do my best not to be, I find myself leaning into it now, filling up the doorway behind me.

"Get out." My voice is low, but it carries across the empty space easily.

The two bunnies flinch, jerking to look over their shoulders toward me. They stare with wide eyes and fear etched into their faces. Good.

"Dad," Hunter says, leaping off the couch to his feet. His face still holds its usual playful grin, but there is a deep furrow between his eyebrows. And that confusion, that anxiety he's feeling is enough to fuel my ire all over again.

I know he'll be asking me about his momma at bedtime tonight. My boy likes to save his tough questions for those quiet moments right before sleep.

"Come on over here, bud," I tell him, taking another measured step into the room.

He navigates through the room like he's playing on an obstacle course, rounding couches, dodging chairs, and jumping over shit someone left on the ground.

I clasp his shoulder and give it a gentle squeeze as I pull him toward me for a half-hug. "Let's go see if we can find Nan."

"She's in the kitchen making cookies."

"Chocolate chip cookies?" I raise an eyebrow in faux surprise, the corners of my mouth twitching as I try to suppress a smile.

His big dark brown eyes sparkle when he eagerly nods his head in agreement. They're the same shade as his Momma's, which is pretty much the only thing he got from her. The rest of him is all me, right down to the little dimple in his cheek.

It's like looking at a miniature version of myself. Sometimes he makes these certain expressions, and he looks just like me. Fatherhood is the most wonderful and terrifying experience of my life. And I was in a fucking MC war for too many years to count.

"Yes, Bobby says they're best right out of the oven," he tells me. His brows knit together with excitement. "And the ones at home come from a package from the store."

If I didn't catch him watching that cooking show on a loop, I'd have no idea who the hell Bobby is. He's one of the chefs on the show, and my five-year-old kid is quoting his advice like they're friends.

It's adorable.

I run my fingers through his hair and pull him close, feeling the warmth of his body against mine. It's one of the small comforts I don't think I'll ever tire of. Not in ten years, not in a hundred.

"Can't argue with that logic. We have to try them fresh out of the oven. Let's go get some." My voice is soft, keeping this conversation private.

I haven't forgotten about the two girls in the room. They'll be dealt with, but Hunter comes first.

"Before dinner?" he whispers, grinning up at me. Any trace of his earlier unease gone, at least temporarily.

"Yeah, bud, one before dinner."

He pumps his fist in the air triumphantly and grabs my hand.

I don't look back at the bunnies behind us. As much as I want to set their shit straight, I don't want to do it in front of Hunter. And I'm over the constant barrage of women trying to use Hunter as some sort of stepping stone to my bed. As if I'd fucking touch one of them anyway.

The women in town are no better, always clamoring over one another to coo over my boy like he's a baby. Like I find that baby-talkin' shit attractive.

I don't.

The smell of freshly-baked cookies hits me in the face in the best possible way as we enter the kitchen. Creamy white walls rose to meet bright white vaulted ceilings with exposed steel beams. Black granite countertops run the length along one wall and a large island dominates the center of the room. There are two sinks, an overflowing tiered fruit holder, and dozens of chocolate chip cookies on cooling racks on the island.

Like one of Pavlov's dogs himself, my mouth practically waters from the scent. They're like a siren song, and I'll bet my bike that anyone who's in the clubhouse will flood the kitchen, begging for a cookie. Knowing my ma, she has two more pans in the oven, enough for everyone to have one.

Behind the island, a gleaming black and stainless steel sixty-inch stove with six gas burners and two convection ovens created the centerpiece for the far wall. On one side, a large stainless steel French-door refrigerator with one of those fancy touch pads on one door. And on the other side is a deep single-basin kitchen sink, its chrome faucet glinting in the overhead light.

Years ago, Gunnar took advantage of his then-girlfriend's access to the open-floor stock at her appliance store. Got everything in here for real cheap.

The kitchen island is home to eight wooden stools, chipped and weathered from years of use. Beyond it are two large dining tables made of solid oak with an eclectic assortment of mismatched chairs. Too many broke, and I got tired of trying to hunt down one to match the rest, so a few years ago, I threw in the towel and let the guys pick whatever random chair they wanted to add. It's enough seating for the brothers who call the clubhouse home, plus those of us who are here most days.

When the whole club rolls in—their wives, girlfriends, kids, and bunnies—we have to bring in extra tables and chairs. But for everyday stuff, this setup works well. Thank fuck we remodeled this place, otherwise, there's no way I'd let Hunter play around in here. It used to be a fucking rundown cesspool on the best of days.

Ma spins around at the sound of our footsteps, her face lighting up when she spots us.

"Well, if it isn't my favorite grandson." She leans over the counter, a yellow printed towel in her hand, and beckons us closer.

Hunter drops my hand and races across the tiled floor, practically launching himself onto the center stool. "Nan! Dad said we could eat cookies before dinner." He rushes his words out like he's afraid I'm going to snatch them back.

"Just one," I remind him. I shift my gaze to the woman standing next to Ma, Helen. "A word?"

She wipes her fingers on the edge of the kitchen towel, then tosses it on the counter next to my mother. "Of course, Prez."

I take a few steps away from her, toward the other end of one of the dining room tables. I don't pull out a chair; this conversation isn't going to take long. I fold my arms over my chest and look out the window.

It's a shit view, just the parking lot to the garage. But at least the sunshine streams through the glass, a welcome change from all that fluorescent lighting.

"Everything okay?" she asks after a moment.

I drag my gaze from the peeling painted lines for parking spots and look at her. She's standing tall, shoulders pulled back and expression expectant but not on guard. I like Helen, I always have. But if I don't enforce the rules, this tentative peace we have will crumble into shit. All it takes is letting one thing slide, and before you know it, everything is fucked.

I exhale and look at her. "Wanna tell me why I just walked in on two club girls I've never seen before tell my boy they're gonna be his new mommy?"

A spark of anger flashes across her face as she murmurs, "Shit." Her expression is pinched, worry deep in the furrow of her brows. "I'll take care of 'em, set 'em straight."

I shake my head a few times, the movement slow and precise. "You know I don't police the girls that run through here. I leave that shit up to you. But they fucked with my boy, Helen, and I can't have that."

"You want 'em gone?" She's not even surprised, her expression and tone even. Understanding.

My arms are still crossed tightly against my chest, but I lift one shoulder in a casual shrug. "What kind of leader would I be if I didn't enforce the rules? And what kind of father would I be if I didn't protect my son?"

She nods, reaching out to lightly skim her fingertips down my bicep. "I understand, Prez. They'll be gone before you leave."

"Good," I tell her, tipping my chin up and stepping backward, out of her reach.

She gives me a barely perceptible nod, her expression unreadable, before turning on her heel and leaving the kitchen. I exhale, uncrossing my arms as I rejoin Hunter and my mother.

Ma's gaze slants to the hallway Helen just disappeared in, her eyebrows high on her forehead. "What was that all about?"

"Just some bunny business." I rest my hand on the back of Hunter's hair, the wild strands sticking up from his cowlick. "How's the cookie, bud?"

"It's the best ever," he says through a mouthful of gooey chocolate and a wide grin.

Ma narrows her eyes at me. "What kind of business?"

I reach over Hunter's head and snag a big cookie off the edge of the rack. "Some new girls said something inappropriate to someone." I cut my gaze to the back of Hunter's head.

"Hmm," she says.

I eat half the cookie in one bite and look at my mother. She busies herself with wiping down the counter, avoiding eye contact with me.

"Shit," I mumble, setting the cookie down on the counter. "What did you do?"

"Jar, Dad," Hunter says.

"Remind me when we get home, yeah?" I started a swear jar around him a couple years ago, mostly to curb my brother's habit of swearing around Hunter. Nova had him for the day while I was at work, and when I came home that night, I found him running around the house with a cape on singing "motherfucker" at the top of his lungs. Nova was on the couch, bent over and clutching his stomach in that kind of laughter that almost hurts.

But sometimes, I find myself contributing to the vacation fund. Though I try to reel my shit in. Hunter's old enough to know better now, but I'd rather he not go into kindergarten next year calling his classmates some creative insults.

"Okay," he replies with a little hum.

"Ma, tell me."

"Well," she starts, wringing the towel for a moment. She sets it down on the counter, smoothing it out. She rolls her shoulders back and regains some of her composure. She looks at me, all earlier guilt wiped clean from her face. "I told them you're looking for a nanny. And, maybe, they got carried away. I don't know."

I grit my teeth and narrow my stare at my mother. "What the hell, Ma?"

"What the hell what, Silas?" she snaps. "You've been living like an ostrich these past couple of months, and now my surgery is in just a couple of weeks. You haven't even interviewed the people I've found for you."

The back of my neck gets hot, and I shift my weight a little. "We have time. And I told you, I'll be fine. He can stay at the garage with me."

She stares at me, her lips thinning into a scowl. "Time is what we don't have, son. I'm getting my rotator cuff fixed, and I'll be out for a month if I'm lucky. Two if it goes sideways. More if there are complications. And a garage is no place for a five-year-old."

My throat burns at the thought of complications of her surgery. So, I ignore it and focus on the other thing she said. "I was in the garage all the time at his age, and I turned out just fine."

She raises both brows, a smirk pulling up the corner of her mouth. "You were there once in a while, but Asher was too little, so you and Lincoln weren't there as often as your father led you to believe. In fact, your favorite thing was to hang out with me in the kitchen. You were my little shadows."

I roll my eyes, but I can't help the small chuckle that escapes my lips. "If you say so."

"Silas," she says, her voice softening as she reaches out to lay her hand on mine. "I just want what's best for Hunter—and you. And you both need someone to take care of him while I'm recovering."

I sigh, the noise weighted. "Fine, you bring me some real options, and I'll pick one. No bunnies though. I mean it, Ma."

She nods and leans back, satisfied with my answer. "You can count on me, son."

"I know," I acknowledge quietly. "Thanks, Ma."

We fall into comfortable silence. Hunter finishes his cookie and chats about nothing in particular, filling the quiet air with a sense of contentment. I can only hope that I'm not putting myself in a shit position by agreeing to do it her way.

11

EVANGELINE

IT TAKES a few blinks before my eyes adjust to the muted lighting inside The Wild Boar. The scent of beer and whiskey linger in the air like it's built into the very foundation.

It's four o'clock on a Monday, but apparently, this is the place to be.

Over half of the tables and booths are full. It's busy here, but not exceptionally noisy. Probably because the ceilings are plastered with that noise-canceling material that absorbs sound.

Edison bulbs in wrought-iron sconces spotlight framed vintage music and concert posters around the room. The floor is made of real wood, scuffed and scratched by decades of footsteps and heavy boots. It's probably a hundred years old, from a time when houses and buildings were built to last generations. They don't make houses with this kind of wood flooring anymore.

The bar itself is a centerpiece, carved almost like a wave along most of the wall to my left. The top is polished wood, oiled enough that the TV's reflection shines on it.

Rustic two-top and four-top square tables fill the space, with the occasional bar-height table thrown in. Black leather booths line the open wall space, some big enough to fit ten people comfortably but cozy enough for an intimate drink.

Across from the bar is a small stage. Two steps off the floor with large speakers on either end and other equipment scattered across it. It's a darkened corner now, but I could see how it would come alive when local musicians played.

I imagine the ambience shifting, doing a one-eighty on those nights it's lit up. From charming and laid-back to electric and charged with energy. Right now, though, it's pretty chill with its charming decor and extensive wall of liquor behind the counter.

My gaze sweeps around the bar. A few couples sway to a melodic slow song while others stand near the stage, talking and laughing with drinks in hand.

I bet it's electrifying when someone's onstage and they play a crowd favorite. I can almost feel the way the energy of the crowd is gearing up, my own heart fluttering in anticipation. I think I'd like to see that.

I slide onto one of the swivel bucket-seat stools at the bar, the black faux leather creaking as I shift my weight around.

"You lost, gal?"

I look at the bartender, an older guy who looks like he's seen some shit in his life. Not surprising considering this is the only bar in town. He kind of reminds me of one of those aging action movie stars from the 80s. He's tall with a barrel chest pushing the limits of his black long sleeved tee. Shaved head, a beard that's more gray than black, and tattoos on the back of his hands.

But his eyes are kind. His expression somehow dubious and soft as he watches me take him in.

I adjust my crossbody purse so it rests on the seat next to my hip, out of the way. "This is the only bar in Rosewood. How'd that happen?"

He tosses a white rag over his shoulder and plants his palms on the edge of the polished bar top. His expression gives nothing away and he deadpans, "Luck."

My brows arch toward my hair and I nod a few times. "Okay. Well, can I get a mojito please?"

They're my go-to drink when I'm out, which isn't all that often. But there's something about the spearmint and the lime that tastes refreshing. And after the last couple of days I've had, I could use a little refreshing. A small respite on this hot summer night.

The bartender tilts his head to the side, the skin between his brows puckering a little. "You new in town or something?"

"Or something," I answer with a nod, my gaze drifting around the bar.

"Huh." He pushes off the bar top and walks down to the other end, presumably to make a mojito before someone at the other end of the bar flags him down.

That's fine, I don't mind waiting. It gives me time to people-watch a bit. I recognize some faces from my time walking around downtown the past couple of days, but most look unfamiliar.

A few groups of people are clustered together at their tables, leaned toward one another in deep conversations, their glasses nearly empty. At the far end of the bar by the restrooms is a couple with their heads bent low, foreheads nearly touching.

I scan the room, my gaze lingering on a group of guys in leather vests at a booth in the corner. My pulse jumps at the thought of seeing Nova again. And my heart races as I search each face in the booth.

But he's not there.

My heart deflates a little, and I can't help but feel disappointed. It's a little silly really, considering I met him once.

"On the house. For the newest resident of Rosewood. Or something." A highball glass clanks against the bar top in front of me, a few drops splashing over the sides. Sprigs of mint and several lime wedges float inside.

My back presses against the chair as I reach for the mojito. "Thank you."

He nods, his gaze lingering on me for a moment longer than necessary. "You waitin' on someone?"

"Nope," I say, popping the P a little bit. "Just . . . exploring."

He nods as if he understands. "Sometimes it takes getting lost to find yourself."

I stare at him for a moment, unsure of what to say. His response was deeper than I was expecting.

"Well, I needed a pick-me-up after the week I've had, and the coffee shop closes at three, so." I hold out one hand, palm up in some half-shrug move.

I take a sip, letting the mint settle on my tongue for a moment. I glance up at the bartender, who's currently bracing himself against the bar top in front of me.

My brows scrunch in confusion. "Why do they close so early? Don't people in Rosewood drink coffee after three o'clock?"

The side of his mouth hooks into a smirk. "Coffee takes first shift, beer is on second, and tequila is on the third shift in Rosewood."

I laugh, the sound laced with both humor and surprise. "Well, I'll keep that in mind."

He taps the bar twice and pushes off. "Holler if you need somethin'."

"Will do," I murmur.

He meanders over to the other side of the bar, and I let my attention drift to the big TV on the wall. It's muted, but the closed captioning is on, so I can read everything they're saying. It's some kind of game show that I've never heard of before, but it seems entertaining.

It's the perfect kind of distraction I needed tonight. The TV at the motel room isn't working properly, so it only gets four fuzzy channels. They said it would be fixed by Friday, but hopefully, I'll be at Magnolia Lane by then.

I just have to drum up enough courage to stay there.

I take another sip of my drink, fiddling with the edges of the coaster. I can feel someone's gaze on me, and I turn to see a guy sitting a few seats down on my right. His elbow is propped against the bar as he blatantly watches me with a serious expression on his face. His sandy blond hair falls over his forehead in a haphazard way, brushing against the thick slashes of his dark brows. He's good-looking by conventional standards, but there's something about him that seems off. Maybe it's because he's wearing a leather jacket and jeans and it's hot enough to cook an egg on the sidewalk outside.

I smile politely, not wanting to be rude—especially when I'm planning to put down some temporary roots here. But I'm not really interested in starting a conversation with him either.

I steal another glance a few minutes later, surprised to find his gaze unwavering. I shift in my seat, hoping a little movement will dislodge his stare.

It doesn't.

I tip my glass back and finish my drink. I can feel a knot forming in my stomach as I realize that I have to pass him as I leave. I'm sure I'm just being paranoid. Too many hours spent with too many true crime podcasts, Cora would say.

Just as I set my glass down, I hear something that stops me in my tracks.

"You lookin' for me, sweetheart?"

Tingles erupt down my spine at the low tenor next to my right ear. I do my best to tamper the relief and swallow the smirk that's begging to be let free. I shift my gaze over my shoulder, enough to see him in my peripheral vision without turning around completely.

"Nah, I'm just having a drink."

He chuckles, this smooth sound like gooey marshmallows on a fresh s'more. "It looks like you started without me."

I lift a shoulder and cave, the urge to drink him in is too strong. He's close, close enough for me to see exactly how rough his five o'clock shadow would feel against my skin. He smells like bergamot and the ocean, and I have to stop myself from running my nose along his neck.

He looks even better than I remembered. Over a head taller than me, despite the bar stool height. His broad shoulders and wind-swept hair. Even the light from the TV behind us casts him in a favorable, blue glow.

A quick flick of my gaze over his shoulder reveals an empty stool where that guy was.

"Oh, did I? Maybe you're just late." I arch a brow, letting the challenge linger in the air between us.

"To a date with you? Never." He smirks, his dimple winking at me. And I swear to god, that goddamn expression of his short-circuits something critical in my brain. He has no business being so attractive.

"If you think we're on a date right n—"

"Nah, you've got it twisted, sweetheart. This is us getting to know one another, giving you time so you feel good about your decision to let me take you out tomorrow." His voice dips low, laced with a simmering promise.

My mouth hangs open, and I feel a blush creep into my cheeks. He stands with an almost intimidating confidence, one hand on the back of my stool and eyes smoldering. I don't know whether to be aroused or amused. Probably both.

"You didn't even ask me out yet," I tell him, shaking my head a little.

"Formalities." He leans in close, his scruff scratching on my jaw and his lips at my ear. "You and me are fated, Evangeline."

"Does that line ever work on women?"

He inhales, his lips ghosting along my earlobe. "This is the first time I've ever said it, you tell me."

Against all rational thought, a smile blooms across my face. I press my tongue behind my teeth, a soft noise escaping my lips. "You're going to have to try harder than that, Casanova."

He pulls back slowly, hovering far enough for me to read his serious expression. "Challenge accepted, sweetheart."

12

EVANGELINE

AFTER ANOTHER MOJITO for me and a beer for him, we set out in search of food. I wasn't quite ready to go back to the solitude at the motel. And if I'm being honest with myself, I'm having entirely too much fun with him.

We kept it light in the bar, and when a couple of guys bearing the Reaper patch came over to talk to him, my stomach clenched. I thought he might've brushed me off. Or worse, turned into a different version of himself around his friends. Loud, crass, flipping from that blend of confident and charming to cocky. I've spent enough time around cocky asshole men to last me a lifetime.

But he surprised me. He said hello and introduced me, but it was a polite brush-off at best. A few words and a couple of nods, then turned back to me. We made small talk and played along with the trivia show on the TV behind the bar until my stomach growled.

"How do you feel about pizza?" He holds the door open, gesturing for me to step outside first.

The humidity greets us, wraps its heavy arms around my

shoulders as I step onto Main Street. The last of the sun's rays claw for purchase on the pavement between buildings behind us.

He flashes me a grin, skirting behind me to stand on my left, closest to the street.

My lips twist to the side in a rueful sort of smile. "We've had a longstanding love affair. Some might even say it was the first love of my life."

He tilts his head to the side, his thick dark blond hair falling over his forehead. "I thought every girl's first love is their daddy?"

My stomach clenches at the mention of my dad. Inevitably, it makes me think of my mom. And the fact that outside of one curt voicemail demanding I answer my phone when she calls, I haven't heard from them since I saw them outside the lawyer's office.

That itself isn't that uncommon. I routinely go months without talking to either of my parents. But after seeing them, despite their chilly reception, I had unconsciously planted a seed of hope.

Hope that whatever Nana Jo left Mom would be enough to thaw her out a little, soften her up into something more maternal, more caring.

But hope is a dangerous thing. And I know better than to let it sprout with her name on it.

I blink a few times, chasing away the drab thoughts of my parents.

"By that logic, your mom was your first love." I pack enough sass that it drips from my words like honey.

"First love?" He taps his bottom lip with his index finger, his face scrunched up like he's concentrating. It's all a ruse, though, his smirk peeking out from behind his hand. "Nah, don't know her."

I cut him a look, my brows raised high on my forehead. "Wait. You're telling me you've never been in love before?"

He dips his chin, tucking his hands into his front pockets as we stroll down the sidewalk. He looks at me from underneath his long black lashes. "Sure I have. But not the kind you're thinking of."

I watch him, my mouth parted and a question on the tip of my tongue. And then I get it. "A dog."

He chuckles, the sound full of mirth. "Nah, we weren't a pet kind of family."

Camaraderie bubbles underneath my skin, a sense of a shared childhood. "Neither were we. I asked for one every year for my birthday though." I let out a chuckle, but it's laced with too much self-deprecation to be joyful.

He cuts me look, sharp and probing.

"Anyway," I start, flicking my wrist in the air in front of me. "Back to your first love. Not a dog. Or a person." I glance across the street at the shops like they're going to give me a clue.

"Not yet, at least." He shrugs, a small smile playing on his lips as he gives me a slow perusal. "Maybe I've been waiting for the right person."

My breath catches at the way his gaze feels on my skin, warming a path that sinks into my veins.

He leans into me, his shoulder brushing mine, and throws me a verbal life raft. Like he can see me treading water with his last comment. "Art."

My eyes widen as I look at him in a new light. My gaze travels down his full sleeve of tattoos on one arm. Curiosity tingles down my spine. "Art?"

His mouth curls into a soft half-smile. "Aye. I spent two years out east at art school, came back home when I needed to, and finished here. Turned it into a career."

"Oh that's amazing. What's your medium?"

His gaze flicks from his tattoos to my face. "Nah, I'm not that kind of artist."

My face flushes for a moment, but I shrug off the embarrassment. I'm not all that artistic, despite Nana Jo's immense talent. None of those genes seemed to land on me.

I clear my throat. "What do you do then?"

"Custom artwork. Motorcycles and cars mostly, the odd boat."

I steal a look at his hands, wondering how dexterous his fingers must be to paint on someone's vehicle like that.

"Not what you expected?"

I flick my gaze up to his face. The skin around his eyes is tight, at odds with the smile on his face.

I take in his expression, my heart lurching at the vulnerability hidden beneath the surface.

My hair tickles my shoulders as I shake my head a few times. I squint, looking at him through my lashes. "I didn't have any expectations."

"Ach, c'mon, sweetheart. The bike. The leather kutte. This handsome face." He pauses to send me a wink and a roguish grin. "You're telling me you didn't have any expectations of me?"

I laugh. "I have expectations about this allegedly infamous pizza, but no, not about you—or this . . . friendship?" Somehow the last word comes out more like a question than I intended.

He tsks. "Ouch. Friend-zoned already?"

I roll my eyes, but it's more playful than sarcastic.

"Aye, it's true. We've got one of the best pizza joints in the country and we're nearly there. Authentic Neapolitan style and everything."

I nod, my stomach already on-board with this plan. "I think the only question left is: what do you like on your pizza?"

He stops suddenly, his head sinking back to bare his face to the sky. He breathes, this loud, noisy exhale that's somehow amused and dramatic. "Evangeline, please don't break my heart so soon."

I stop in front of him, tipping my head up to watch the amused curl of his lip.

"If you tell me you eat fruit on your pizza, I'm going to have to reconsider my earlier proposal."

My heart stutters over the word proposal, my mind sinking into flashes of lace and rings and white dresses.

Which is ridiculous.

I blink and force my mouth to curve into a smirk. "You know, peppers are technically a fruit."

His head falls forward into something neutral, a teasing sort of sigh slipping from his lips. He starts walking again, as if my answer allowed him to move again. "Bell peppers. I'll accept that," he says with a nod.

"But," I say, elongating the word as we cross the street. "I do love pineapple."

He clutches his chest, right over his heart in a dramatic sweep of his arm. "You wound me, sweetheart. Twice in one night. First, death by friend-zone and then pineapple. What a way to go." He sounds like he's lamenting, a sort of musical quality in his teasing voice.

A laugh bubbles up from my chest, the sound bouncing off the brick walls of the buildings around us. I can't help but feel a sense of ease around him, like we've known each other for years instead of a few hours.

"So, ready to dive into something personal yet, sweetheart?" His tone is casual, matching his speed as we stroll down Main Street.

I want to be annoyed with the pet name, I do. But there's something about the way his tone drops when his tongue curls around that word. It causes a shiver to run down my spine and my heart to race.

"I don't know, should I be afraid?" I tease, glancing from him to the sidewalk in front of us.

A group of teenagers are outside one of the coffee shops, standing in a loose circle, talking and laughing.

Nova chuckles, a deep, rich sound that makes something in my lower stomach clench in the best way possible. "Nah, you don't ever need to be afraid with me. But I'm just curious about the person that I'm going to be spending all my time with."

I peek up at him from the corner of my eye, my heart skipping a beat at the idea of spending all my free time with him. Something I seem to have an abundance of lately.

But I don't let myself get too carried away. This isn't the plot of some romcom, even if this town feels like it was plucked straight out of one, the hero included.

"Well, what do you want to know?" I keep my tone light, content to see how this plays out.

He hums, pretending to mull over a question like he hasn't had it ready for the last thirty minutes. "Let's start with something easy. What brought you to Rosewood?"

My gaze drops to the perfectly square cement sidewalk. "My grandmother left me her—oomph."

Something hard crashes into my shoulder, stealing my words and sending me careening into Nova on my right. I stumble to the side, but I don't fall completely.

"Oh, shit," someone murmurs from the left.

I can barely hear them over the thundering of my heart, my adrenaline spiking so quickly, if not briefly. I'm not a clumsy person usually, but I didn't want to eat pavement in front of Nova and everyone else walking around downtown.

"You okay, Evangeline?" His voice is a low rumble next to my ear, his hands spanning across my ribs.

I nod, swallowing down the tremble in my throat as I steady myself. "Yeah, just lost my footing for a second there. I'm fine though."

Nova's hands linger as I straighten up, slowly falling away. He takes a step, but not behind me. No, he pulls the ultimate protective gestures and steps in front of me.

"Shit, I'm sorry about that," a guy says, hands outstretched toward me. He's late teens, shaggy brown hair and face twisted in a wince.

"It's fine." I wave him off.

But the kid doesn't step back. He doesn't take his gaze from Nova in front of me. He tilts his chin down a little. "No disrespect meant, Casanova."

I see a flutter in the side of Nova's jaw, but that's about all I can see from this angle. After a long tense moment, he nods. The kid visibly exhales, taking several quick steps behind him.

There's something off about the whole encounter, but I don't have time to question it. The scent of freshly baked bread and fresh garlic permeate the air, distracting me from my curiosity.

13

EVANGELINE

I FOLLOW MY NOSE, stopping in front of The Slice. Just around the corner on one of the side streets off of Main. Rustic, weathered bricks and wrought iron details give the pizzeria a modern take on old world charm. A cobblestone pathway connects the sidewalk to the entrance, three tables on either side making a small courtyard.

A hand-painted wooden sign sticks out of an overflowing barrel of bright flowers next to the door. The Slice written with a cursive flourish in white. Soft strings of Edison bulbs illuminate the space above each cluster of tables, creating an inviting ambience.

A bell above the door jingles as Nova opens it for me. The second he steps foot inside behind me, someone behind the counter yells his name.

Nova ghosts his hand along my lower back as he stands next to me. "Marco, what's up, man?"

One of the two men behind the counter flashes us a grin as he dusts his hands off on a white apron tied around his waist. He has a mop of dark curls tucked underneath a black beanie. Flour handprints and smudges dot his pants and there's what looks like pizza sauce splatter on the sleeve of his white The Slice tee.

Marco braces his palms on the counter and leans forward. "Usual tonight? Eddie here will ring you out, but I'll put your order in now." He jerks his head to the side, where another employee, Eddie, stands behind a cash register and takes care of the customers ahead of us.

Nova presses forward, his palm now resting on the small of my back. What about that space makes these traitorous tingles erupt? "Nah, not tonight. Thanks, though. We're just going to grab a few slices for here."

Marco's grin turns sly as he glances between the two of us. "All right, all right. I got you, Nova." He winks, tapping the counter twice as he leans back. "Eddie'll take care of ya. But you holler if you change your mind."

Nova nods once. "Thanks, Marco."

WE SETTLE in at one of the tables in the corner outside, a light breeze rustling the flowers in the surrounding planters. The red and white petals dance, their stems bending left and right.

Nova sets our plates in the middle of the table, and I set our drinks down beside them. The scent of fresh tomato sauce and melted cheese fills my nose. He nudges my selection toward me, the slice of pepperoni and pineapple big enough to almost spill over the edges of the plate.

"Thanks for dinner," I murmur. "You didn't have to do that."

"Please, it's nothing," he says, pulling his two pieces of sausage, pepperoni, and mushroom pizza closer to him.

The crust is crispy on the outside and chewy on the inside, with just the perfect amount of sweet and tangy tomato sauce and melted mozzarella cheese.

"Besides, it's all part of my grand plan to woo you."

I choke, sputtering a little at the ease he said that. Nova pushes my ice water closer to me, a wrinkle forming between his brows.

I accept the cup and take a drink, willing my heart to slow down at the spike of adrenaline. I blink a few times. "Sorry, went down the wrong way or something."

He looks at me, something mischievous glinting in the corner of his gaze. He tucks into his own dinner and we eat in comfortable silence for a few minutes. The ambiance of the pizzeria and the soft chatter of the other people around us all adding to the cozy atmosphere.

He breaks the quiet with a soft chuckle. "You know, I don't think I've ever wooed a woman before. How am I doing?"

I grin, taking another bite to give myself time to choose my words carefully. "I've never been wooed before, so I can't say for certain."

"Bullshit." He leans forward with a chuckle.

I wipe my greasy fingers on a napkin and tip my chin up. "What? It's true."

He looks at me for a moment, his gaze sweeping my face and falling down the slope of my neck and back up again. "A gorgeous woman like you? That's a damn shame, sweetheart." His voice is low, a rich tenor of promise and heat.

I feel heat rise to my cheeks, but I force myself to hold his gaze. "I guess it takes the right person."

His eyes flare for a moment, the air around us vibrating with tension. Understanding flashes across his face, his expression melting into a self-assured grin. He swipes his thumb across his bottom lip, dragging his lips into one of those panty-dropping smiles I've only read about in books.

A tiny worry furrows into my consciousness, whispering that

I'm over my head with him. But the moment passes as quickly as it came, and I push the thought away.

Truthfully, I don't know what I'm doing. I'm cautiously optimistic about my time in Rosewood. Following some instinct to stop living my life weighed down by the expectations of others. To be more spontaneous and say yes to more invitations. To stop worrying about judgment cast by people who don't deserve a say in my life.

To choose fun for the sake of it.

Bathed in the moonlight and fairy lights, Nova looks like a six-foot-two tattooed embodiment of fun. Carefree, playful, flirtatious, creative.

And so goddamn attractive it makes my thighs clench every time he sends me a flirty wink.

It's too tempting to resist.

He's too tempting to resist.

No, that's not true. I could resist his allure. But I don't want to.

Decision made, I hold my hand out, palm up. "Give me your phone."

The lights above us cast a warm glow over the table. The temperature cooled down into something much more bearable since we got here. There's a slight breeze that wisps through the courtyard every five minutes or so. It's perfect outside. The stars light up the sky far above us, the low hum of laughter from everyone outside.

I'd have to be senseless to not feel the romanticism in it all. But maybe I'm caught up in the thrill of flirting.

"Why? Trying to see if I'm talking to other women already?" He arches a brow, slowly reaching into his pocket.

I blink in surprise. "Do your dates go through your phone often?"

"I thought you said this wasn't a date," he quips, sinking his teeth into his bottom lip.

"It's not." My retort lashes out quickly, but it does nothing to cool the heat in my cheeks.

"I'm not." He lifts a shoulder, his teeth releasing the hold on his lip. "Talking to other women." His thumb sweeps across the screen of his phone, and a second later, he sets it in the palm of my hand, unlocked. He holds my gaze the entire time. "And no, I don't make it a habit of giving anyone access to my phone."

I nod and school my expression into something neutral like that news doesn't please me. It's an irrational thought, and I brush it aside. Instead, I add my phone number in his contacts. My thumb hovers over the name, internally debating if I should save it under something quirky or memorable.

But in the end, I just type in my name.

As I hand his phone back, our fingers brush against each other, sending a jolt of electricity up my arm. I try to ignore the sensation as I watch him lock his phone and tuck it into his pocket without looking at it. My heart thumps wildly inside my chest, anticipation swelling inside.

The silence between us stretches out, neither of us wanting to break it. It's comfortable, though, not awkward.

He's the one to finally speak up. "You know, I never did get to finish that question earlier. What brought you to Rosewood?"

I take a deep breath, trying to keep my voice steady at the topic change. I thought for sure he'd call me out on giving him my number. "My grandmother left me her house in her will."

"I'm sorry for your loss," he says softly, his hand hovering over mine.

I nod, not trusting myself to speak. The memories of my grandmother still hurt. Even though it's been a whole year, it feels like I've been missing her in my life for much, much longer.

The moment is broken by the sound of his phone chirping in his pocket. I don't know what's more surprising: the fact that he has his phone on any noise at all or the fact that it's a chorus of what sounds like chirping chicks.

He pulls out his phone and checks the notification before letting out a sigh. "I hate to cut this short—"

"It's fine." And it is. I was going to head home soon anyway. Somewhere between the first mojito and now, I decided that tomorrow is the day I start going through Nana Jo's house.

My house.

He stands up from the table and reaches out a hand to help me up. I take it, feeling the same jolt of electricity as before. "Let me walk you back to your car."

I let him pull me to my feet, enjoying the way his hands feel on me more than I probably should. He rests his fingertips along my back the entire walk back to The Wild Boar, ushering me around townspeople strolling around downtown. We don't talk much, the mood shifting quicker than I understand. But it's just as well, there are plenty of people to look at, even at this time of night.

"I'm just right there." I tip my head to the left, indicating my car parked alongside others at the curb.

He stops, turning toward me. His eyes meet mine, the blue seeming darker in the nighttime, before slowly dropping to my lips. Instinctively, I swipe my tongue across them.

He makes a noise in the back of his throat, low and muted. Pained. The air surrounding us thickens, anticipation sounding across my skin like a chorus line of tap dancers.

He sinks his fingers into the hair at the nape of my neck, letting them tangle in the wild strands. The heat from his palm warms my skin, and I unconsciously arch into his hold.

Nova leans in as he tilts my face toward him. My lips part on an exhale, my heart thundering in my ear, and I wait.

Those two seconds feel like an eternity, but finally—finally—

his lips press against mine. They're soft, plush—gentle. A sweep of his mouth along mine.

It's a prelude. A promise of what's to come.

The kiss is still slow and languid, as if we have all the time in the world. As if we're not standing on the sidewalk in the middle of downtown.

As if this isn't our first kiss but our thousandth.

His mouth moves over mine, coaxing my lips to part further. The kiss deepens, our bodies pressing closer and closer together. I can feel the hard planes of his chest against mine, the heat of his skin seeping through the thin material of my shirt.

We break apart, exhaling quick pants of air, the silence between us heavy with unspoken words.

"I'm sorry. I have to go," he murmurs an inch from my mouth.

I nod, still trying to catch my breath from the best kiss of my life. "Yeah."

He leans in once more, dragging his lips across my jaw, until he reaches my ear. "Goodnight, sweetheart."

"Goodnight," I whisper as he pulls away.

I watch as he walks backward, toward The Wild Boar. A grin tugs up the edges of his mouth. It's a smile that's joyful and slightly smug. With the way that man just kissed me, I'll allow a flash of his ego.

He pauses outside the front door of the bar. "Get inside your car, Evangeline" he calls, his dimples popping out.

I startle, coming back to myself. My cheeks warm as I walk toward my car. Just before I slide into the front seat, I look over my shoulder.

He's still there, waiting to make sure I get in.

I hate the way it only endears him to me more. At least that's the lie I'm telling myself.

WELCOME TO ROSEWOOD

IT'S YOUR FAVORITE NEIGHBOR, ***and I'm back with the juiciest gossip in town. It's the moment we've all been waiting for since we bid one of ours adieu last year.***

Magnolia Lane has the lights on. And rumor has it, a new Carter girl is in town. Permanently. The late Josephine Carter was always busy around town, and it seems her granddaughter will be too.

Hold on tight, my dear neighbors, for the plot thickens. Rosewood's newest resident was seen downtown arm-in-arm with one of the Reapers. And not just any Reaper either, but a St. James Reaper.

Can you feel the anticipation thickening in the air? Will she secure a coveted place on the back of a bike? Or will she disappear as swiftly as Delilah's apple pie at the summer festival?

Only time will tell.

Until next time,
—Rose

14

BANE

"NICE OF YOU TO JOIN US." I lean forward, the front legs of the chair I'm sitting in slamming to the concrete floor.

"Yeah, well, next time you take the meeting. Some of us have shit to do," Nova grumbles as he sinks into the chair across from me. He leans to the side, looking around me toward the kitchen behind us. "He's not even here yet."

I glance at the clock on the wall next to me. "He had to make sure Hunter was asleep. He'll be here in a minute. "

That's about how long it takes to get from their house to mine. Living next door to my cousins has its perks, and that is definitely one of them.

"He could've brought him here. That kid's ability to fall asleep anywhere is a superpower."

"Remember when he fell asleep at Lockwood Park?" I laugh, the memory of him curled up at the top of the playground, right in the little cubby space at the beginning of the plastic slide.

Nova chuckles too, his eyes lighting up the way they always do when we talk about the five-year-old ball of energy in our life.

"Yeah, and Silas had to climb all the way up there to pick him up. He must've been, what? Four?"

"He was three-and-a-half and we had taken him to the beach all day. He was exhausted by four o'clock," Silas says by way of greetings, striding into the room.

"That's right," I say around a grin. "That's right about when he started his nap strikes."

"Dark days, brother, dark days," Nova says, his shoulders shaking in a faux shudder.

Silas glares at both of us, pulling out a chair and sinking into it. His mouth pinches into a frown. "We don't talk about those days. We agreed."

"Of course. I would never talk about the six months you spent driving him around, listening to Taylor Swift on repeat just so he would take a thirty-minute nap." I manage to get the whole sentence out. Barely. My lip twitches, and I know once Nova breaks, I won't be able to hold it in either.

"And we would never talk about the day you started singing her songs without even thinking about it," Nova says. Laughter swallows up the last few words, and that's all it takes.

I let my amusement free, the chuckles lifting some of the perpetual weight around my neck. "What was it? *Exile*?"

"*All Too Well*," Nova says.

Silas plants his elbow on the table and points his index finger at Nova. "First off, why do you even remember that? And secondly"—he points between the two of us—"you're both a bunch of assholes."

He drops his hand to the table, fiddling with the baby monitor in front of him. It's the same one he's had since Hunter was a baby, giving him a video feed of his room.

"Yeah, yeah. Let's get into it. I'm beat." Nova sighs, letting the laughter fall.

Silas arches a brow, his gaze on the monitor. The sound is off, but there's a volume indicator on the bottom of the screen. "Tired from a day spent drinking?"

Nova scoffs and rolls his eyes. "Fuck off, Silas. I was working on the Blake order this morning."

"Phase one or two?" I ask.

Nova's talent is unmatched, not only in our area, but quite possibly the whole country. That guy has more creative talent in his fingertips than some people ever have in a lifetime. He's good. Too fucking good to be stuck in Rosewood.

But he doesn't see it that way. He chose to come back home, help put together the dream the three of us have had for the compound and the Reapers since we were kids.

"One," he says. "All the file said was red, no animals. Do you know how many options that gives me?"

"Too many," I murmur with a nod. "But you can do it, man. There's a reason your clients book out a year in advance for your work. You'll figure it out."

"I always do," he says, his gaze on me.

"Back to The Wild Boar," Silas says, tapping his fingertip against the top of the baby monitor. "I don't want to leave Hunter alone too much longer."

I jerk my chin toward the direction of their house. "He's fine. You've got eyes on him, and you're sixty seconds away if he wakes up."

Silas looks at me, his face drawn tight and worry etched along his brow. "A lot can happen in sixty seconds."

"Aye, but not to Hunter and not to us. We're triple protected behind security and fences," I assured him.

"Eddie called us in because he's noticed an uptick in out-of-towners in the last two weeks. At first, he chalked it up to tourist season, people visiting local family members," Nova says.

"Why didn't he tell us his concerns sooner?" I ask.

Nova lifts a shoulder and lets it fall down. "Fuck if I know.

But if I had to guess, I'd say he wasn't sure. Until tonight. When he caught some assholes dealing in the back of the bar."

I lean forward in my chair. Tension lines my neck instantly. "Who?"

"Eddie didn't recognize 'em, no visible affiliation. But he remembers seeing Crestview on one of their IDs when they ordered a round."

"Motherfuckers." I grit my teeth and shake my head.

"We don't know that yet." Silas continues to tap his finger on the top of the monitor, his speed getting quicker. "Not every asshole in Rosewood is a Reaper, so we can't assume the same about the Hell Hounds."

"No, but we can assume that if they're pulling shit at The Wild Boar, then they're either testing our boundaries, seeing if we're still strong enough to hold 'em. Or they're looking for trouble. Trouble we're not in the business of fixing anymore." I keep my voice calm, despite the anger swirling inside of me. It rises like a wave, growing bigger and bigger each time.

We put everything we had into ending the war and getting out of the game. It took Ray—my uncle, their dad, our president—and it nearly took Nova. We lost too many brothers during those years. And I'll be damned if all our sacrifice was in vain.

We may have taken ourselves off the board, but they're mistaken if they think we're out of commission.

We just remade the board.

One where we prosper, mostly above the board finances, and live without the constant threat of bloodshed. We created a new kind of living, a brotherhood born of camaraderie and not coercion. The Hell Hounds could have followed suit. But they chose to stay rooted in the old ways.

I mull over ideas on next steps, trying to find the flaws in each and adjusting. "I'm happy to send them a reminder of our agreement."

"Nah, not yet. Check-in with Redford first, see if he's noticed anything. Where are the guys Eddie caught now?" Silas asks.

Sheriff Anthony Redford was a year out from his retirement now. We've always had an understanding between us, but we grew into an arrangement once we pulled the club out of the shit right about the time Hunter was born.

But all that's gonna change when he retires and his protégé, Ethan Bellfleur, steps in as sheriff. I caught him trying to throw his weight around just two weeks ago, the pompous dick.

Nova runs his hand across his jaw. "Said we were his first call. Didn't have the manpower to restrain both of the guys, and they split when he called me."

My gaze narrows on him. "And why did he call you and not me?"

Nova looks at me, his jaw flexing. "Am I not a Reaper? A St. James?"

I settle back into my chair, folding my arms across my chest and settling in for the shit he's trying to stir.

I don't answer his questions, they're rhetorical and we all know the answers. But he got out, for a couple years at least. And Silas and I did our best to shield him from all the shit that was flying daily when we were growing up. So it's yeah, he's a Reaper, but he's more a modern-day one. And that's something I'm grateful for, even if he doesn't understand it.

The shit I've seen—the shit I've done—it haunts me if I let it. I'm glad he wasn't here for those years.

I keep my face neutral, not giving anything away. "Usually I field those calls, that's all I'm saying."

He nods slowly, but the tension still lingers. "Probably because I was just there."

"When, just now?" Silas narrows his eyes at his younger brother.

Nova rolls his head slowly, looking at Silas with a carefully blank expression. "Why don't you just say what you want to ask me?"

I watch them, my gaze ping-ponging between the two like it's a tennis match and not a casual conversation between brothers.

Silas's brows cave in, and a moment later, he offers him a small nod. "You told Ma you were meeting someone at The Wild Boar."

Nova exhales through his nose, the sound thick with exasperation. He shakes his head, the corner of his mouth curling into a smirk, and I already know whatever comes out of it will rile Silas up.

"Man, you need to get laid."

And there it is.

Silas sits up straight, tension vibrating his body like it's a live wire. "We're not talking about my sex life."

15

BANE

"SEX LIFE?" Nova says somewhere between a scoff and a laugh. "Now I know you've been talking to Ma too much. Say it with me brother: fucking."

Quick as a snake strike, Silas leans over the side of the table and tries to push his shoulder. Nova blocks him, and the chairs scrape against the wood floor as they try to fight for dominance.

Normally, I'd be all-in for their stupid show of affection, but it's been a long week and it's fucking Monday.

"Are you done yet?" I bark out the question, loud enough to break through their ribbing.

"Yeah, yeah," Nova says, brushing invisible lint off his shoulder. "I'm just saying: Silas needs to get laid, then he won't be so worried about my sex life." He mocks the last two words, sending Silas a pointed glare.

"So, you admit it. You're seeing someone. I hope it's not one of Helen's girls. I had to kick two out of the clubhouse just last week."

Nova's head rears back, mouth parted and eyes wide. "Jesus,

man, no. Give me a little credit, yeah?" He flicks his gaze to me. "Don't we have more important things to talk about?"

I dip my head in acknowledgement. Usually, it's Silas keeping Nova on track, so this role reversal is new. "Aye, when you were there, did anything seem off?"

Nova presses his shoulders into the back of the chair, stretching his legs out in front of him. "It's a Monday night, normal crowd. No one stood out."

"What do you think?" I level a look at Silas. He's the president of the Reapers for a reason, even if he doesn't think he deserves the title. "Should we call a meeting?"

He runs his hand across his jaw, scratching it almost absentmindedly. "Nah, not yet. But tell a few of the guys and start doing patrols. Nothing official, but I want eyes on the town at least four times a day. Especially the perimeter. Look for anything suspicious, places they could be holding up."

I nod my agreement, drumming my fingers along my leg underneath the table. I pause, looking at my cousins. "Who's gonna tell Aunt Dixie?"

"Not it," Nova says instantly.

"What are you, five?" Silas scoffs.

"Maybe, but you'll still break the news to Ma that the Hell Hounds are back and sniffing around. You know she doesn't believe in don't shoot the messenger," Nova says.

"We don't even know if they're back. Everything we have is circumstantial," I interject.

I watch the way they look at each other, like they can communicate telepathically or some shit. No matter how close the three of us are, there will always be something that ties the two of them tighter. Every once in a while, a little speck of jealousy worms its way into my veins, leaving a path of anger and longing in its wake.

Sometimes I wish I had that kind of connection with someone. A sibling. But then I remember who my parents are and those ugly feelings dry up quicker than the beer tent at the summer festival. It might've made my life easier, but I can't imagine subjecting another person to that kind of childhood. I scraped by thanks to these two assholes.

Cousins that feel more like brothers. Men who helped me up when I needed it and stood next to me even when I said I didn't.

Them and my aunt.

And that's enough.

I let my fingers settle their rhythm on my leg. "I'll let her know. She can't go into her normal smothering, not when she's got surgery in a couple weeks and Hunter to look after."

"It's because she's got Hunter that she will. If you think she was bad when we were growing up, it's nothing on her with a grandbaby," Silas says. "That woman is a bear when she feels threatened."

"Nah, not a bear. An elephant." One of those fierce African elephant mothers. They go to great lengths to protect their young.

When I was in eighth grade, mono tore through our school. It laid me out for two weeks. My old man was on the road a lot, running shit for Uncle Ray. Aunt Dixie came to check on me a few days in, took one look around, and when she didn't see my mom, she took me with her.

From that moment on, I always had a room at Aunt Dixie's. It became my safe haven. Her brand of affection wasn't ever the cookie-cutter shit you saw on TV, but she showed it in other ways. Actions more befitting our lifestyle with the Reapers, especially when we were growing up.

I still remember the look on her face when she stormed the Hell Hounds favorite bar. A daughter of one of their patched members set Nova up, flirted with him long enough to set the trap. He got nine stitches that night.

He was seventeen.

Aunt Dixie looked like hell on wheels that night. Stormed up to their bikes outside their bar and took a knife to their tires. Pulled out a tire iron and remodeled the bike of the girl's father.

It wasn't retribution so much as a warning. A first and final strike.

She had the entire club behind her, but she may as well have gone solo for the cloud of rage she floated on. She wrote her message with every flick and swing. Expressing her emotions in destruction.

Even though we squashed our differences with the Hell Hounds years ago, and they seemed to benefit from our retirement, Aunt Dixie never forgot. Still quick to pull the trigger on anything to do with the Hell Hounds, especially if it involves violence.

I nod a few times. "Well, maybe we put her on need-to-know. No need to stir that pot prematurely."

"That crazy woman," Silas grumbles. "If she gets a wild hair and does something and fucks her shoulder up even more, her doctor is gonna riot."

The thought of anyone talking to Aunt Dixie like that brings a smile to my face. "I'd pay to see that," I murmur. "She'd hear him out and then she'd hand him his own ass, and he'd say thank you by the time she was done."

Low chuckles fill the room.

"Yeah, well, he's the best surgeon in five counties, so unless you two wanna start this process over again, we better hope she's not going to sneak off and wreak havoc on the Hell Hounds," Silas says.

"By the way, I heard about your little deal with Ma," Nova says with a grin.

Silas groans, letting his head fall backward to look at the ceiling.

"What deal?" I ask, glancing between them.

Nova smirks, folding his arms across his chest. "The one where she got his grumpy ass to agree to a nanny."

"About fucking time," I grumble.

Silas snaps his head forward and glares at me. I accept his shit with a deadpan expression of my own. I've had more than enough practice on how to deal with his moods. And they're all varying shades of annoyed.

"What? You know it's true. I love Hunter, but that boy is a St. James through and through. Your ma can't keep up with him and run the front office for the garages."

"Plus, she physically can't lift anything for like six weeks while she recovers," Nova says.

"Why do you think I agreed to it?" He runs his hands over his head, letting his palm hook the back of his neck. Stress tugs the sides of his mouth into a frown.

"Yeah? And how many did you say no to already?" Nova asks, but he says it like he already knows the answer.

"Under our new agreement? None." Silas looks entirely too smug about that.

I narrow my eyes on him. "And when did this agreement happen?"

"Two days ago," Nova deadpans.

"Not important," Silas says at the same time as he waves his hand dismissively. "What's important is that we keep an eye on this, quietly for now, yeah?"

"Yeah. No moves until we have a better understanding," I agree.

Silas raps his knuckles on the table and pushes his chair back. He swipes the baby monitor with one hand and pushes his chair in with the other. He looks at me, the side of his mouth twitching. "Good luck with your call tomorrow."

"Asshole," I grumble to his back as he walks out the way he came in, a chuckle following in his wake.

Nova clamps his hand on my shoulder, patting it a couple of times as he walks toward the door. "You workin' tomorrow?"

"I'm always working."

"Yeah, heard that. See you at the garage," he calls over his shoulder.

The back door closes with a soft snick, punctuating their departure. I sit at the table for another few minutes, listening to the silence of the house echo around me.

I let my mind spiral out all the different scenarios in which the Hell Hounds incite a fight. None of them end well, but that's the nature of our world. Violence is always lurking around the corner, waiting to pounce when we least expect it.

I shake my head, clearing the thoughts away. There's no use getting worked up over something that hasn't even happened yet.

One day at a time, that's all I can do.

16

EVANGELINE

I PUSH open the door connecting the garage to the back hall of Nana Jo's house—my house.

God, that's going to take some time to get used to.

Love and longing roll over me with the first step. Everything looks exactly the same. I don't know why, but I'd thought it might look different. Cleaned out, maybe.

But it's the same. Nana Jo is still firmly stamped in every piece of this room, right down to the mismatched hooks on the wall to my left. Her favorite quilted jacket is still hanging on the first hook, the magenta bright against the cream colored walls.

Grief swells up inside of me, a tidal wave of emotion. It's not the unending sadness I thought it might be. Threads of love and gratitude braid around the grief. All blanketed by a sense of home. The one place that I always felt accepted.

Magnolia Lane was a safe haven for me once. And I have a feeling it just might be that again.

Determination floods my system as I make my way through the back hall into the kitchen area. It runs almost the length of the house along the back, bleeding right into a casual eating area.

The formal dining room shares a wall with the back hall, separated from the kitchen by a set of six-paned glass French doors.

In all the summers I spent here, we never once ate in the formal dining room. She preferred to spend time in the kitchen, eating her breakfast at the round blonde oak table or snacking at the island or drinking her coffee on the back patio.

She always said a house should be more than wood and paint. It should be a *home*, a reflection of the people who live in it. And she lived most of her life in this house, got married and raised her children here.

But as I look around, it's not *just* Nana Jo's life reflecting from every shelf and inside every cabinet.

Grandpa Dalton is here. His old banjo on the built-in bookshelf in the living room. I can almost hear the twang of the strings and the deep rumble of his voice as he'd sing a made-up song. His record player and vinyl collection that we still added to after he was gone.

A bouquet of dried peonies from Aunt Hazel's garden.

And me.

So many pieces of me.

Framed photos of me with Nana Jo and my cousins. An old wooden orange box full of our flea market finds. A hand-painted tea set for two, a vintage music box that never quite worked right, kitschy salt and pepper shakers, a set of quirky needlepoints.

We spent countless hours perusing flea markets and yard sales, always hunting for the perfect thing to bring home. Sometimes we turned it into a game. Who could find the most random thing or who could get the best thing for under ten dollars.

I take a deep breath, spinning in a slow circle around the living room. The memories soothe the ache in my chest. I know I'll always miss her, but this house is still filled with her love, even now. And I know even after I add my own touches to it, that will never change.

I'M on hour three of cleaning out the living room, sweat dampening the back of my neck and my back starting to ache from the constant up and down. But the first thing I did was go through Grandpa Dalton's vinyl collection and make sure the record player works.

It's hot as hell in here. I thought about turning on the air conditioning, but it really needs some fresh air in here.

Suspicion wrinkles my brow every time I think about how relatively clean it still is inside. It's not like I expected it to be reclaimed by nature or something, but I didn't think it'd be so . . . normal. Sure, it's a little dusty and the air is weird and stale, but overall, it looks like it's been empty for a month, not a year. I keep expecting to come across some mail or paperwork clueing me in to who's been looking after the inside of the house. But so far, it's been mostly old birthday cards and a handful of magazines.

I've separated everything into piles. Things I'm going to keep over by the velvet chaise, everything I think someone in the family might want by the bookcase, and then everything else in one big area in the middle of the room. All of those things are open for anyone to take, otherwise, I'll donate them.

Or maybe I'll have a yard sale of my own. It could be a sort of tribute to Nana Jo, considering we must've gone to hundreds of them over the years. A small smile tugs up the side of my mouth at the idea. I kind of like the notion that a girl and her grandma might stop by *my* yard sale and find treasure of their own.

My phone vibrates on the coffee table next to me, pulling me from my yard sale day dreams.

> Unknown Number: How do you feel about seafood?

I blame the heavy emotions of the day for the slow speed it takes to connect the dots. But when I finally do, I can't resist the urge to tease him, just a little bit.

I sink my teeth into my bottom lip and absently swipe away the perspiration on the back of my neck. I snag my iced latte from the table and settle into the couch. I drink the last dredges of my coffee for flirtatious courage.

Me: Who is this?

His reply is instant, like he'd been watching his phone.

Unknown Number: your man

Me: Charlie?

Unknown Number: who the fuck is Charlie

Me: my man?

Unknown Number: you're not as funny as you think you are, sweetheart

A giggle slips free without my permission. It's that damn use of a nickname. I can almost hear the way he says it, all low and seductive.

Ugh.

I'll admit, I'm *not* feeling my most comical right now. I've been cleaning and organizing for hours now, and that would be enough even if I hadn't stayed up until one o'clock in the morning watching *Sons of Anarchy* on my phone. I guess you could say I was feeling curious.

Me: I don't know. I'm feeling like Charlie might be my man after all the time I spent with him last night.

He doesn't reply right away, and I try not to read into it too much. I glance at the ornate metal clock on the wall and realize with a start that it's already noon. He's probably working, and maybe he only had a few minutes to chat.

Or maybe he didn't realize I was teasing?

I dismiss that thought almost as quickly as I have it. I like what I know of Nova, which admittedly isn't that much, but he doesn't seem like the type of guy to run away from a little misunderstanding. Even if it was deliberate on my end.

I tap the edges of my phone for a minute before I go into our text and save his contact information under Nova. I exit out of everything and toss my phone to the spot next to me on the couch. Right as I push to stand, my phone vibrates again.

Giddy anticipation pricks at my fingertips, and I turn it over to see a notification with his name on it. I feel like a teenager again, that same sort of fluffy light feeling swirling around inside my stomach.

Nova: There are only three possible Charlies in Rosewood right now. One is 75, one is married, and the other is accounted for.

My mouth parts, shock stealing my words completely.

Me: I have so many questions. How do you even know that?

Nova: It's a small town.

Me: it's not that small!

Nova: it is when you've lived here most of your life

Me: You didn't really check, did you?

Nova: and if I did?

Me: That's . . . I don't know, kind of crazy

Nova: only for you, sweetheart.

I feel my cheeks flush at his words, and I quickly look around the room to make sure no one is here. I'm still alone, Simon and Garfunkel singing about silence in the background.

Me: You don't even know me.

Nova: I know enough

I bite the inside of my cheek and stand up to pace a little bit. Was Cora right about him? Is he bad news? Or does he just flirt in a unique sort of way?

I find myself nodding, bolstered by the idea that he might've been riffing off of me. Maybe we're both bad at tease-flirting on texts.

I stop and let myself imagine saying no to him, not spending any more time together. Disappointment sinks like a weight in my gut.

Okay. There's my answer then. I throw Cora's caution to the wind and text him back.

Me: There's good seafood in Rosewood?

Nova: Technically, Tide & Table is in Glendale, right outside Rosewood.

Nova: They have the best pan-seared scallops on Tuesday nights.

Me: I'm cleaning out my grandma's house tonight.

Me: but I'm free tomorrow

Nova: I'll pick you up at 7

Me: I'll meet you there.

Nova: Don't trust me, sweetheart?

I tamp down the urge to giggle, rolling my lips inward for a moment. My hair falls off of my shoulder, brushing against the screen of my phone. I trap a breath in my lungs as I tap out a reply.

Me: you gotta earn it first

Nova: oh, I'll earn more than that

I exhale, amusement riding my senses. He better live up to the expectation he's creating, or I'm going to be so disappointed.

My fingers flutter across my lips as I remember the way his mouth felt on mine. God, how was that only last night?

Me: promises, promises

Nova: I always keep my word

The record stops, the staticky scratch echoing around the room. I toss my phone to the couch with a grin and cross the room to rifle through the vinyl.

I find the perfect record to play and get back to work, a noticeable spring in my step.

17

BANE

NOTHING CLEARS my mind quicker than a ride through the backroads of Rosewood. The sun starting its descent into the horizon, bathing everything in that forgiving golden glow.

Out here, I can see for miles on either side of the road. It's mostly residential, the plots of land large enough that you can't just cross your yard and grab a cup of sugar from your neighbor. Not like it is on the compound. If you lived out here and you needed something quick, you'd be fucked. Especially if your neighbor wasn't home. It'd take you ten minutes from your door to theirs—*if* you drove an UTV. Or a golf cart, like the Merriweathers do.

But looking at these properties, I get why people decided to live so far away from each other. Every yard is landscaped by both man and nature. Pines, cypress, and ash trees, some tall enough to dwarf the houses they surround. Flowering bushes and manicured lawns. Vegetable gardens and acreage left to grow wild.

The houses themselves are generally architecturally impressive and run the gamut of style. Traditional and modern takes on the farmhouse, Southern cottages, the occasional colonial.

I can see the appeal. Your own space to shape and mold into your tastes.

Silas gave me the green light to build whatever I want on the compound a couple years ago, but I continue to stay in the house next door instead. It's enough for me.

We've got more land than we know what to do with, and even though it's considered Reaper property, technically, it's St. James land. Reginald St. James, our great-grandfather, bought the land all those generations ago. And now it's ours—mine, Silas's, and Nova's—as stipulated in our grandfather's will.

Living next door to my cousins isn't so bad though, even if I'm in my parents' old house. We're not far from work or the clubhouse, and Aunt Dixie's a stone's throw away too.

Sometimes I feel like I'm fifteen again, holding up in one of their spare rooms like my own house isn't twenty feet away. Nova always tells me to just move my ass in. Called us three men and a toddler for a few years for how often I spent time over there.

Silas has a two-story farmhouse with white siding and wide pillars supporting the roof. Large windows in almost every room and a wraparound porch.

It's not unlike the style I would choose for myself, honestly. But the truth is, I don't fucking know what I want to do with any plot of land. So, I just keep going back to the beige colonial that reminds me of how shitty life can be, regardless of how many coats of fresh paint I put on.

And no matter how many times Silas tells me the land is just as much mine, it doesn't *feel* like mine. Not when there are so many secrets sucking up all the oxygen at the compound.

So, for now, I'm good in this house.

If I built my own thing, who knows where it would be and how long that would take. Plus, it would eat away at the time I spend with Hunter too. That kid is a bright spot for all of us. Silas tells everyone that Hunter saved his life, but I'm inclined to think he saved us all.

He's technically my cousin, but it's easier for him to understand if I call him my nephew too, so that's what we do.

Since I have uncle status, I have the pleasure of indulging every weird idea his five-year-old mind comes up with. Especially the ones that I just know give Silas gray hair.

Light to my left catches my attention. Mrs. Carter's property is lit up like a Christmas tree. Her porch lights, yard lights, and what looks to be every single light inside the house are on.

"What the fuck," I mumble, slowing my speed.

Mrs. Carter died last year, and as far as I know, her house has sat untouched the whole time.

Rosewood loves their gossip. No way someone moves into Mrs. Carter's old place without anyone hearing about it.

Unless it's the Hell Hounds making a move.

But just to make sure I don't give some new homeowner a heart attack, I hit the button on my watch and lift my wrist closer to my face.

"Call Aunt Dixie," I say, pitching my voice over the sound of my engine.

"Calling Aunt Dixie," the automated voice repeats a second before I hear the line ringing in my right ear. These earpod headphones were a fucking game-changer.

She answers on the second ring. "How's my favorite boy?"

Her familiar greeting tugs up the corner of my mouth, like always. I don't care that I'm well into adulthood and she says it to Silas and Nova too.

"Good, Aunt Dixie. Listen, I was out for a drive and I noticed all the lights are on at Mrs. Carter's old place. Did someone move in?"

"No, not that I heard. And I was just downtown this afternoon. Not to mention, Debbie was running her mouth for fifteen minutes while I waited for my coffee. I'm sure she would've jumped at the chance to spill that kind of tea."

"Huh. Okay. I'm going to check it out." Maybe something happened with the electric company. Or maybe it's some assholes playing in a dead woman's house.

She's quiet for a second, and I just know her wheels are spinning. "Spill it out, Lincoln St. James."

I wince reflexively, the weight of her using my full name in that tone of voice.

"Nothing confirmed yet, but we're keeping eyes on anything that could link back to Crestview."

There's a moment of dead air before she seethes, "Those motherfucking Hell Hounds."

"It's preliminary at best, so don't go marching over there just yet." I do my best to keep my voice even, a hint of persuasion.

She voices her displeasure, some rustling coming through on the line. "And you think they're squatting in Josephine's old place?"

I hesitate a moment. "The thought crossed my mind. It's been empty for so long, the timing seems suspicious."

"Hm. Where are the other two?" she asks.

"At the garage, I imagine. I needed a break and someone needs to do a sweep."

"Alright," she says on a sigh. "Be careful."

"Always am."

"I know, I know. But I like to remind you." I can hear the smile in her voice.

"I'll let you know what I find, if anything." I pull into Mrs. Carter's driveway, slowing down.

"If you don't, I'm going to show up at your house later." It's a promise and a warning.

"I will." I hear three quick beeps, signaling she hung up. I love that woman, but damn if she doesn't ever say goodbye properly on the phone.

I coast my bike to a stop in front of the closed three-car garage. Muffled music seeps through the house as I shut off my engine. My boots crunch over loose stones as I cross the driveway and climb the three steps to the wraparound porch. Considering it's been left untouched for a year, it's not in bad shape.

The noise is louder here, and I recognize the unmistakable notes of The Pixies. I hesitate in front of the big window next to her door, peering inside. A flicker of movement catches my eye, but I can't see what or who it is past the lacy curtains.

I lift my fist to knock on the door, but it's already ajar. I push it open slowly and peer into the dim foyer.

"Hello?" My voice echoes off of the empty space, save for a small eggplant-colored console underneath an ornate oval mirror. The scent of stale lavender permeates the air and my nose twitches.

No one answers, but I'm not all that surprised. Music blares from the record player in the living room to my right. I keep my footsteps silent, dark amusement prickling the back of my neck at the song.

I enter the living room, and I'm taken aback by the sight before me. The velvet chaise lounge in the picture window, the built-in bookcase along the left wall stuffed with books, and the uncomfortable-looking modern floral-patterned sitting chairs all frame a scene. And a mountain of stuff, loosely circling the room. Stacks of books, piles of trinkets, vases and picture frames.

And in the center is a dark-haired woman bent over. She's wearing a long black skirt and a bright pink cropped tank top. Her cascading hair obscures her face, but I feel a flash of awareness in my body that I've only felt a few times before.

My heart skips a beat like some fucking cliche, and before I can second-guess myself, I take a few strides toward her.

"Hey," I call out in my friendliest voice, reaching out to get her attention.

My palm rests on her shoulder for the barest second before she stands up and spins around with catlike reflexes and a startled scream.

Pain explodes across my nose, and I fall to my ass with a resounding thud. Stars flash across my vision and the unmistakable warmth of blood sludges over my top lip. I pinch the bridge of my nose to stem the bleeding and look between my fingers at the woman before me.

Straight into a pair of brown eyes so dark and deep that I could trip and drown in them. I had fallen into them.

Once.

Years ago, surrounded by sand and summer breeze. I dove headfirst, utterly captivated by her.

It's her.

The one from the beach.

My girl.

Lightbulbs flicker on in rapid succession, or maybe that's just my brain restarting after she rang my bell with . . . "What are you holding?" My voice comes out a raspy laugh.

"Are you—are you laughing?" Her voice hits that certain level of incredulity that has my lips twitching again.

"This is going to be a helluva story to tell our kids one day, baby girl," I murmur, voice low.

"What?" Her hands hang by her side and she leans toward me, and I get a whiff of something sweet, like sugared figs or caramelized honey. Her gaze flicks between my eyes as she bites the corner of her lip, this little wrinkle forming between her brows. "Shit. Maybe you have a concussion."

I tip my head back a little further, keeping my gaze on her. "Nah, I'm fine. I've had plenty of concussions in my life, and this ain't it."

"Are you sure? Maybe I should take you to the hospital?"

"Nah, no hospital, but could I get some paper towel or napkins?" I wink at her.

"Yes, yes, of course. Stay here." She straightens up and drops the makeshift weapon, leaving me sprawled out in the middle of Mrs. Carter's rug.

All of the things to take me down, who knew it would be a fucking scented candle.

I let my head fall back and chuckle. It's a good thing I'm alone, because absolutely no one would ever let me live this down if they knew.

18

EVANGELINE

"SHIT, SHIT, SHIT." I hustle through the house, swerving around the furniture and hopping over a box of questionable pantry items until I'm in the kitchen. I rip the whole roll of paper towel off the little holder on the counter and dash back to the living room.

My adrenaline is still going strong, making my fingers tingle. Oh my god, what if I broke his nose? Or gave him a serious head trauma?

I skid to a stop next to his knees, offering him a handful of scrunched-up paper towels from my fist. "Here, put this on your nose. I'm so sorry. I didn't mean to hit you so hard. Even if you kind of deserved it for just walking into a stranger's house."

He takes the paper towel from me, but his eyes stay trained on mine. "It's okay, baby girl. I've taken worse hits."

I stare at his dark brown eyes, the color stark against the bright white covering half of his face. There's something familiar about him. Did I see him at The Wild Boar? I shake my head a few times. No, no way. I'd definitely remember someone like him.

He looks like he walked off of one of those movie sets, the

one where it's a bunch of insanely good-looking people who are playing regular Joes in a small town.

The skin around his eyes wrinkles, like he's smiling underneath all the blood rapidly turning the paper towel red. It's enough to snap me out of whatever haze I was stuck in.

Reality slams down around me with the grace of a hail storm. My heart thumps inside my chest, adrenaline flooding my veins.

"Actually," I draw the word out, standing up and moving two steps away in an instant. I glance around the room, looking for something I can use as a weapon, which is ironic if I think about it too much. "What *are* you doing here?"

"The door was open." His voice is muffled, but he doesn't make any sudden moves. If anything, he reclines against the chaise couch. One leg bent, his elbow resting on it as he tips his head back, his other leg casually straight in front of him. The soles of his black boots are only inches away from my bare feet, the soft pink polish on my toes a sharp contrast.

Black leather and ballerina pink.

The irony of it all is not lost on me. I'm still clutching the roll of paper towel like it's a lifeline, my stomach churning with a mix of fear and adrenaline.

"But that doesn't give you the right to just waltz in like you own the place," I snap, my voice rising in pitch. I feel off-balance, like I can't get enough air into my lungs.

He tilts his head to the side and pinches the lapel of his leather vest between two fingers, tugging it up so I can see the Reaper patch. Like that's an answer.

I shift my weight to my back foot and glance at the skull and crossbones emblem, noting the rectangular white patch reading Vice President underneath.

"You're one of the Rosewood Reapers?"

My fingers itch to grab my phone. But that's not what

surprises me. It's the fact that my knee-jerk reaction was to ask Nova and not Cora.

Probably just because he's a member. Yeah, that's why. Definitely.

He nods, his eyes never leaving mine. "That's right."

I fold my arms across my chest and move back another step until my calves bump the box behind me. It's full of random trinkets I thought my cousins might want. They chime at the contact, and my shoulders hitch toward my ears as I anticipate the sharp sound of breaking porcelain.

Thankfully, it never comes. I shuffle to the side so I don't break anything or fall, but I end up tripping over a velvet throw pillow shaped like a piece of hard candy.

I yelp, my arms windmilling to keep my balance. My feet get tangled up in everything on the floor, and I pitch to the side. My eyes slam shut, a silly reflex I've had since I was a kid, and I brace for the pain of landing on a collection of hard and sharp-edged things.

But it never comes.

A pair of strong hands settle on either side of my waist, steadying me in an instant.

I gasp, my eyes flying open and seeing the vice president of the Rosewood Reapers on his knees in front of me.

My heart pounds, and I'm a little embarrassed. But then his hands smooth over my sides, and my gaze snaps to his hands. They settle more firmly on the natural curve of my hips, and I have the strangest thought like they belong there.

I let myself follow the line of his arm, appreciating the way the veins pop against his colorful tattoos of each nearly-full sleeve. His shirtsleeves strain against his biceps, like he's never missed a day at the gym.

My mind drifts to wonder what else he could bench press with muscles like that. My gaze slides over the lapel of his kutte, up his tanned throat, where I see the black edges of a tattoo peeking over the collar. His Adam's apple bobs as he swallows, and I decide right then and there that such a specific part of anatomy doesn't have any right being so attractive and alluring.

"Mrs. Carter was a friend of the club, so I check on the place sometimes." His voice comes out all low-pitched and gravelly.

Or maybe that's because he's quite literally on his knees in front of me. Hands banded around the sides of my hips, closer to my belly button than my ass. But he might as well be touching my bare ass for the way it feels. Warm, possessive, like a brand.

The scent of dark golden amber and the woods after it rains fills my nose, and I try not to make it obvious when I inhale again.

His breath is warm against the sliver of skin between the hem of my tank top at the top of my skirt.

"Oh-okay." I stumble over the word, shaking my head a little. It's those eyes and that low tone, like he spent the night sipping whiskey. It's meddling with my brain, turning me into the kind of woman who doesn't push a stranger away. The kind of woman who wonders how that deep voice would sound in my ear.

"I got you, baby girl," he whispers. It's low enough that if I wasn't straining to hear him over the thunderous beat of my heart, I would've missed it.

I stand frozen for a second, my brain trying to process what just happened. Did he really just call me *baby girl*? And why the hell does desire pool low in my belly instead of panic or disgust?

And all of a sudden, like one of those flash floods, a memory slams into me.

"Hold onto me," he murmurs, his breath tickling the sensitive skin of my inner thigh. He settles my left leg over his right shoulder.

I thread my fingers through his hair, reveling in the softness of it. "What if I fall?"

Nerves roll around in my gut like I've got a belly full of snakes. I'm not scared, not really. But I am a little nervous. I've never done anything like this before—and I didn't think my first time would be in public.

Well, kind of. We're not that far away from the bonfire party at the end of the beach. Far enough that no one can see us, but close enough that I can still see the blazing orange flames.

"I got you, baby girl," he murmurs, trailing his lips across my skin. One hand wraps around my thigh, anchoring it to his shoulder. And the other one palms my hip, steadying me. "Let me make you feel good, yeah?"

I swipe my tongue over my bottom lip, my pulse racing so fast, my skin feels sensitive. "What about you?"

He looks up at me, his dark lashes framing equally dark eyes. I decide he looks like some kind of fallen angel, except instead of wings, he has arms full of tattoos.

"Me?" He arches a brow, his lips curving into a sinful smile. "There's nothing I want more than to eat this pretty pussy all night. Every fucking night. So, be a good girl and hold on to me, yeah? "

I curl my fingers into his hair, and he sends me the most carnal grin I've ever seen. If sex was a smile, it'd be his.

I blink, the memory fading as quickly as it came. My entire body trembles, and I nod a few times. Definitely too many to be considered a normal response, but I can't help it.

I'm pretty sure I gave my virginity to the vice president of the Reapers on the beach eight years ago.

19

EVANGELINE

HE WAS the first person to ever go down on me, and honestly, it was still the best I've ever had. I don't know if that's a testament to his skills, my inexperienced eighteen-year-old self. Or the string of really shitty boyfriends since then.

He was also the first person I slept with. And in *public*.

I guess he got *a lot* of my firsts.

But oh, holy fucking shit, I can't believe it's him.

It *is* him, right?

Sweat beads along the back of my neck, and I resist the urge to drag my hand across it.

No. It's definitely him. I'd remember the shape of those lips—and the way they feel on my skin—anywhere. All those cliches are real: a girl never forgets her first.

My fingers tingle with the urge to snatch him up and kiss him, the memory of our night together riding me hard. But that would be crazy and awkward and—*oh my god*, why is he *looking* at me like that?

Eyes half-open, shadowed under a fringe of black lashes, lips parted, jaw flexed. It's the kind of expression a man wears before the last threads of his control snap and he kisses the daylights out of you.

It's the look *he* wore before he ruined me just a little bit, just like he promised all those years ago.

There's a part of me—a big part—that's low-key freaking out. Like internal organs malfunctioning freaking out.

My heart beats so hard, it feels like it's going to fly right out of my chest, like it's a trapped bird, desperate to flee its cage.

My gaze bounces from one of his eyes to the other, looking for some kind of understanding, a spark of recognition.

But his eyes are bottomless pools of intensity, offering me nothing. No, that's not right. They're giving me a peek into the depths of his possession. I don't know how else to explain it, but that's exactly how it feels. I keep waiting for him to say something, but the silence stretches between us, neither one of us jumping in to break it.

Nana Jo didn't raise a chicken though, so I roll my shoulders back—as much as I can when he's still holding me like that—and dive in.

"What did you say?" Okay, so it comes out more of a murmured question than any kind of accusation, like someone might have if a seemingly random stranger just called them baby girl.

But even though my brain says he's definitely a stranger, my body begs to disagree. And my heart is too busy recovering from the adrenaline surge to weigh in.

He stares at me for a beat before he blinks. It's a slow sweep of his lashes, and when he opens them, it's like he's erased it somehow. He lets his hands slide over my hips. It lasts a single second before he's pushing to his feet.

I swallow, my throat suddenly dry. If I thought him on his knees was seductive, it's ten times more to have him towering over me like this.

Lips pursed a little, brows low over his eyes—eyes that are busy raking over every inch of me. I swear I can feel his gaze like a soft caress. Broad shoulders filling my vision and nearly blocking the sunlight of the room behind him.

His dark hair falls forward, and if he shifts forward just a little bit, we'd be touching. Somehow the fact that we aren't touching heightens everything. The inch of space between us feels charged with unspoken claims and swelling desire.

He clears his throat and takes a big step backward. He bends down to snag the forgotten bunch of paper towels and wipes along the side of his nose.

I point my index finger toward him, circling it around the air a bit to encompass his face. "I'm sorry about that, by the way." I wince, my shoulders hiking toward my ears for a second. "But also, not *that* sorry, because you did walk in my house and scare the hell out of me."

He laughs, this low chuckle that rumbles around the room. "It's fine. Bleeding's stopped, it's not broken. No harm."

I nod, a single strong dip of my chin. "Well, good. So, what did you say? A few minutes ago?"

He glances away for a moment, the laughter sliding off his handsome face. He brings his gaze back to mine, and I already know he's going to lie. It's written all over his face. More precisely, it's the way he carefully arranges it to this blank, sort of neutral look.

"I said 'I caught you.'"

My brows sink low over my eyes, a grin tugging at the corner of my lips. I'm not sure what amuses me more: the fact that it's really him or that he's lying. That is definitely *not* what he said.

I incline my head toward him, folding my arms across my chest. Curiosity wraps around me like a warm blanket, and I'm content to see how this all plays out.

"Well, thanks. I would've definitely fallen and probably

broken Nana Jo's collection of"—I hike a thumb over my shoulder, toward the stuff on the floor—"special vases." My voice trails off and both of us look at the six vases to my right. Six distinctly phallic-shaped vases.

He grunts, his lips twitching. "Mrs. Carter had eclectic taste."

"We liked to go to estate and yard sales together. Sometimes we would see who would find the most, uh, *eclectic* thing." I tilt my head to the side, letting my arms fall to my sides. "And Nana Jo was competitive when the mood struck."

He nods slowly, his lips doing that twitching thing again. "I'll bet."

"You said she was a friend of the club? What does that mean? How did you know my grandma?"

He slips his left hand in the pocket of his jeans. "It's a small town, and Mrs. Carter had been here a long time."

"Her whole life," I interject with a slow nod.

"Well, I don't know how much you know about the Reapers, but we take care of everyone here in Rosewood," he says.

My mind flashes back to the episodes of that motorcycle show I binged on. Are they some kind of vigilante justice group? I look at him with a new understanding.

I press the inside of my cheek between my molars as I realize something. "So I should expect more Reapers to walk right in my house?"

He tenses, his whole body freezing for a second. "I'll make sure they know you're here."

I don't know what I was expecting, but whatever it was, his response wasn't it. I expel a breath and force a small smile.

"Well, good. Because there's a lot of work to be done here, so I'll be here for the summer at least. And I won't always have a candle handy. Next time I might have a frying pan," I deadpan with a smirk.

"Noted," he says, the side of his mouth hooking upward.

"I'm Evangeline." I extend my hand toward him. And I can't help it if I'm pushing him a little bit under the guise of politeness.

He slips his large palm in mine, and it's like every cliche love story I've ever read is playing out in one handshake. My palm prickles like sparks poked my skin, the hair on my arm stands up like there's a buildup of electricity.

I glance from our clasped hands, following those delicious tattooed arms all the way up to get snared in his gaze.

"I'm Bane."

With two words, every romantic notion and fantasy that I didn't realize I was stockpiling comes crashing down.

Those tiny seeds of hope that I had unconsciously planted all those years ago on that beach just spontaneously combusted. They float all around me, falling slowly to ash, invisible except to me.

Disappointment fills my feet with lead, cementing me to the floor.

Because the guy in front of me? He's hot as fuck with a real bad boy vibe and possessive streak that would probably make me beg for more.

But he's not him—my guy from the beach.

His name was Lincoln.

20

EVANGELINE

"SO HOW WAS THE FIRST NIGHT?"

Cora is entirely too chipper for eight o'clock in the morning. Her voice bright and loud in my ear. I switch her to speakerphone and set the phone on the island behind me.

A yawn steals my reply, stretching my mouth wide as I open one side of the refrigerator. It's a modern touch in the otherwise farmhouse chic kitchen. French door style stainless steel with a flex door in the middle and the freezer on the bottom, plenty of room in all three sections. Surprisingly, it wasn't as gross as I was expecting. My apartment back in the city was vacant for three months before I moved in, and I needed a hazmat suit to clean that kitchen.

But I guess Mr. Robert wasn't kidding when he said everything was taken care of.

The fridge, the island, and sink were the only things I cleaned in the kitchen last night. The rest I plan to tackle today. That and get some food. Because the fridge might be clean, but it's painfully empty. I think I have a protein bar in my purse.

I didn't have the energy to get groceries last night, not after all the sorting and the awkward encounter with Bane.

God, I still can't believe it wasn't him. Memories can change over the years, warp and grow fuzzy. Nostalgia can embellish them and details can fade. But still, I could've sworn . . .

Maybe he has a brother? Shit, it could even be a twin brother.

"Jesus," she says with a chuckle. "Didn't you get any sleep? I can literally hear how big that yawn was. Can you catch someone's yawn over the phone? Because—"

The rest of her sentence is muffled behind a yawn. I laugh, even if it's sleepy and weak.

"Guess that answers your question. Besides, it's normal to be tired after the emotional trip yesterday."

"I told you to wait for me, and I'll do it with you. It's not fair to ask you to clean out Nana Jo's entire house alone. I'm actually surprised she didn't have anything in her will to stipulate that. She seemed to be so meticulous about everything else," she says.

I open one of the cabinets next to the fridge. It's full of magazines, cookbooks, mail, and random papers. "Yeah, who knows. I'm sure she had her reasons though. And you have a life here—a job and commitments. I don't expect you to drop everything because I suddenly decided to move here for the summer. I'm perfectly fine alone."

She sighs. "I know, but I wanted to help."

"I know, and I love you for it. But I didn't really want to wait. Spending money on a motel seemed like a waste when I have a perfectly good house to sleep in." I thought I'd had a comfortable savings account, definitely enough to stay at the little motel longer. But that was before I inherited a house—and all the costs associated with owning a house. I'm trying to be smart about my finances, at least until I find another job.

"Yeah. How was it sleeping there?" She's quiet, and I can

hear the hustle and bustle of the bakery she works at through the line.

I pull out a stack of papers and stuff from the cabinet, set it on the island, and start sorting it into keep and trash piles. "I slept on the big couch. The house isn't nearly as dusty as I was expecting, but still. I want to clean it up first. Get fresh sheets and all that stuff."

"Now shopping I can help with. I've been meaning to grab a couple things I need from Glendale. We can go tonight, grab some dinner, make a whole night of it. I'll call Abby, even though I doubt she'll say yes. I swear, she works more than the rest of us combined."

I smile, thinking of Cora's youngest sibling. Abby and I should've been the closest, considering we're only ten days apart. But despite us all being relatively close, we never bonded like Cora and I did.

Though that probably has more to do with my mother and her incessant need to turn everything into a competition—and then promptly win. Aunt Hazel was due with Abby a few days before my mother, but because Virginia Carter never does anything by half measure, she convinced a doctor to induce her early.

"I'll pick you up at four. Then we'll have plenty of time to shop. Abby should be able to meet us for dinner by seven then, if I can convince her to come," she says.

My hand hovers over the newspaper renewal notice, and a line of tension zips down my spine. "Oh shoot, I, uh, already have plans tonight."

"What? With who? Actually, you know what, I'm not even surprised. Only you could make friends with someone after seventy-two hours in a new town." She sort of huffs the words out, and I'd bet that protein bar in my purse she's rolling her eyes with a half-smile on her face.

Just like I'm almost positive she's going to lose all that amusement in about two seconds.

"Yeah, about that. It's kind of a date." I wince, the words rising in pitch towards the end like I'm asking a question.

The line is quiet, long enough that I look at the screen to make sure we're still connected.

She sighs, this noisy exhale that somehow sounds both exasperated and annoyed. "Please tell me you heeded my advice and you're not, in fact, going out with a Reaper. With *Casanova*."

My own annoyance rises to meet hers head-on. "Fine, I won't. Just like I won't tell you that I had a Reaper in my house yesterday. A *different* one." I lay it on thick enough that she can probably feel my sarcasm like a heavy layer of sunscreen. "Who was honestly so hot I'm starting to wonder if there's something in the water in this town, because this man was—"

"Details, Eve. I need details. Now."

I fiddle with the corner of a gardening magazine in the trash pile. "Well, it's kind of a funny story actually."

She scoffs. "I'll be the judge of that. Stop stalling."

"Fine," I say on a sigh. "I hit him in the face with Nana Jo's Tahitian vanilla candle."

"You *what*?" she sputters, incredulity lacing her words.

I bristle a little, the back of my neck getting hot. I glance around the kitchen, pointedly not at the phone. Even though she can't see me, I still feel bad about the whole bloody nose thing.

"Well, he surprised me. Walked right in the house and everything. I happened to be holding that candle, and Cora, let me tell you. That man fell like a bag of rocks." I can't help it, a little giggle slips free as I remember the look of utter astonishment on his face as he stared at me.

"Oh my god," she says through a fit of giggles. "That's honestly not at all what I was expecting you to say. What happened then?"

"Well, it's a little funny now, but at the time, I was seriously freaking out. He started bleeding, and then I nearly fell face-first as I ran to get him a paper towel."

She's full-on belly laughing now. That kind of amusement that builds bigger and bigger, and I bet she's going to start that wheezing thing she does when she laughs so hard, she can't get enough air.

"Then he saved me from breaking Nana Jo's dick vases."

And there it is. The high-pitched wheeze filling the kitchen. It's so contagious, I find my own amusement rising to hers.

"God, you should've seen his face though. Even with a busted nose, that man was so hot. All broody and masculine. He looks like the kind of guy who would chop wood just for fun, ya know? Ugh, and then I thought he looked familiar, so I couldn't get it out of my head that I knew him. I'm sure I made a weird situation even more awkward, but he was cool about it. He didn't exactly run out of here, but he didn't linger either."

"Oh my god, Eve. I've got tears, literal tears. That's the best story I've heard in ages. You know who would love that kind of thing?"

"Nana Jo," we answer at the same time.

"Yeah, she would've loved everything about it," she murmurs, her words laced in laughter.

"Especially the Reaper." I waggle my brows.

"Ugh, do I even want to know who it was? It better not be that asshole Jagger." Her volume drops, warning threaded into her words.

The doorbell rings, a soft three-tone chime echoing through the house. I push off the island and walk toward the front-door.

"Nah, it wasn't. Hey, you're not here, are you?"

"What? No, I'm at the bakery."

"Someone just rang the doorbell," I murmur.

"Well, there's your first clue. You know I'd walk right in. Who is it?"

My lips twist to the side in a smirk. "That's true. Hang on, I'm going to see who it is."

The shape of a man is visible through the frosted glass panes on the front door. I can make out dark hair and dark clothes, but even right in front of the door, the details aren't clear. I make a mental note to look into front door options.

I open the door, and my breath catches in my throat. Standing on the faded doormat is Bane, a big white pastry bag in one hand and a brown tray with two iced coffees. He's wearing his black Reaper kutte over a plain black tee, his medium-wash jeans molded to his thighs in a way that pretty much guarantees they're hugging his ass perfectly. His hair is slightly disheveled, like he ran his hands through it once too many times today.

"Thought you could use some help. I brought breakfast," he says, lifting up both hands a little.

My lips part, and I keep my gaze on him when I tilt my face toward my phone. "Cora? I'm going to have to call you back."

21

BANE

AS FAR AS peace offerings go, I'd say it was a slam dunk. But she's just staring at me, her eyes wide and face soft.

It's the same expression she had when she stumbled into me at that bonfire beach party. It's a look that makes my chest feel tight, like I'm not sure if she's my salvation or my next obsession.

Like she thinks I might be *her* salvation.

I was spiraling then, and she unknowingly threw me a lifeline. She offered me the one thing I never thought I'd have again: hope.

In that moment, standing on her doorstep, I knew why I came back. Why I'd likely continue to keep coming back. It wasn't because she was arguably the most beautiful woman I've ever laid eyes on. Or because we still have some kind of intrinsic chemistry that's impossible to ignore.

It was because she'd made me feel alive. She probably saved my goddamn life that night.

I take a step forward, closing the gap between us and lifting up the bag of pastries. "Breakfast?"

"Oh, um, thank you. That's actually kind of perfect. I don't have any food here yet. Come on in." She uses her grip on the door handle to swing the door open wider, gesturing with her other hand clutching her phone.

She's wearing another long flowy skirt, black with big blue flowers scattered all over and a slit up the side that flashes a glimpse of her smooth, suntanned skin. And a white graphic tee knotted to show just a hint of her stomach.

Her hair is rolled into a messy bun on the top of her head, tendrils already falling out sort of haphazardly around the sides of her face.

Her smile is small but warm, like she's pleasantly surprised to see me but maybe a little confused too. Welcome to the fucking club. I don't know why I'm here except for the fact that she's here. And this is a big ass house, too big for one person to go through it.

But mostly, I couldn't stop thinking about her last night. Embarrassment clung to my skin like perspiration every time I thought about the name I gave her.

It felt like I was lying, even though I wasn't. Even though it shouldn't fucking matter because I never even knew her, not really. And yet, I've slotted her as a turning point in my life.

Like a moth to a flame, I can't help but be drawn to her. The jaded pieces of me maintain that our time together was coincidental, shit was turning around already.

But there's a small voice, a whisper really, that says it was all her.

I guess I can consider this surprise visit necessary information gathering.

Yeah, that's exactly what it is. Just collecting data so I can make an informed decision on what to do next.

Anxiety eases her tight grip around my chest with that thought, and I can breathe a little easier.

"Nice place." I want to shove the words back into my mouth

the moment they escape. Making fucking small talk now? What the *fuck*.

She laughs, this low, breathy sound that echoes around the hallway before the kitchen. "You mean the living room in the front that looks like a tornado ripped through it? Or this?" She stops in the doorway to the expansive kitchen, her right hand fluttering in the air a little.

I pause next to her, just behind her shoulder. Her perfume wafts up to me, the scent of sweet cherries and vanilla wrapping around me like a dessert cloud. "I guess it's a good thing I came to help, yeah?"

"So, is this part of some Rosewood welcome wagon or something?" She looks at me over her shoulder as she walks into the kitchen, curiosity bright in her gaze.

"Sure." I look around her kitchen, my attention snagging on the piles of things around the counters.

"Well, that's nice of you. I bet you don't get too many new residents though. I remember Nana Jo saying it's a pretty tight-knit community." She clears her throat, and my gaze snaps to hers. "Sorry about the mess. I decided to start in here today." She shoves a pile over, making room on the island.

"Should I be worried about any more candles?"

She flashes me a grin, though it's tainted with a grimace too. "How's your nose?"

My nose twitches like just the mention of it was enough to send a phantom pain lancing through the tender area.

I set the pastry bag and coffee tray down in the small square of available space. "It's fine, really. Here." I pull one of the coffees free from the tray and hand it to her.

Her fingertips land on mine for a moment, and I want to punch myself in the face for the ridiculous thought that skitters across my brain. How much I like the way her touch feels on my skin. Like I'm some goddamned teenager, not a grown-ass man.

She takes the iced coffee from me, and I try to ignore the rush of heat that floods my body at the contact.

She recovers first, pulling the cup toward her and rotating it to read the drink's symbols on the side. "Oh, thanks. What, uh, is this?"

"A chai latte with a shot of espresso."

Her head snaps up, her gaze boring into mine like I just offered the correct answer to some magical riddle.

EVANGELINE

"Oh," I breathe out. My nerves are sparking inside my body, sending these little waves of pleasure into every inch of my skin. "I love a good chai latte. Thank you."

That's an understatement. Dirty chai lattes are my absolute favorite drink.

He glances around the room, unable to meet my eyes for a few moments. "Lucky guess, I suppose."

"What are the odds?" I murmur before taking a sip. Oh, *yum*. It's a vanilla chai blend with just a hint of spice and the espresso is smooth and nutty.

It's basically the best combination ever. Seriously, what *are* the chances he randomly picked my favorite drink?

Bane chuckles, the sound both deep and light at the same time. I can feel my cheeks warm in response, and I turn toward the impressive stack of assorted papers covering the counter.

"Well, *Bane*, let's see what other magic you can work, yeah?" He pointedly ignores my emphasis on his name. I'm not even sure why I did it.

"I don't know about magic," Bane says, his lips turning up into a smirk. He leans his palm flat against the counter, his gaze raking over the mess in front of us. "But it looks like I got here just in time."

I roll my eyes, but it lacks any real heat. "My knight in shining armor."

He nods. "Sure, if by armor you mean a V-twin engine and 1450cc of raw power and torque of shining chrome."

My mouth parts and I stare at him. "I honestly have no idea what any of that means."

Bane laughs, his eyes dancing with amusement. "I'll show you sometime."

"Okay. I'll hold you to that." I look at him from underneath my lashes, trying to see if he meant that the way I'm definitely taking it. I can't help the accompanying flutter in my stomach at the thought. He's hard to read, his face expressive but not entirely open.

"We should get started," he says, voice low. He glances my way as he says it.

I reach for the top of the stack. "Right. I thought I'd go through all this stuff. It's mostly recipes Nana Jo pulled out of magazines and random pieces of mail. As tempting as it is to just toss all of it, I want to go through and sort everything. Just to make sure I don't accidentally throw away a photo or family recipe or something."

He moves to stand across from me. "Makes sense to me."

We sort through papers in comfortable silence, organizing the chaos together to the sounds of soft music coming from the record player.

"What about this?" He holds up a manila envelope, sealed shut with thick black tape. My name scrawled in Nana Jo's handwriting across the front.

My heart begins to beat faster as I take it and turn it over in my hands, feeling the weight of the contents inside.

I look up at Bane, whose eyes are already on me. His expression is intense, brows drawn in tight. "What is it?"

"I'm not sure. I've never seen it before."

He slides a pocketknife from his pocket, thumbing it open and leaning over the counter in a move too quick to track. A flick of his wrist, and the black tape parts.

"Oh, thanks," I murmur. I peel back the envelope and peer inside. "It's a bunch of cards."

I pull one out at random, an illustrated giraffe wearing a birthday hat on the front and my name scrawled in unfamiliar handwriting inside. That's it.

Confusion weighs my brow down.

"I don't get it. Where did these come from?"

"Maybe your grandma bought one of those huge boxes of greeting cards and wrote a bunch out for future birthdays," he muses.

"Yeah, maybe." It doesn't really look like Nana Jo's handwriting, but it's hard to tell. I stuff the card back inside the envelope and set it on the top of another stack.

"Old receipts? Keep or toss?" He pinches some paper between his index finger and thumb, holding it up for me to see.

"Oh, uh, I guess toss. Unless it's from this past year, because I'm still a little confused about some of the details Mr. Robert told me."

"I can help you if you have any questions. I oversee the books at the clubhouse."

"Oh, that would be great." Butterflies stir in my belly, their soft wings fluttering against my insides. I tilt my head to the side, locks of fallen hair brushing against my shoulder. "You sure you're not my knight?"

He smirks and shakes his head, dismissing my comment. "Where are the garbage bags? I'll take care of the trash pile for you. You probably don't know this, but Rosewood takes their recycling pretty seriously."

"Ah, yes, I did know that. Bags are behind you, under the sink," I tell him, pointing toward the cabinet where Nana Jo put all her cleaning supplies. "I used to spend all my summers here when I was younger."

He turns around and bends over to sort through the cabinet. "I feel like I would've remembered seeing you around town."

I completely miss whatever it is he said, drowned out over the sound of my heart beating too fast at the sight of him.

Because *damn*. The man can wear the hell out of a pair of jeans. Honestly, how can he even move so easily in jeans that tight.

He stands up, and my gaze snaps to his. I can feel the heat my cheeks are radiating, even though I'm pretty sure he didn't catch me.

I swipe my tongue over my lips. "What?"

He smiles, his plump lips spreading wide into a genuine grin. He lets his gaze rake over me. "I said I feel like I would've remembered seeing you around town."

"Would you?" It's a whispered challenge, one that slips out before I even realize it.

22

NOVA

THE BELLS CHIME as I push open the heavy door of Sugar & Spice Bakery. It's always busy here, and not just because it's one of two bakeries in town. But their food is genuinely delicious.

It's just a shame that one of their head bakers hates my guts. To my credit, she hates me on principle, not because I did anything personally.

I pull a number from the red ticket dispenser by the door and stand behind the handful of people waiting to grab pastries and coffee.

My phone vibrates in my pocket, and I pull it out. I swallow down the groan at Silas's name flashing across the screen.

"What's up," I answer.

"Where are you and where the hell is Bane? Why am I the only one at work right now? And I thought you were going to look after Hunter today, give Ma a break."

"Jesus, man, did you even take a breath?"

"No," he snaps. "I don't have time to take a breath. There's shit we need to discuss, and it's best talked about in person, yeah?"

My stomach clenches. Silas only ever gets cagey about talking on the phone when it's club business. "Shit."

"Shit is right, brother. I'm going to need you. Tonight."

Fuck. "What's the threat level?"

I know he thinks I'm being flippant, and I'll never move up in the club if I don't take this shit seriously—something he's told me numerous times. But Rosewood is so squeaky clean now. Sometimes we get pulled in for stupid shit that the sheriff's office should handle.

He sighs. "I need you to visit some friends of ours out west. Tonight."

Everything inside of me freezes. "How west?"

"Not far. Maybe three hours or so," he replies evenly.

I exhale. So not those *friends*. Thank fuck because the Black Serpents might be allies, but it's reluctant as best.

But wait. Three hours west is prime Savage Souls territory. Or it was until we ran most of them off. My heart kicks inside my chest, anger unfurling inside my gut like a poisonous plant.

"I thought we were out of the game. You tryin' to move us back on the board?"

There's a beat of silence. "I'm going to pretend you didn't just insult the fuck out of me."

I run my hand over my face and expel a breath. "Yeah, shit. Sorry." I don't need to tell him that I panicked a little bit. There's no way in hell he's forgotten all the shit Savage Souls did by not aligning with us all those years ago.

"Look, I'll give you all the details later. But I need you and Bane on this."

What he means is that he doesn't trust anyone else to handle it. A fissure of pride worms its way into my bruised heart, filling one of the many, many cracks with warmth.

"Yeah, alright. I'll swing over a little later. I thought Ma said she was taking Hunter to the beach today though, so I made other plans."

"Fine," he says with a sigh. "She did, but I thought it might be too much for her."

I snort. "I would love to be there when you tell her that it's too much for her to take her grandbaby to the beach."

"I meant about her shoulder, asshole," he grumbles.

My number is finally called, and I glance up to see one pissed off Carter girl. If I hadn't seen her with Jagger last year, or with my girl last week, I would've assumed that's her standard expression. Guess I'm just special.

"Yeah, I know. Look, I gotta go. I'll see you later, yeah?"

"Sure. And if you find Bane, tell him to call me back. That asshole has been dodging my calls since yesterday."

"Will do. Later." I end the call and stuff my phone into my pocket as I stroll toward the bakery case.

"Morning, Carter." I greet her with my most charming smile, laying that shit on real thick.

"No," Cora says, pointing her index finger at me.

My smile stays firmly in place as I look at her, arching my brow. "Can't a man buy some doughnuts?"

"Sure. At the Cookie Jar," she says flatly.

"C'mon now, Carter, you know Sugar & Spice has the best glazed croissants in a fifty-mile radius."

She matches my expression, her eyebrow up and her mouth curving into a smirk. "I'm going to tell Melanie Cleary you said that."

Melanie Cleary owns the Cookie Jar. She's around Ma's age and makes some of the best cookies I've ever had the pleasure of eating. But she doesn't do doughnuts, so I don't care if Carter runs her mouth about that.

I only smile at her. "I'll take a half dozen today."

She holds my gaze for a beat, before blindly reaching behind her to grab a white box. She folds it into shape and stares at me, apparently done talking.

I look at the rows and rows of doughnuts. "I'll take a glazed croissant to start. And one of your bestsellers, whatever that is."

She bends down and grabs an elephant ear pastry and puts it in the box. There's no way in hell that's their bestseller, but alright. It's fucking delicious and I'll eat it if Evangeline doesn't want it.

Carter arches her brow, daring me to question her. I just keep my smile and continue to order.

"Alright, a chocolate long john, a Boston cream, and one of your favorites."

Her gaze snaps to mine, anger overruling her decision to ignore me. "If you think asking my favorite doughnut will make me like you, you're wrong."

I tuck my hands into my pockets and lift my shoulders in a shrug. "Nah. But I am heading to meet your cousin, and since I know you wouldn't tell me her favorite if I asked, I figured I'd get a variety. And maybe I'd get lucky and her favorite is your favorite."

"I thought I told you to steer clear of my cousin, St. James," she practically seethes my name, slamming the box on the top of the bakery case.

I pull my hand out of my pocket and run the pad of my index finger along my brow. "Ah, you did. But see, the thing is, Carter"—I flash her a grin—"I'm shit at taking orders. Just ask my ma."

Carter's eyes narrow, and for a moment, I think she's going to hand me my box of fried dough without a comment.

"You're a real asshole, you know that?" she sneers at me, sealing the white box with a big Sugar & Spice sticker.

I lift my shoulders, fixing a nonchalant smirk on my face. "That's what they keep telling me."

I'll be damned if I ever let someone see how their shitty, unwarranted opinion of me affects me. Especially not Coraline Carter, Reaper-hater extraordinaire.

I grab the box off the case and take it to the cash register by the door. I hand the girl behind the counter some cash, and just as I'm about to turn and leave, I hear Carter call out my name.

"St. James." Her voice snaps through the bakery, several customers turning to watch the exchange.

"If you hurt her, I'll make sure you regret it for the rest of your life," she says, her eyes flashing with warning.

"Don't worry, Carter. I don't plan on hurting her. In fact, I plan on doing quite the opposite. Long, detailed, time-consuming plans." I arch a brow and leer at her, just a little. Enough to rile her up.

"Get the fuck out of here before I regret my decision to forgo violence today."

I push open the door, the bell tinkling above my head mixing with my laughter.

23

EVANGELINE

A KNOCK SOUNDS at the front door when I'm inside the walk-in pantry. I've been wiping down the shelves for the last twenty minutes while Bane takes care of what he called *the garbage and recycling situation*.

I honestly don't even know what that means. I've been studiously avoiding that one side of the garage since I got here and silently praying that there hasn't been garbage decomposing in there for a year.

I'd thought it might be weird, having him here. Intellectually, I understand that he's a stranger. But emotionally, he doesn't feel like one.

And that's a whole kettle of confusion I haven't really had time to process yet.

"Coming," I yell, pitching my voice toward the front of the house. I wipe my wet hands on my skirt and quickly walk toward the front door. "Be right there!"

I swing open the front door, expecting to see the mailman or maybe even Cora, ready to chew me out for not calling her back.

But instead, it's Nova.

More specifically, it's Nova holding a white box of pastries in one hand and a to-go tray with two coffees in the other.

"Nova." My eyes widen in surprise. Delight pricks along my nerves, sending tingles down my spine.

He grins, his eyes crinkling at the corners. "Hey, sweetheart. I thought I was being clever, but it seems my cousin beat me to it." His voice is soft, but not calm. There's a band of steel underneath all that quiet tenor.

My mouth falls into a frown. "Cousin?"

His brows arch toward his hair, but the look on his face isn't nearly as innocent. "Oh, didn't Bane tell you? We're related."

I shake my head a few times, trying to process the fact that he's here. And apparently related to Bane, who I'm still trying to figure out.

"Huh. Must've slipped his mind, I guess. Come on in." I step back, holding the door open for him.

"Must have," he mutters, stepping into the house.

"Here, I can take one of those," I murmur, reaching for the box of pastries. "That's so thoughtful of you. At this rate, you're going to spoil me."

"Good," he says, ghosting his palm up my back and resting his hand on the nape of my neck. "I want to spoil you in all things, Evangeline."

His breath warms that secret spot behind my ear, the one that elicits a shiver down my spine in the best way. It sends my mind straight into fantasies of other ways Nova could spoil me.

Primarily with his hands and tongue and dick. Lots and lots of it.

I shake my head a little bit, scattering those dirty thoughts away. I'm not even sure where they came from, only that ever since I came to this town, I've been letting myself get carried away with emotions. All kinds of emotions. And actively leaning into things that sound fun.

And what could be more fun than Nova and Bane? If Cora was here, she'd probably flick water at my face and tell me to cool off.

But luckily for me, she's working for the next three hours.

I turn my head, just an inch or so, bringing our mouths close together. "Maybe you could start tonight." It's an invitation, one I hope he accepts.

He groans, the pained sound practically vibrating against my lips.

"Am I interrupting something?" Bane drawls from somewhere near the kitchen.

I jump what feels like eight feet into the air, but is really closer to two inches, splaying my hand over my heart. "Jeez, you scared me."

I feel a flush warm my cheeks and spread down my neck like I got caught doing something.

I glance at Nova to see him leveling Bane with the most serious, bordering on hostile expression I've ever seen. I blink and it's gone, replaced with an expressionless neutrality.

"Bane," he says, tipping his chin up. "What are you doing at my girl's house?"

The question rolls off his tongue like water, smooth and easily. But behind the calm of his voice lies an edge of steel. There's possession and challenge in those words.

If I wasn't standing so close to him, I might be able to brush it all off under surprise or shock. But I can feel the tension radiate from him as if it were a physical force, his biceps practically trembling with it.

It's so much more than a simple question.

"Your girl, huh?" Bane reaches his arms up to the top of the door frame, a lazy stretch that reminds me of a panther in the jungle.

The hem of his shirt rides up, revealing an inch of completely tattooed skin above his jeans.

If I didn't know any better, I'd say he was trying to get me to ogle him. On purpose.

"Something to say, cousin?" Nova flashes him a grin, all teeth.

Bane presses forward, his shoulder muscles flexing in the most distracting way. "Nah, just didn't know you laid claim to her. That's all."

Nova takes a step forward. It's not big, but it might as well be a gauntlet for the way Bane reacts. He drops his arms, letting them hang loosely at his sides.

The way he said the word *claim* makes me think it has a different definition than what I'm used to. And I decide I've had enough. I haven't actually had enough caffeine to try to puzzle out their relationship or attempt to read between the lines and decode the things they weren't saying.

I walk toward the kitchen, pausing between the two of them. "Should I get Nana Jo's yardstick? There's one in the pantry." I glance at both of them with an arched brow.

As expected, they stop glaring at one another. Instead, switching those neutral sort of expressions to me.

I wave my hand around a little, indicating the space between them. "You know, so you guys can measure your dicks and then work through . . . whatever this is."

Nova breaks first, the side of his mouth curling up into a grin. He chuckles, the sound genuine even if a little mischievous. He steps into me, trailing his fingertips down the middle of my back.

"Are you trying to get a glimpse of our cocks, sweetheart?" Nova practically purrs.

Heat sears my cheeks and my heart stutters for a beat.

"What? No. *I'm* not looking at anything. The yard stick is for the two of you."

Nova breathes a laugh into my skin. "Nah, no need, sweetheart. We don't want to embarrass my cousin. He's sensitive about those things."

"Real mature, Nova," Bane says with a scoff.

I step out of Nova's hold, not because I don't enjoy the way his hands feel on me. I was trying to clever and cheeky, but I guess I walked into that one. I should've known better than to try to diffuse a weird pissing contest by bringing up dick size. I swear no man can resist the topic.

"Women really aren't all that impressed by a bunch of dudes bragging to one another about how many inches they have." There, got us back on track.

I shake my head and set the second doughnut delivery on my island. I slide my finger underneath the flap to tear the sticker and open it up, enjoying the blast of sugar-fried dough in my face.

I tilt my head to the side, remembering the exception as sort of an afterthought. "Well, unless they have a micropenis."

Which by the way, is exactly what it sounds like. Cora had the pleasure of finding that out from experience, which she promptly made me experience secondhand years ago.

"Excuse me?" Bane says.

"Back up, sweetheart. When did you see this tiny dick exactly?" Nova asks.

Am I imagining it or was there a sort of growl to his voice? Come to think of it, Bane did that growly thing too.

I spot my favorite smushed up against the side of the box. Excitement zips through me. Twenty-six years old, and still, the promise of baked goods excites me as much as it did when I was six. Honestly, maybe more.

"Oh, it wasn't me. Cora dated a guy with a micropenis, and

then she made me relive it with her. Honestly, I felt kind of bad for the guy, even though he was kind of a jerk," I explain while I swipe my index finger along the side, scoop up the chocolate frosting and lick it off.

I hear a grunt and lift my head to see Bane and Nova still as statues in front of me. They both radiate the same level of intensity, but that's about as far as the similarities go.

"What?" I murmur, picking up on the shift in the room. "Is it the micropenis thing, because—"

Bane steps forward, blocking out my view of anything else except him. "Shh, stop talking about dicks, baby girl," he says, pitching his voice low.

What happens next feels like time somehow slowed down and sped up.

Bane presses his thumb to my bottom lip. Not harshly but with enough pressure that my heart stops for a second. My gaze flies to him, but he's laser-focused on his thumb. More specifically, his thumb *on my lips*.

My hand, the one that I just licked frosting off of, drops to his wrist. I don't push him away, the need to know what he's going to do next pounding in my veins.

I don't wait long.

He drags the pad of his thumb across my bottom lip with enough pressure to send dozens of electric sparks flying. They travel down to pool low in my belly.

He tips his chin down and finally, our eyes lock. There's a wildness to his gaze that I haven't noticed before. I feel like we're opposite ends of two magnets, drawn to one another by some otherworldly force.

He steps forward, the pressure of his thumb parting my lips slightly. I'm practically panting now, my breaths coming in a slow rolling wave.

I swallow, unable to look away, unable to think of anything else except him. I feel it then. A shift between us. Something more than the heat and sparks of two people attracted to one another.

24

EVANGELINE

"BANE," Nova snaps. His voice lashes out like a whip, cracking the air between us.

I startle, unconsciously tightening my grip around Bane's wrist.

"It's alright," Bane says quietly, brushing his thumb softly across my lip now.

It's such a stark contrast to the pressure a moment ago that it makes me a little weak in the knees.

His dark brown eyes search mine, the ring of amber bright and intense. And after a moment, he pulls away. "You had some chocolate," he says, pitching his voice louder.

I don't look at Nova's reaction, my focus glued to Bane as he brings his thumb up to his mouth. He slowly sucks the trace amount of chocolate off, his lips lingering a moment longer than necessary. My heart flutters wildly in my chest, and I'm suddenly overwhelmed with a sense of familiarity.

His tongue lashes out to swipe the gooey marshmallow from the side of his thumb. I hold his gaze, the bonfire casting orange shadows along his face.

God is he hot though.

The unruly dark hair, ruffled by the warm breeze off the lake. The sharp jaw and those pouty lips. But it's his eyes that keep drawing me back in. Depthless and dark, like I could spend an eternity by his side and still never reach the bottom.

My heart skips several beats, and I realize that I'm in trouble.

Big trouble.

"I dare you to tell me that isn't the best goddamn s'more you've ever had," he says, handing me a perfectly crafted graham cracker treat.

I take it from him, the marshmallow oozing out the sides. I take a bite and close my eyes in delight. "It's so good," I mumble.

"I told you," he says, eyes twinkling with mirth.

"I believed you, but I also wanted to see your skills in action." I smirk and swipe my tongue along the side of my mouth, searching for the sticky remnants.

"Here, let me help you," he says with a chuckle, stepping right in front of me.

My dessert euphoria fades into something much more carnal as he palms the side of my neck, his thumb resting underneath my jaw. He tips my head back and leans in close.

Close enough to feel his breath waft over my parted lips. He angles my face to the left an inch and presses his lips against the very corner of my mouth.

His tongue flicks against my skin, and my knees feel weak at the sensation.

"You missed a spot." His lips brush against me with every syllable, and I think it might be the very best feeling I've ever felt.

"Bane," Nova snaps again.

His voice propels me out of the memory I was reliving and thrusts me back into the present.

In Nana Jo's kitchen with two very tall, very intense, very attractive men.

Bane shrugs Nova's hand off his shoulder, never taking his

gaze from mine. I blink a few times and swallow down all those pesky lusty feelings the memories of that night bring up.

He must read something in my eyes because he offers me a small nod and steps back. "I'll be in the garage."

"Okay." I don't know what else to say. Because honestly, what the hell is happening right now?

Not that I'm not eternally grateful for the help here, but there's tension between them that I wasn't expecting considering they're cousins. And work together.

But I'm struggling a little to make sense of it all. How could they both feel so familiar, yet remain strangers all the same?

I take a deep breath and try to shake off the awkwardness of maybe having a moment with Bane while Nova was three feet away.

This day has been a series of weird turns, and it's not even halfway over.

Bane turns around and heads toward the door to the garage without another word. Before he can leave, Nova calls his name. Bane stops but he doesn't turn around, tension holding his back ramrod straight.

"Check your phone, man. Prez has been trying to get ahold of you. He sent me to find you, so I wouldn't make him wait too long. You know how he gets," Nova says.

Bane nods, and I watch him pull his phone out of his pocket a second before he disappears into the garage. I switch my focus to Nova and try to shake the feeling that I'm missing something.

He's watching me closely, his gaze searching my face for *something*. I'm not sure what he's looking for, but I can feel my cheeks heat under his perusal.

"You okay?" he asks, his voice gruff and low.

I nod, not trusting myself to speak when my mind is in a freefall. It's spinning with all the possibilities of what this could mean.

For me, for them, for us.

I haven't known Nova long, but I understand enough to realize that he's not an idiot. He definitely picked up on the moment between Bane and I.

But I have no idea where that leaves us. Does he care? Is he jealous? Does he not want to see me again? Am I spiraling for no reason?

I don't ask any of these questions though. I take the easy way out and focus on the other thing he said.

I clear my throat and glance to the left. "I'm fine. So, uh, your president?" I ask before I rip off a piece of my doughnut and take a small bite. I admit, I'm curious about the inner workings of their motorcycle club. Namely how it compares to my very limited understanding that's most definitely based on fiction.

"Aye, that's part of why I came over." He's still serious, looking at me like I might disappear if he takes his eyes off of me for even a second.

"You mean you didn't want to spend your day helping me clean out magazines from the early two-thousands?" I tease, smiling at him and shaking my head a little.

He steps in close to me, and my body mirrors his without thought. "I would gladly spend all my days with you, sweetheart. Helping you clean out this house or otherwise."

I'm not sure if he's laying on the charm thick or if he's serious, but mostly, I'm relieved that he isn't ditching me and running out the front door.

"But unfortunately, I have to rain check our date tonight."

Okay, I guess I spoke too soon.

Disappointment sours the chocolatey treat in my stomach, and my shoulders hitch toward my ears a little. I force myself to smile, even if it feels a little off. I decide to give him an out.

"Don't worry, I understand." I wave a hand in the air, the one still clutching my doughnut, and take a small step back.

His brows cave in and he eliminates the space I just created. "No, I don't think you do. When Prez says jump, we don't even ask how high. We just fucking leap."

His gaze ping-pongs between my eyes, searching for some kind of understanding. I don't know what he finds because don't really get how everything works. Yet. But I 'm a fast learner.

I nod, my mind already decided. "Okay."

"I'll make it up to you." His voice goes low and soft.

I quirk a brow at his promise. "Really?"

"Of course I will." He pushes a stray lock of hair behind my ear. "And sweetheart, I always keep my word."

Shivers tiptoe down my spine, anticipation tensing my muscles. That promise sounded entirely different than the first one.

Or maybe that's wishful thinking.

"But until then, you've got me. Put me to work." He flashes me what I've started calling his trademark smile, his dimple popping out to play.

It takes literal effort on my part not to swoon when I see it.

"In that case, can you help me wipe down the top shelves in the pantry? They're a little too tall, and I can't find Nana Jo's step ladder."

I spend the next two hours working alongside Nova to spiff up Nana Jo's kitchen so I can transform it into something of mine. I let my mind wander a bit, imagining the different things I could do to renovate it.

Bane comes in occasionally, but for the most part, they don't interact much. Really, it's a little different between me and each of them too. Not bad exactly. But off. And not at all how they've been around me before, when it was just the two of us.

I tuck all that information away to examine later, when I'm not so tired I feel like I could sleep for three days. Maybe it's a good thing we had to postpone our date after all.

25

NOVA

I SIGH and resist the urge to check my phone for the tenth time in the last two minutes. It'd be pointless anyway. It's not even my real phone, it's a burner.

It's been a while since we had to do any recon like this, and even now, it's not really that bad.

The air conditioning kind of works, the TV gets decent channels, and the room is clean. It's certainly better than other places we've had to hole up.

But that was before.

I glance out the inch of window not covered by the two dingy gray curtains. It's just enough space to see the buildings across the street and nothing more. It makes me feel a little suffocated, honestly.

I've been stuck in this box of a room with my cousin for days. Normally, I rather enjoy Bane's company. I mean, he spends more time at our house than his own, so it shouldn't be this awkward between us.

But that was before he nearly kissed my girl. In front of me.

The only thing—and I do mean only—that stopped me from physically removing him from her space and her house was the fact that she didn't seem upset.

I'd bet my bike that she wanted it.

Everyone always assumes I'm this big ladies man, a new girl in my bed every day and sometimes a few at the same time.

But no one talks about Bane. That asshole has a way of charming women without even trying. I used to be impressed by him—I looked up to him and my brother.

And I probably would still if he wasn't vying for my girl's attention. Bane never does anything he doesn't want to, and he never does shit by half measures.

It's not a matter of if but when. And I hate the thought of having to compete with him for her attention. For her affection.

Jealousy coils in my gut like a snake, swirling and twirling until I give it an outlet to strike.

I'm not a fucking idiot, I know the kind of shit they say about me around town. Most of it is rumors, but it's not like I ever tried to dispute them.

I mean, they call me Casanova for fuck's sake. I used to hate it, but I've sort of embraced it over the years.

Hearing the nickname fall from Evangeline's lips gives me a whole new appreciation. Second only to the way she'll scream my name when I bury my head between those creamy thighs.

I've been doing my best to not think about her, but it's proving harder than I thought it would be. The way she looked at me when I told her I had to cancel and leave haunts me. Her disappointment was so acute, I felt it echoed inside my own chest. Which is a fucking weird sensation for me.

I drum out some random rhythm on the table, losing myself in the vibrations it makes on my fingertips and continue to stare out the window. I've got another hour before we switch.

Four hour shifts allow each of us not to get too fatigued. Believe it or not, staring out a window all day gets tiring, even when loud action movies play in the background.

Two bikes pull into the parking lot of what should be an abandoned warehouse. We should know, we were the ones who torched it and drove the Savage Souls MC the fuck out of town.

A moment later, a box van pulls in behind them. Shit.

"We've got movement," I murmur.

"Who?"

"Two bikes and a van. Bikes are idling and the van is pulling into a spot in the front."

"Shit," he mutters.

The bed creaks as he slides off of it. A second later and the sound on the TV is gone.

Bane crosses the room to stand behind me. "Is it the Savage Souls?"

I squint, trying to discern any symbols I recognize. "Hard to tell from here, but they're definitely wearing something."

"I don't know what would be worse: if those motherfuckers crawled out of whatever hole they've been living in for the last five years or if it's some new MC trying to stake claim."

We're three hours west northwest of Rosewood, in what we started referring to as a diamond point. There's four cities surrounding Rosewood that roughly make the shape of a diamond. And all four have either MCs of their own, ties to the various cartels, or both.

When we stopped offering safe passage through our territory, shit got uncomfortable. And when we pulled out of the game altogether, it was nearly volatile.

We have an understanding with three of the four points, and the fourth remained empty.

Until now, it seems.

Two guys come out of the warehouse and get in the back of the van, both of them wearing kuttes too.

Bane tenses beside me. "Shit. It's them. I recognize their shitty emblem on the back."

My brows cave in and I squint harder. "How the fuck can you see that from here?"

"You need to get your eyes checked, man. Let's go. We need to see who they're meeting, what they're up to."

I know nothing less than irrefutable proof will convince my brother to take action. He'll never risk the club—or Hunter—unless he has no other choice.

We leave the motel room without another word, and I twist the lock behind me before the door slams shut. I don't have anything valuable in there, but you never know.

Bane gets behind the wheel of the black pickup truck, and a few seconds later, I slide into the passenger seat. It's one of the handful we use for shit like this. One of the perks of the club owning a garage, I suppose.

"Ready?" Bane glances at me as he drives out of the parking space in front of the motel room we've been staying in.

He always backs into parking spaces. Said those few seconds it takes to reverse can be the difference between life and death sometimes. And considering the shit I've lived through isn't half of what he's experienced, I'm inclined to follow his lead.

Even if I'm annoyed as fuck about him trying to move in on my girl.

I tip my chin. "Let's get this shit over with."

We get on the interstate, the van a few cars ahead of us. Bane and I are quiet as we follow the van, the low hum of the engine the only sound in the cab. It's a few more minutes before they take an exit for Silverstone.

I glance at Bane. Anxiousness is visible in the crease of his brow, his mouth curved into a frown. His hand is clenched around the steering wheel, knuckles white.

And I know he's come to the same conclusion I have.

My eyes flicker between him and the van. "Should I call the Prez?"

He shakes his head. "Nah, not yet. We don't know anything. Could be a coincidence."

A dry laugh slips free and I run my fingers through my hair. "C'mon, man, you're the most superstitious motherfucker I know. You can't tell me it's a coincidence."

"I'm not superstitious," he grumbles.

"Okay, sure," I say slowly, bobbing my head a couple of times. "But you do believe in signs, right? Like when you see crows circling overhead or when you hear a howling dog."

Bane snorts. "That's not superstition, that's just common sense. Crows circling overhead usually mean something's dead nearby, and a howling dog can signal danger. It's just being aware of your surroundings."

I roll my eyes. "Yeah, because that's not superstitious at all."

I don't bring up the fact that years ago, he went into the fortune teller's tent at the annual summer festival downtown a surly fuck who was hell-bent on destroying his life. And twenty-four hours later, he was a changed man.

Like he was the old Bane.

No, like he was Lincoln.

I don't know what the fuck she said to him, and he never told me no matter how many times I asked, but something happened in that little purple tent.

So, yeah, I kind of think he's full of shit.

He shoots me a withering look before turning his attention back to the van. We follow them through the little town until they pull up to a seedy-looking bar on the outskirts.

Three Crowns Tavern.

"What the hell are they doing here?"

Three Crowns Tavern isn't affiliated with anyone, last we checked. Sure, we're not in the game anymore, but that doesn't mean we don't stay afloat with information.

And this particular bar has always been a neutral of sorts, despite being in overlapping territory. Savage Souls and Hell Hounds always left it alone.

My brows draw together as Bane pulls off to the side of the road and kills the headlights. "Whatever it is, I doubt it's good. No one brings that many men in a van for a casual night at a bar," he says.

We don't have to wait long.

The van idles in front of the bar, parallel to the side with three tall, tinted windows. Bane and I watch in silence as the side door opens, and three men step out, each one wearing black leather kuttes.

I lean toward the dash, craning my neck to get a better look. But I can only see a corner of the back. "Is that a tail?"

"Fucking Hell Hounds," he growls.

I swear under my breath when one of the guys steps around his buddy, giving me a full view of his kutte. And it's not the same as the other guy.

"Motherfuckers," I snap, my voice low. "Hell Hounds are in bed with Savage Souls now."

"Maybe, maybe not. Could be a friendly meeting."

I glance his way, narrowing my eyes. "You don't really believe that, do you?"

"Weirder shit has happen—"

He never finishes his sentence. All three men pull out semi-automatic guns and open fire on Three Crowns Tavern.

Bane shifts the truck into gear, pulls onto the street, and does an immediate U-turn all in the span of ten seconds. The tires squeal in his haste, but I don't think the need for stealth is high anymore.

Not when we saw two different clubs come together to destroy peace.

26

EVANGELINE

I WALK down Main Street and wiggle my fingers to dissipate the lingering adrenaline. My car just decided to stop working ten minutes ago.

While I was driving.

In the middle of the road.

Thank god I'm in Rosewood and not back in the city. I can't even imagine how bad that accident would've been. Thankfully the only thing that's bruised is my ego when I screamed like a child.

And promptly shouted a lot of creative swear word insults to no one in particular as I navigated my car to the side of the road.

I check the time on my phone and quicken my pace, dodging a group of teenagers outside the smoothie place. I grab my hair at the nape of my neck and twist it loosely to toss over my shoulder. I knew I should've worn my hair up today, but my waves were actually laying so nicely that I wanted to embrace them.

I didn't take into account the scorching hot sun today. The hair on the back of my neck stands up, and the sensation of being watched rolls over me.

I glance over my shoulder, expecting the girls I passed to be staring at me but none of them are. I look over my other shoulder, letting my gaze dart around for anyone that might be looking at me, shielded behind my big black sunglasses.

I don't see anyone outright staring, but there are people walking everywhere. Downtown Rosewood is always busy, and doubly so during the summer months.

It's probably just my anxiety playing tricks on me. I was supposed to be at the restaurant to meet Cora three minutes ago. I know she won't really care that I'm late.

But punctuality is one of those things my mother drilled into me too many times. And when I'm stressed, I find myself slipping back into those bad habits.

I exhale and pull open the door to Lunch Box, which ironically is open for lunch and dinner. Air conditioning blasts me in the face, the whirring sound all I hear until I open the second door into the actual restaurant.

Decorated with vintage diner decor, the Lunch Box is an adorable restaurant. Black and white photographs and framed vinyl records hang on the walls, ornate sconces, and classic red vinyl booths.

It's about half-full with the late lunch crowd, soft murmurs and crooning fifties music on the speakers. It smells like a burger cookout in the best way, and my mouth waters a little.

I pivot on my heel by the hostess stand until I see Cora waving her right arm high in the air.

"Eve, over here!"

I smile and make my way to the booth on the other side of the room, against the front windows.

"Damn, babe. If I didn't know any better, I'd say you were a Rosewood native," Cora practically crows. She whistles and waggles her brows.

I stop in front of the booth, plant my hands on my hips, and slide my right foot forward. I look down at Nana Jo's cowboy boots, pivoting on the ball of my right foot to showcase the bright colors to Cora.

They're the kind of boots you wear when you want to make a statement. I'm not entirely sure what my statement is yet, but I know I want to make one.

I sink my teeth into my bottom lip, insecurity blanketing some of my bravado. "Are they too much?"

"On you? Never," Cora says with a wink.

"You sure?" My eyes find hers, searching for sincerity underneath the gentle teasing.

"Positive. I love this laidback style you've adopted since you got here. It's more you than any of that frilly shit your mom makes you wear."

"She doesn't make me, Cora. I'm not a child." I scoff and drop my arms and slide into the seat across from her. The red leather creaks under my shifting weight.

"Eve, you know I love you, right?"

Her serious tone causes my shoulders to tighten with tension. Uneasiness wraps around my neck, squeezing tighter. "Should I be nervous?"

She reaches across the table and curls her hand over mine. "I love you like you were my own sister, but your mom." She pauses to blow out a breath.

"I know," I whisper quickly. Dread coils in my gut at whatever shitty thing my mom has done. Maybe it has something to do with Nana Jo's will or some argument she had with Aunt Hazel. But it doesn't really matter what she's done, because I can't change any of it. And I'd just as soon not hear about it. Not when I'm already feeling bummed out.

She shakes her head slowly, regret painting her features. "Look, I'm just going to say it, okay? Your mom, she's fucked up. She fucked you up—and your sister too."

"Why are we talking about this?" I shift in my seat, withdrawing my hands from Cora's grip to fold them tightly across my chest.

"Hey, no. Don't do that. That's not—shit." She sighs and runs her hand through her hair. "Your mom is a shark in the boardroom, right? She's one at home too."

"She's more like an orca," I mutter.

Her lips part and her brow bunches up over her bright blue eyes. "What?"

I flick my hair over my shoulder and fiddle with the ends of my curls. "Did you know that sharks will flee their favorite, several-generation-old spots when an orca whale simply swims into it?"

She tilts her head to the side and looks at me. "No, how do you know that?"

I lift a shoulder into a careless shrug. "Saw it on a docuseries about the ocean."

I'm downplaying that a bit. I might've gotten a bit obsessed with ocean life last summer after I saw this girl on social media free-diving with sharks. It was wild.

"Right. Well, actually, yeah, that works. Aunt Ginny is *definitely* a killer whale, an apex predator for sure. But Eve, you're not a shark. You're like an adorable otter, just swimming along and loving life."

"Okay," I drag the word out, confusion muddling up this analogy. "I think."

"Okay, so this analogy got a little out of hand. But all I'm saying is that it's good to see you more like yourself. And in jean shorts and cowboy boots, too!"

I glance under the table at them, their brightness vibrant even in the shadows. "I do love these boots. I always have."

"I'm just really happy you're staying in Rosewood, and not only because I get to see you whenever I want. But I'm happy *for* you. Because I think this is going to be good for you. Really good."

I feel my shoulders relax a little. "I think so too."

"I've missed you, Eve," she whispers. And I just know she's not talking about physically seeing me.

My eyes sting with unshed tears and my throat tightens. I didn't expect the conversation to take this kind of turn. I look at her, blinking several times to clear my vision. I reach across the table and clasp her hand. "I've missed me too."

Her eyes well up with tears, the two of us looking at one another with small, matching grins. We pull apart, and I swipe my index finger underneath my lower lashes, catching any stray tears.

"Gosh, you got all of that from some boots?" I laugh, this watery flutter of amusement.

She leans back against the booth, her lips twisting to the side. "Well, I have been binging some excellent shows. I'm practically an armchair psychologist now."

A laugh sputters out of me, and I look at my cousin with enough love and affection to fill this entire restaurant.

"Let's order our weight in French fries and milkshakes. Will you tell me all about your date with *He Who Shall Not Be Named?* I've been patiently waiting for you to tell me about it, but it's been three days, and I'm not a saint, babe."

27

EVANGELINE

"SO, HE JUST *GHOSTED* YOU?" she asks, her face screwing up in disbelief. It smooths out quickly, too quickly, really. "I'm going to kill him."

"Should I be alarmed by how quickly you go from confused to murderous?" I'm only half-joking.

Cora has always been fiercely protective of me, and I love her all the more for it. But I don't want her to get into any trouble.

I spent the last three days binge-watching that MC TV show in my free time, and my mind keeps flashing to what happens to people who meddle in their shit.

I *know* it's fiction, and that the Reapers aren't even remotely the same. Just like I know Cora wouldn't actually kill him, but she'd definitely talk shit.

And I'm a little on edge already.

"Don't distract me. I'm busy. Plotting."

"Yeah, well, it's not that big of a deal." I drag my French fry through the pool of ketchup on the plate. Our waitress, Debbie, gave us a mountain-sized portion of French fries to split, just like Cora requested.

Cora flicks her hand in the air, as if she can bat away my words. "That's bullshit, Eve. You were *excited.*" She pauses and holds her hand up, palm facing me. "And don't try to deny it. You'd only be insulting me." She stares at me, one brow arched in warning.

"I wasn't going to deny it." I lift my shoulders and let them fall back down, swirling my fry around once more.

"Even though I told you not to get involved with them. They're nothing but womanizing manwhore crybabies."

I rear back and look at her, brows arched high on my forehead. "Jesus, Cora," I say, keeping my voice low. "There are people around us."

She sighs like it's such a burden to not talk shit about the Reapers. "If he were here right now, I'd tell him straight to his face. I warned him you know." She pauses and points a fry at me.

"What? When?"

"A couple days ago, when he came in and got doughnuts for you." She shrugs and pops the fry in her mouth.

"Oh, duh. I should've realized that when I saw the box. But I was distracted by—"

"All the dick?" she deadpans.

"No, jeez. I didn't see anyone's dick."

"But you want to." It wasn't a question.

My cheeks heat without my permission. "What? I don't know. I mean, maybe. Yeah. Have you seen those men though? Bane's arms—I'd let him toss me around *for sure.* And don't get me started on the way Nova kissed me." I fan my face with my hand and roll my lips inward to stave any more rambling. "Wait, what was the question?"

"I didn't ask one," she says with a snort. "I just made an observation."

I toss the ends of my hair over my shoulder with a playful huff. "Well, whatever. Anyway, it's fine."

"Fine. But just know that I'm not saying I told you so because I love you."

I roll my eyes with a small scoff. "He didn't ghost me, not really. He told me he was leaving town for a few days. Besides, it's good timing since my car decided to die."

"And he can't text while he's mysteriously out of town? Seems pretty suspicious to me," she says, her lips pursed in a frown.

"What's this one-eighty now? First you were against me having anything to do with any Reaper, and now you're rooting for it? Pick a side, babe." I toss a baby fry toward her.

She snatches it off her little saucer plate full of ketchup and plops it in her mouth. "I did—yours."

"You're the best, you know that?" I flash her a wide grin.

"Oh, I do, but please, keep reminding me," she says around a laugh. "Also, you need to get your car into a mechanic. You can't be staying at Magnolia Lane without a car. If something happened, the closest neighbor is like a mile away. And Nana Jo swore Mrs. Keppner took her hearing aids out after four o'clock just so she didn't have to listen to Mr. Keppner's running commentary on their nighttime shows."

I laugh at the picture she's painting. I haven't seen the Keppners yet, but I do kind of remember Nana Jo telling us some stories to prove her theory.

"Yeah, I will. It died like right in the middle of the road, about a block away. I coasted into a parking spot, thankfully. And then I walked the rest of the way here. I was going to tell you right away, but *someone* distracted me with cowboy boot psychology." I level her with a pointed mock-glare. There's no real heat in it, but I can't waste an opportunity to tease her a little.

"Gosh, that's scary. You're lucky nothing worse happened. And it hasn't been acting weird at all before today?"

I shake my head. "Nope, nothing. I know it's an older car, but

I'm hoping I can still get it fixed. But I'm going to look for a job. I don't want to drain my savings, ya know."

She lifts her head and pins me with a look. "Does this mean you're moving to Rosewood permanently?"

"Maybe." My voice warbles in a weird way. Truthfully, I don't know if I want to stay here permanently or stick to my original plan of only being here for the summer.

She leans forward, her smile bright and eyes wide. It's almost childlike in its unadulterated glee. "I vote yes, move into Magnolia Lane permanently!"

I laugh, not at all surprised she'd say that.

Her palms splay flat on the table as she leans forward even further. "Think about how fun it would be for you to decorate Magnolia Lane. There are so many rooms, and I'm sure you'll want to keep some of Nana Jo's stuff. But, Eve, no one expects you to not make it your own, ya know? This could be perfect for you."

She's brimming with excited energy, talking faster and louder than before. It's infectious in the best way.

"We'll see, okay? I'm not saying no. First, I need to get my car fixed, then, I'll look for some work."

She sits back into the booth, deflating a bit, like someone pulled the air from her. "Shit. I don't think you're going to find an interior decorating firm within a hundred miles. Not one that's deserving of your style, at least."

"I know." I already knew I'd have to pivot. Truthfully, I've been thinking of getting a job for the summer anyways. I don't want Cora to feel like she has to entertain me while I'm here. And I kind of like the idea of a routine, something fun even.

"You already know you have a job with me when I open my bakery, but that's not going to be for a while. I can ask my boss, Shelbi, if she can squeeze you in if you want," she offers.

But her face pulls into a grimace, and even if I wanted to work with her, her expression tells me it's not going to work.

Cora has been dreaming about opening her own bakery for years. We've talked about it several times since we found out Nana Jo left her the money to do it.

I'm beyond excited for her and so proud my ears burn.

"You know I'm there if you need me when you open yours up, Cora. But I was thinking something a little different." I lift a shoulder and let it fall down. "But I'm not going to even worry about that until I get my car fixed, ya know?"

"Sorry to interrupt, girls, but I couldn't help but overhear you're having some car trouble?"

I look up from my plate of fries to the woman standing at the end of our table.

Half of her long dark blonde hair held back at the nape of her neck with a black claw clip, small winged liner at the corners of her dark blue eyes, and the most beautiful shade of rose painted on her smiling lips.

I wipe the corner of my mouth with my napkin, my cheeks warming. "Oh, I'm sorry. Was I talking too loud?"

"No, you weren't, honey, but I was sitting right behind you. And since I happen to own a garage, I thought I'd introduce myself. I'm Dixie and I own RCGC here in town." She extends her hand to me, and I notice her nails are painted the same shade as her lipstick. I absently wonder if that's her signature shade.

Nana Jo used to get her nails done every week, and while she loved to get different colors, she had a signature shade too.

Big Apple Red.

I always thought it was ironic because Nana Jo never liked big cities. She went to New York City for the shows and the food, she'd say, but she'd always leave because there were too many people for her.

I shake her hand. "Oh, I love your nails. Do you get them

done in town?" I don't remember seeing a nail salon in the downtown area.

She pulls back and flicks her wrist to examine her nails. "It's a newer place over on Taurus, at the Oasis. Tell 'em Dixie sent you, and they'll hook you up."

"Oh, that's so nice of you. I'm Evangeline," I tell her, touching my hand to my chest and then gesturing across the table. "And this is my cousin, Cora."

She looks between Cora and me with narrowed eyes. "You Ginny's girl?"

It takes me a second to respond, my mother's rarely used nickname catching me off guard. "Yeah, one of them. You know my mom?"

Dixie shifts her weight to her right, her hip jutting out like she's settling in for a story. "Your mom and I go way back."

"No kidding?" Cora asks, her brows reaching toward her hairline. "Were you friends with my mom too?"

Dixie shakes her head, a few pieces of her blonde hair falling to frame her face. "Nah, Hazel was a couple grades ahead of us. But Ginny and I were thick as thieves since grade school. Until life took us down two different paths, as it often does."

My lips part and I look up at Dixie with a new perspective. I've often wondered about my mom's childhood.

"Wow. I had no idea." I've never met any of my mom's friends before. The only version of her I've ever known has been almost friendless by choice. Unless we're counting those weird work frenemies she has.

"You look just like her, you know," she murmurs, her gaze tracing my features. "All except for your eyes. You've got your daddy's eyes."

I can feel my eyes widen as she dropped that little piece of information. "You know my dad? I thought he went to school in upstate New York."

She lifts a shoulder and lets it fall just as quickly. "Met him a few times when your mom came to visit. How's she been?"

"Good," I answer automatically.

It's my go-to response and it flows much easier than the truth: *I have no idea because she doesn't think to include me in her life. She never really has.*

I clear my throat. "When's the last time you saw her?"

"She spent an entire summer here when your sister was a toddler. That was, gosh, I don't know, probably twenty-six years or so ago."

Huh. My mother will never win any sort of mothering or parenting awards, but I'm pretty sure she wouldn't just leave a newborn several states away. I doubt Nana Jo would've allowed it.

So it must've been before I was born.

Or when she was pregnant.

Now I'm tasked with the shitty job of breaking it to this nice woman that my mother is awful and she's never once mentioned Dixie to me.

I shift in my seat. "Oh, I didn't know she came back here then. She never mentioned it."

Dixie smiles. "Don't worry about it, honey. I'll let you girls finish your lunch. Bring your car down to RCGC this afternoon. I'll have one of my boys take care of you, yeah?"

I straighten in my seat. "Really? You have availability?"

"I'll make room for ya. Consider it a friends and family favor," she says with a wink.

I bite the inside of my cheek. "Oh, shoot. Would I be able to get it towed to your garage? Because I don't think it'll start. It sort of died about two blocks down."

"No problem, honey," Dixie says, waving a hand dismissively. "I'll send one of my guys to tow it to the garage. I just need your keys."

I'm already rifling through my purse for my keys. I unscrew

the car key from the rest of them and drop it in her waiting palm. "Thank you so much. I'll be right over after we pay."

"Don't rush on our account. You girls have a good day now," she says, tapping the key in her palm a few times. She turns around and makes her way out of the restaurant.

As soon as she's out of earshot, Cora leans over the table and hisses, "That's the ultimate Reaper old lady."

28

SILAS

"YOU DID *WHAT*?" My eyebrows knit together and my eyes narrow.

My mother calmly continues her process of shutting down the office for the day. She stacks colorful Post-It notes on top of one another and puts them in a little compartment in some desk organizer thing I bought for her last year.

"I told Evangeline you'd give her a ride home," she answers without looking up from her task.

"Why?" It's practically a growl, but I'm too irritated to check myself.

She gives me her attention then, a steely glare through her eyelashes as she pauses her tidying up. *Shit.* I know that look. Almost thirty-one years old, and I still respond to my mother's *look.* I hold in a sigh and prepare myself to withstand her sharp tongue.

She slowly stands up straight, her left hand sinking into her hip. She lets her face fall into something we used to call her bull-shit look growing up. As in if she's giving you this look, she's tired of your bullshit.

"Do I need to check in with you before I make a decision inside this office in this company I helped build from the ground up?"

I exhale a breath, my cheeks puffing out slightly. "Of course not—"

"Great," she interrupts me, resuming her end-of-day organizing. "So then you're going to take this nice young woman home since her car won't be done until tomorrow."

"I have my bike, Ma."

"Good thing you live so close then. Go grab your truck," she deadpans, but I swear to god, her eyes fucking twinkle.

I glance at my son in the small room attached to the office. He's sprawled out on a big bean bag chair we bought just for him, playing with plastic dinosaurs. "But Hunter—"

"Hunter is more than fine with me for another twenty minutes while you take this new customer home. She's new in town, and I told her we'd take care of her." She looks at me, a single arched brow and mouth pursed into a straight line. "Are you going to make a liar out of me, Silas St. James?"

I run my hand through my hair and grab the back of my neck. "Nah, Ma. I'll take care of it, yeah?"

She beams, a smile so wide you'd think I just told her I'm sending her on some all-expenses-paid cruise, not taking someone home.

"I know you will, honey. Now, go on and get the truck. Let's not keep her waiting." She practically shoos me out of the room with a flick of her wrist.

"Yeah, yeah. I'll see you later." I push open the door, still surprised she pulled the middle name card. That shit always works on me.

Which is probably why she does it.

Whatever. I'll just take her home and then wash my hands of

the whole fucking thing. Evangeline sounds like the name of one of Ma's bowling club friends.

I shield my eyes from the sun the moment I step outside. Someone to the left calls my name out, and I toss up a hand in greeting. I can't stop, not only because I've been hired out like some courtesy driver, but I see some girl circling around my bike.

Dark hair in some messy knot on the top of her head, cutoff jean shorts, and her white tee tucked into the front. And the loudest pair of fucking boots I've ever seen.

Hot pink with turquoise accent cowboy boots.

Helen's fucking girls are getting bold, I'll give them that. I grit my teeth at the prospect of having to kick another one off property for a while. If they can't follow the rules, then they can't be here. It's that simple.

And everyone knows better than to touch someone's bike. It's like the first fucking rule here. My annoyance ramps up further when she leans over to look at the handlebars.

"Didn't your momma teach you not to touch things that don't belong to you?" I pitch my voice loud enough to carry the ten feet that separate me from my bike.

She flinches, yanking her hand back to her chest quicker than I can track. "Shit, sorry."

She pushes her sunglasses up the bridge of her nose. They're big and black, covering too much of her face. I don't recognize her at all.

"You new here or something?"

"Yep," she says, rocking on to the back of her heels. "She told me to wait out here."

I tilt my head to the side. "Helen told you to wait by my bike?"

She cocks her head to the side. "Well, no. Not exactly."

My patience runs thin and I step closer to her. "You don't touch anyone's bike unless they give you permission. That's the first thing she should've told you the moment you stepped onto the compound."

She brings her hand up to shield the sun from her eyes as she presumably looks at me. It's then I notice how small she is. Not tiny but not what I would call tall either. She looks like she'd fit perfectly under my arm.

I shake that errant thought away the moment I realize what I was doing.

"Got it?" I press, letting some of my frustration leak into my voice.

Her brows hike above her sunglasses. She pivots on the balls of her feet, looking from left to right. "Sure thing. I was just waiting for—"

I lunge over my bike and clasp her arm, right above her elbow. "Back up," I grunt and gently move her elbow several inches away, out of range of my bike.

My brother would call me dramatic, but he's never had someone bump into his bike and have it eat pavement before. That shit is painful—in time and money.

"Sorry, sorry," she murmurs, stepping back another foot.

Her cheek grow pink under my scrutiny, and I feel a twinge of guilt. Maybe I was too harsh.

My hand slips from her arm, the pads of my fingertips trailing down her soft skin. A weird buzzing sensation travels from my fingers, up my arm, and sinks into my skin like an electrical current.

"It's fine." The words slip past my clenched jaw with a grunt. I cross my arms across my chest, curling my fingers into my palms to erase that weird tingling sensation.

"I was just curious. I've recently discovered this show, and I—"

"Don't tell me, started watching that biker show and now you wanna ride on the back of some asshole's bike and live out your fantasies?" I droll, arching a brow underneath my black baseball cap.

You wouldn't believe the amount of bunnies that run through here with the same fantasy. It's wildly unoriginal. Maybe if I was ten years younger and didn't give a fuck about where I stuck my dick, I wouldn't care.

Fuck, I don't even know why I'm that irritated now.

"And I was wondering if I could ever ride one," she continues her train of thought like I didn't interrupt her.

I uncross my arms and twist my hat backward, looking across the parking lot to the brothers smoking by the cluster of picnic tables by the clubhouse.

At least they're not close enough to bear witness to whatever the fuck is happening now.

I feel her gaze on me, hot and sharp. And then I do something stupid. Something only overheating could cause. I've spent too much time outside today, I'm sure of it.

"You wanna go for a ride?"

The words fly out of my mouth too fast, like I was scared or something. Which is ridiculous.

She rears back a half-step and tilts her head to the side. "Right now?"

I fold my arms across my chest, feeling better with my weird olive branch. She'll say no, and I won't feel so bad for making an assumption about her. And then I'll carry on with my day and try to forget about her pouty lips and her long legs.

Fuck, just thinking about her legs has me stealing another glance at them.

"You got something better to do?"

I want to kick my own ass. Why the fuck am I pushing so hard? I've never had a woman on the back of my bike—including Hunter's mom.

And yet here I was, practically begging this stranger. I've

never begged a woman in my life, and I can't explain what's happening. Only that it is and I can't stop myself.

She grins, and she looks different. Not younger, but more carefree. Joyful. My lips curve into a frown, and for some reason, her smile only widens.

I'm citing heat stroke. That's definitely what's happening to me right now.

"Sure, I'll go for a ride." She tucks her hands in the back pocket of her jean shorts. The move puffs up her chest, almost like she's putting 'em in the spotlight. Or maybe that's my sex-deprived mind playing tricks on me.

I shift my weight to the other foot and cock my head to the side. "You ever been on a bike before?"

"Nope, sure haven't," she says, rocking back on her heels.

"It's easy. Just like—"

"Riding a bike?" she interrupts me, a laugh tumbling out of her rosy lips.

"Yeah," I grunt, rounding my bike with my helmet in one hand. "Something like that. Just hold onto me and follow my lead, yeah?"

I step into her space, one hand reaching up behind her and plucking her scrunchie between my thumb and index finger. I pull it out of her hair slowly, giving her plenty of time to stop me or do it herself.

But she doesn't. She holds perfectly still as her long hair tumbles around her shoulders. And then I do something stupid. I look down at her, which would be fine except for the fact that she was already looking up at me. All doe-eyed, rosy lips parted.

That fucking look makes my cock stir in my pants. Which is not what I fucking need to be feeling right now.

"Here, put this on." I scowl at her, shoving the scrunchie on my wrist in one jarring movement, and lower my helmet over her head. I fiddle with the strap, adjusting it underneath her chin.

My fingers brush the line of her jaw, and I hear her sharp intake of breath.

And I guess I need to add that to the growing list of shit that turns me on. What a fucking bullshit list too.

Jean shorts, bright as hell cowboy boots, that doe-eyed look, and her quick inhale.

"This is your helmet?" she asks.

"Aye," I grunt my response.

"Then what are you going to wear?"

"I'll be fine, we won't be going that fast. Just follow my lead, yeah?" I turn away from her before I do something more befitting my younger brother and take her back to my designated room inside the clubhouse.

"What if I want to go fast though?"

I straddle my bike, blinking several times to clear the image of her long legs wrapped around my waist and her demanding I go faster in an entirely different scenario.

My cock throbs inside my jeans, a painful reminder of how little action he's seen lately. I try to think of bland shit like golf and numbers and deli sandwiches.

But then I feel her hand on my shoulder as she swings her leg over and settles into the small seat behind me.

Oh for fuck's sake.

This was a bad idea. All I can focus on is the way her body feels so fucking perfect behind mine.

"I'm Evangeline, by the way," she says.

I shake my head a little. I guess Ma is trying her hand at matchmaking now.

29

EVANGELINE

HE TURNS his head to the left and my mouth brushes against his neck. Tingles spread across my lips like wildfire, and I inhale sharply.

"Silas," he says, voice low.

"Silas," I repeat softly. It comes out as a whisper, and I'm almost positive he doesn't hear me.

Which is good. No need to add any more awkwardness to this whole exchange.

My face heats when I think of the way he caught me ogling his bike. I was just so curious, no one seemed to be around, and I'd never really taken the time to look before.

When Dixie told me she'd have someone drive me home while my car stayed here, I kind of expected someone . . . different.

Definitely not this tall drink of water.

Seriously, with the sun behind him, casting long heat waves over everything in its path, he looked like some kind of bad boy god striding across the parking lot to absolutely corrupt me.

And I was absolutely going to let him.

Obviously. I mean, he offered a ride and I barely let him get the words out before I agreed. I almost don't care how eager it makes me.

Now I'm convinced there's something in the water in Rosewood. There are far too many good-looking men walking around. Most of them seem to be tied to the Reapers, so maybe it's a motorcycle thing. Maybe that's my type and I've been going after the wrong men all these years.

He didn't drive a motorcycle, my mind helpfully supplies.

I shake my head, scattering all thoughts of my mystery man away. There's no place for him right now, not when I want to give *Silas* all of my attention.

God, that *name*. It rolls off the tongue like a prayer, and I idly wonder what it would sound like in a very different situation.

I carefully shift my weight and rest my boots on the little foot pegs. I glance from one side to the other, looking for the little bars. Isn't there supposed to be handholds on this thing too?

"You okay?" he asks, his voice low.

"Yeah, just wondering what I'm supposed to hold onto." I'm still looking over the side, my hair falling down and blocking my vision.

"Just hold onto me," he says gruffly, placing my palm on his side. "You'll be fine."

I nod, gripping the sides of his shirt with both hands as he brings the bike to life. I can feel the heat of his skin through his shirt, and my fingers slide up and down just the barest inch. A jolt of electricity shoots through me, and my fingers still.

The vibrations course through us both, a steady hum that feels strangely erotic between my legs. Or maybe that's because I've spent too much time in my head lately.

He walks the bike backward until we're facing away from the garage before finally releasing the clutch and pushing off with one foot.

We crawl through the connected parking lots, slowing to a stop before the sidewalk at the garage's driveway. He drops his leg to the ground as we wait for a handful of cars coming from the left.

Anticipation brews in my gut, sending little bubbles floating through my body. I squeeze my thighs together. I adjust my hold on his shirt, and he lets out a huff.

He turns his head and grabs my hands, pulling them until they rest on his abs. "Tighter, Evangeline. Move with me. With the bike, I mean, and you'll be fine."

I take a deep breath and nod, my chest now pressed tightly against his back.

He releases the clutch, and we pull into traffic. We cruise down the street, fast enough to feel the wind tugging my hair but not so fast where I'm clinging to his back like some kind of monkey.

I look from left to right, noticing all the people around. Rosewood is by far the most active town I've ever been in. There are always people out and about, walking downtown, playing in the parks and on the beach.

Silas's hand ghosts along my thigh, grabbing my attention immediately. He turns his head toward me. "Ready?" he asks, pitching his voice louder.

"Always."

I lean in closer and splay my fingers wide over his abs. And then I try my best not to think about how it feels like he has a six-pack underneath his tee.

The engine roars as we accelerate. We turn left, away from downtown, and a moment later, the two-lane road turns into a four-lane highway.

The wind whips around us, and I feel a lightness in my chest like I haven't felt in years. The bike leans into every turn, and I can feel the power of the engine beneath me.

Laughter peals out of me like fluff from a dandelion, scattering in our wake.

"Oh my god! This is amazing," I yell.

My smile is so wide my cheeks pinch a little. But I don't care. What's a little discomfort when you're faced with this incredible feeling?

The world around us blurs together as we fly down the highway, at least that's how it feels. I feel like I'm having an out of body experience, floating high above the ground and simply letting the winds carry me.

I watch as the trees blur together, a rolling green wave of life. And I find myself suddenly overwhelmed with gratitude.

I tuck my head behind his broad back, resting my cheek on his shoulder blade and close my eyes. Not that I can really feel him with the helmet between us.

For a moment, I forget where I am and who I'm with. I forget about my complicated relationship with my parents, and my deteriorated one with my sister. I forget that I was fired last week and that Nana Jo left me, and I've been untethered ever since.

All I know is the warmth of the body in front of me, sheltering me, and the feeling of weightlessness that makes my soul feel light.

The air is rich with the scent of juniper and honeysuckle. The sun is warm but not unbearable on my skin.

This—this is what freedom feels like.

He eventually slows, and I open my eyes to find that we've reached the outskirts of town. He pulls into a little rest stop and stops in a parking spot along the edge.

His booted feet drop to the pavement, and his left hand reaches back to rest on the middle of my thigh.

Jesus, his hands are big. His thumb slips between my leg and his hip, and his hand nearly covers the entire side of my thigh. It makes me feel safe and feminine.

The calluses on his palm scratch against me, but it's the good kind. Like scruff scraping against the delicate skin of my inner thighs.

He keeps his palm there, and my heart skips a beat. Tingles erupt from underneath his touch, sprinkling down and sinking into my veins.

The feeling is almost overwhelming, my thighs trembling. His thumb moves in small half-circles, sweeping across the sensitive skin of my outer thigh.

"You okay?"

"I'm amazing. That was . . ." I trail off, unable to find the right word for how wonderful it felt.

I flex my fingers against his abs, and I feel them contract. It was probably an involuntary movement, but I can't resist the urge to do it again. Just to see what he does.

My fingers wiggle a little bit, and his free hand covers both of mine with a low grunt, stilling them.

"That's enough exploring for one day," he says. I swear his voice is deeper than it was two minutes ago.

I bite the inside of my cheek and nod. "Okay."

"Tell me where you need to go," he demands.

Oh. Right. We're not out for a joy ride just for the sake of it. He's taking me home because my car is at the shop.

I clear my throat. "Oh, uh, I live on Magnolia Lane. The big white house with the three-car garage and the little porch."

"Aye, I know it." He taps the back of my hand twice. "You need a break?"

I shake my head. "I'm good."

His one hand leaves mine to grab the handlebar, but he leaves his palm around my thigh for the entire drive to my house.

WELCOME TO ROSEWOOD

IT'S YOUR FAVORITE NEIGHBOR, ***and I'm back with the juiciest gossip in town. Just when we thought things couldn't get any hotter, our very own president was seen cruising through town with an unnamed woman on the back of his bike. Looking exceptionally cozy.***

Do you hear that, dear readers? That's the sound of hundreds of hearts screaming as their dreams of tying down the illusive St. James brother go up in flames.

Fear not though, for there are two more St. James men. And dozens of Reapers. You can take the Reaper out of danger, but you'll never take the danger out of a Reaper. And who doesn't crave a walk on the wild side?

Until next time,
—Rose

30

EVANGELINE

"ALRIGHT, honey, it'll just be a few minutes if you want to take a seat. They're in the middle of something right now, but they'll have yours up front in a few minutes," Dixie says, grabbing a clipboard from a nail in the wall next to the desk. She plucks the papers free from the clip, adds the sales receipt I just signed, and staples it all together.

"I'm okay standing for now," I reply quickly. And I am, but mostly, I don't want to be caught off guard if Silas walks in.

After he pulled into my driveway and carefully helped me off his bike, he waited until I went inside and shut the door before he left.

And I'm having a hard time reconciling that almost gentlemanly gesture with the gruff way he spoke. It piqued my curiosity, I suppose.

Not that I need to be *curious* about another man.

My silent phone burns a hole in my back pocket. But I resolved to wait for Nova to text me, so that's what I'm going to do. And if he never does, well, then, I'll just move on.

"Thank you so much, Dixie. I'm so glad you could get me in and fix it so quickly."

I look around the little office as I tuck the receipt into my back pocket. It wasn't nearly as expensive as I thought it would be, but I'm not complaining.

I note the almost coastal vibe of her office, something I wouldn't have necessarily thought of for an auto shop.

Pale blue-gray walls, rattan basket with a lid in the corner, a sand-colored vase with dried sea grass on the little shelf along the back wall. A glass jar less than halfway full of seashells sits next to her computer monitor on her desk.

"You like sea-shelling?" I ask, glancing out the front window to see if they've pulled my car around yet.

"Oh these?" she asks, picking up the vase I was looking at. She smiles at it like she's reliving a memory. "My grandson likes to collect them from the Paddock beach. He used to line them up along the edge of my desk, but they kept falling off and breaking. So we got this vase, and now, everyone is happy."

"That's sweet. How old is he?"

She sets the vase back down on her desk and flashes me a smile. There's a little twinkle in her eye that wasn't there before. "Five going on fifteen, I swear. We spend a lot of time together. I know I'm biased because I'm his grandma, but he's the best child."

I chuckle. "I'm pretty sure Nana Jo used to say that about me."

"She did, you know."

I cut her a look for a second, before it smooths out into a small grin. "I keep forgetting that Rosewood is a small town."

She nods. "Aye, it is. But Josephine's grandbabies were her pride and joy. We went to the same nail tech, got to know each other over the years. And I didn't want to say anything the other day in front of Coraline, but your grandma talked differently about you."

My chest aches but in a good kind of way. Like the way your body aches after an intense workout, but you know something good is going to come from it.

I take a step closer to her. "She did?"

Dixie nods slowly, a soft smile on her lips. "She talked about you like you hung the moon. Said you were always the leader of her troop of grandkids, despite you being the youngest."

I feel tears prickling the corners of my eyes and I blink them back. Grief hits me in the strangest ways sometimes.

"My cousin Abby is younger than me by a couple weeks," I mumble after I clear my throat a little.

"She always thought you'd end up working with kids. Said you had a way with them, kindness when others didn't. She was real proud of you, honey."

I smile, blinking away the moisture in my eyes. "Thank you for saying that, Dixie. It means a lot to me."

She reaches over and pats my hand. "Of course. Life has a way of taking us down unexpected paths, doesn't it?"

I nod, feeling a little emotional. "It sure does."

She withdraws her hand and scoots around the desk. "Let me go check on what's taking them long. Can you do me a favor and just keep an eye on my grandson?"

I pull back and look around the small office. "What? He's here?"

She jerks her head toward the glass door to the right. "He's in there while his daddy is busy in a meeting. It was another office that sat collecting dust, so when Hunter was born, I had the boys convert it into a safe place for him to be when I'm here."

"I bet he loves it."

"The guys sneak him vending machine snacks when I'm not

looking, he gets to watch practically any movie he wants, and he has a whole bin of toys." She says it all like she was saying duh.

I laugh. "Yeah, it sounds like it would be fun for him. Sure, I'll go say hi just so he knows who I am."

She pats my shoulder. "That'd be wonderful. Thank you, Evangeline."

She disappears through the glass front door leading outside, and I make my way over to the back of the room. I can hear the soft murmur of a child's voice, almost like singing. And my heart swells with a sudden longing.

I don't know what it is about kids that makes me feel this way. I can't explain why my heart squeezes and flutters when I spend time with them.

I spent almost every winter break for a decade teaching an expression of movement dance class for elementary-age kids. Outside of my summers in Rosewood, it was the only other place that came close to feeling like I belonged.

I press down on the handle and the door creaks open. Inside, a small boy with deep brown eyes and a mop of disheveled brown waves sits on a bean bag chair in the corner.

He looks toward the door, holding a green dinosaur toy mid-air. A Disney movie plays from a small TV on the opposite wall.

"Hi, I'm Evangeline."

His eyes grow wide and his lips part. "Evangeline? Gosh, that's a lot of letters."

I laugh. "Yeah, you're right. It was hard for me to learn them all when I was about your age. My friends call me Eve."

He nods and sets his dinosaur down. "I already know how to spell my name. H-U-N-T-E-R." He recites the letters of his name with a wide grin.

"That's really impressive, Hunter. You're so smart. Your grandma had to step out for a second, but she asked me to watch you. Do you mind if I join you?"

"Sure. Wanna watch this with me? It's getting to the good part," he says, eyes glued to the TV.

I take a step inside the room and sit down against the wall. "What are you watching?"

"Moana!" he exclaims. "Nan loves movies with music, so we watch a lot when I'm here."

"Oh I love musicals. I used to be in one when I was little. Learned how to dance that way."

"My dad says he's too old to dance, but sometimes he'll dance with me in the living room."

"That sounds fun. I bet you're a great dancer."

"I am," he says, nodding seriously.

I smile at him, feeling a warmth spread throughout my chest.

The door opens and Dixie steps in. "Well, look at you two getting to know each other."

I push to my feet, swiping a palm over my backside on reflex. "Hunter was just showing me a movie."

Dixie smiles, love shining from her gaze as she looks at him. "That, I believe. Your car's ready, honey."

"Perfect. Thanks again, Dixie. I really appreciate it." I pivot to look at him and offer him a little wave. "Nice to meet you, Hunter."

He jumps to his feet and waves with his whole arm. "Bye, Eve!"

I wiggle my fingers and follow Dixie out of the room.

"I hope he wasn't too much trouble," she says, breaking me out of my thoughts.

"Not at all. It was only a few minutes," I reply, shaking my head with a smile. "Besides, I like kids."

Dixie stops before she opens the door leading to the parking lot and turns to me. "Evangeline, before you go, I have a job offer for you."

31

EVANGELINE

I RUN my hands over the soft material of my long black skirt. I already double-checked to make sure my shirt is okay before I left the house. It would be just my luck to walk out with a big tooth-paste splat in the middle of my chest.

I didn't know what to wear to an informal interview for a nanny position with the woman who used to be my mom's best friend. Who also happens to own the garage my car was fixed at.

And who is apparently the queen old lady of the Reapers.

I honestly don't even know what that means, but Cora was adamant that Dixie is like the *queen bee*. So, you know, that only fuels my anxiety.

But I'm here.

Nervous and a little sweaty, but here.

Her proposition yesterday seemed more like a dream job than anything. Hanging out with Hunter and making more money in a week than I made in a month at my junior position at Pine Valley Design?

Piece of cake.

I adore kids, and this particular kid was pretty easy. But

sitting in a little office watching a Disney movie is a far cry from what we'd do most days together.

Hence, the trial-run interview.

I bite my lip as insecurity wafts around me, twirling my anxiety up into a little ball. Maybe I should've worn jean shorts instead?

No, this is fine. I have black bike shorts underneath, and I can always tie up the sides of the skirt, on either side of the slit, if I need to. It would look a little silly, but I seriously doubt a five-year-old will care all that much.

I climb the stairs of the gray and white farmhouse style home further back on what Dixie called The Compound. Like her neighborhood has a proper title or something.

It's a beautiful home with a spacious front porch adorned with a couple of chairs and some potted cacti. The door creaks open before I even knock, and Hunter stands on the other side of the screen, smiling so bright and wide, his little cheeks squish up.

"Eve, you made it!" he exclaims.

I grin, feeling some of my anxiety slip away. "I wouldn't miss a day to hang out with you."

He presses his nose to the screen. "Nan said you're gonna babysit me today because she has to go get a new shoulder soon. Because she broke hers."

I chuckle and rock back on my heels a little bit. "Well, that's true. Your grandma has to have shoulder surgery soon, which makes it hard for her to do all the fun things she wants to do with you. So that's why she asked me to come over."

Hunter nods, his head dipping slowly like he's thinking it over. "Okay. Wanna play cars with me? Or Go Fish? Oh, I know, we should play in Nan's backyard! She has the best tree swing. It's way better than the swings at the park. Nan has lots of movies here too. We can watch one and then sing along together!" He leans his hands into the screen, palms flat next to his face. "Let's dance together!"

I laugh. His enthusiasm is contagious. "That sounds like a lot of fun things. Maybe we should make a list?"

"Hunter Alexander St. James, I know you're not pushing out my screen again, are you?" I hear Dixie's reprimand before I see her.

Hunter's response is instant. He pulls back from the screen like it's going to burn him, jumping a foot back. He tucks his hands behind his back and spins to look at Dixie. "Sorry, Nan!"

Dixie appears then, her blonde hair swept up in a clip at the back of her head. She's wearing a black draped tank top, black leggings, and black sandals. Her clothes might be dark, but her smile is sunny and bright.

She casts a pursed-lip look at her grandson, who looks at her with a contrite expression. I get the feeling this is a common topic here.

"Come on in, honey," she says, opening the screen door for me. "Let's chat a bit before Hunter steals you for the rest of the day."

"I'll go get my cars ready," Hunter says over his shoulder, already running down the hallway.

I follow Dixie inside, noting the cozy living room with a plush gray sectional couch and a large TV on one wall.

"Let's go to the kitchen. I hope you like sweet tea lemonade. I just made a fresh pitcher," she says, tossing me a smile over her shoulder.

"I do." Nana Jo loved the combination, and while it's a little sweet for me, I'm not about to turn it down now.

The kitchen is bright and airy, with white cabinets, quartz countertops, and a huge island in the center. There's a rustic blonde farmhouse table in the dining area off the kitchen with a matching bench seat and chairs. It's large enough to seat twelve.

And I just realized that I actually have no idea who Hunter's dad is or how many kids Dixie has. I didn't even think to pepper Cora for the information.

But that's mostly because I've been avoiding her. Just a smidgen. I'm terrible at keeping secrets, and I rarely keep anything from her.

But I didn't tell her I was coming here today.

The way I see it is there's no point in getting her riled up if it doesn't end up working out.

"Have a seat." Dixie taps the backrest of a stool at the island before she skirts around to the other side.

"Oh, sure, thanks." I pull out the stool, tuck my skirt under my butt, and slide onto it.

"So our situation is a little tricky, as I'm sure you can imagine," she says, bracing her hands wide on the island.

I'm not sure I understand, so I don't say anything. She must read as much on my expression.

She smiles. "Do you know who Hunter's dad is?"

My cheeks flush, and I feel a little silly now that I didn't ask Cora. "To be honest, no, I don't, I'm sorry. I figured I'd meet him today."

She nods, her smile growing. "He won't be here today, but hopefully I will convince you to come back tomorrow."

I chuckle. "I plan on coming back, Dixie."

"Just wait until Hunter runs you around all afternoon. That boy has more energy than any of my boys ever did." She says it fondly, like she doesn't really mind all that much.

"Well, I'll have to come up with some energy-burning things to do," I muse, my mind already drifting to all the things I'm going to google when I get home.

"Alright, honey. For now, you'll watch Hunter at my house while you two get acquainted. I'll be around if you need anything. And then my son will hash out the schedule with you in the next couple of days."

I nod a few times. "All of that sounds good."

She pushes off the island and busies herself by pouring two glasses of iced tea lemonades.

"Here you go, honey." She places a tall glass in front of me.

I accept the glass. "Thank you. And thank you for this," I tell her, circling my finger in the air to encompass me being here.

"Of course. I wasn't exaggerating about Josephine singing your praises to everyone who would listen—and even those who wouldn't."

"Alright, Eve, I've got all my cars lined up in my room," Hunter crows as he runs down the hallway, heading straight for me.

"He's here so often, I turned one of my spare bedrooms into one just for him," she says over the rim of her glass.

My heart aches in the best way, Dixie's affection evident in everything she does for Hunter. It reminds me a bit of the way Nana Jo was with me. And it endears me to their family even more.

I set my glass down on the island and turn to Hunter. "I hope you have a Beetle because I have the perfect idea for a car show."

Hunter slides his small hand in mine and practically drags me down the hallway, doing this excited jump-hop-tug thing the whole way.

And my heart aches a little bit more.

32

EVANGELINE

I'M STROLLING down Main Street, heading toward the coffee shop. I'm in the mood to indulge, and even though I ended up having a blast the last time I went into The Wild Boar, I know Nova isn't here. And that takes some of the fun out of it.

By all rights, I should be tired. As much fun as I had with Hunter today, there was a thread of low-level anxiety that clung to me all day. It's nerve-wracking knowing someone is watching you.

So I call the one person I know is always up for some celebratory food and treats. Cora answers on the second ring.

"Where are you?" I ask, a literal pep in my step.

"I'm at home. Why, where are you?" Cora asks. She sounds busy, like she's walking around her house or something.

"I'm downtown. Wanna meet me for coffee?"

"Babe, please," she says with a scoff. "Not all of us can sip espresso at midnight and turn around and fall asleep twenty minutes later."

I grin, unfazed by her sass. "Okay, dinner then?"

"Sure," she says, dragging the word out. "You're awfully chipper. What's going on? Did you find Nana Jo's secret treasure or something?"

I pause at the corner, waiting for the walk sign to flash. "Nana Jo has a secret treasure?"

Cora laughs, it's light and musical. "No, I was kidding. But seriously, what's with the good mood?"

I was going to wait until I saw her to tell her, but this works too. Maybe a little time to cool off from her initial annoyance will be good for her. "I found a job that I think is going to be perfect."

"Oh, yay! That's great news. Now you can stay in Rosewood forever," she sing-songs the last word.

I chuckle and glance across the street to all the people in line at Uncle Harry's Custard. "You're always trying to find ways to keep me here."

"Duh," she deadpans.

"I'm going to nanny Dixie's grandson. She approached me about it when I took my car in the other day, and I spent the whole afternoon with him today. Kind of like a test run hands-on interview thing." I pause, smiling when I recall Hunter's beaming face when we turned Dixie's backyard into an obstacle course. "It was a lot of fun. And Hunter is adorable."

I'm caught up in my happiness that it takes me a second to realize that she hasn't said anything.

"Cora?" I pull away my phone and make sure we're still connected. Four bars still. "Hello?"

"Do you realize who you're nannying for?" Cora's voice hits that high pitch that tells me she's one step away from tumbling off whatever cliff of incredulity she's balancing on.

I knew she'd react loudly though. Her feelings on the Reapers in general are well-known. So I let it bounce off of me with a shrug.

"Yeah, Hunter," I tell her, but I'm distracted by the familiar form walking toward me.

Short dark hair, dark enough that it looks black from this distance. Straightened within an inch of its life and hitting just below her chin in a chic bob. A black blouse with soft ruffles along the neckline, tucked into pin-straight, wide-legged black slacks.

I miss whatever Cora says, because there, on the other side of the crosswalk, is my sister.

"I'm going to have to call you back." I pull the phone away from my ear, my thumb beelining for the end call button.

Cora's disgruntled voice is the last thing I hear before I end the call.

The light turns green, the sign flashes *walk*, and my feet carry me across the street quickly. My thoughts around my sister are complicated on the best of days and harmful on the worst.

"Lizzie," I call out before I clear the crosswalk.

She folds her arms across her torso tightly. The points of her French stiletto nails digging into her biceps.

"Elizabeth," she snaps, her head tilted high so she can look through her oversized black sunglasses and literally down her nose at me.

Two inches taller and two years older than me, my sister *Elizabeth* is more like my mother than I ever will be. Cold, calculating, ruthless in her profession.

When we were much, much younger. She was Lizzie, my friend. But that didn't last long.

I don't even know why I still try to hold onto that long-forgotten version of her. Of our relationship. Sometimes I wonder if I made it up like lonely kids who have make-believe friends.

Staring at her now, we're strangers.

Two women born of the same parents and miles apart from one another.

"What are you doing in Rosewood, Elizabeth?" I do my best to keep my voice even.

"I was touring in Europe when Grandmother's will was read. This is the only time I could come back." She flicks her fingers in the air, keeping her arms wrapped tightly around herself.

"Oh, okay. Well, I'm glad you got to come back." I don't know what I was expecting. I really don't.

Except that's not entirely true.

I don't know why, but I guess I thought she was here to see me. Like maybe she heard I was staying in Rosewood and wanted to see me on the most neutral territory the two of us have ever had.

"Is that all you have to say?" Lizzie raises an eyebrow high above her sunglasses, her voice dripping with condescension.

"What do you want me to say?" I ask, my frustration leaking through.

She sucks her teeth as she presumably stares at me. "I want you to tell me why Grandmother left you Magnolia Lane when Mom has been promising it to me since I was eight. Do you have any idea how much money it's worth?" She's nearly seething by the end of that little speech.

I bet she'd be horrified to know she has a vein throbbing along her temple right now.

I sigh, unimpressed by her antics. My sister is a world-renowned violinist. So talented that she has companies competing for the chance to pay her thousands and thousands of dollars to tour with them. What the hell does she care about money?

"I don't know, Lizzie," I say, my voice heavy with the emotional load it always seems to have whenever she's around.

"*Elizabeth,*" she barks, emphasizing her name.

I continue like she didn't interrupt me, "Mom shouldn't have promised you something that wasn't even hers to begin with. I didn't even know about it until Mr. Robert told me."

She scoffs. "Right, I'm so sure Little Miss Perfect, Innocent, and Sweet Evangeline had no idea, huh?"

Her words are biting and her expression is cut from stone, sharpened with the intention to cause as much damage as possible.

I clench my jaw and try to hold back the anger that's bubbling up inside me. It's always been like this with Lizzie. She always has to find a way to make me feel small, like *I'm* an inconvenience.

"What do you want from me?"

"I want you to give me Magnolia Lane. It should be mine. I deserve it," she says, her voice firm. She tilts her head back and drops her shoulders like she expects me to cave in immediately.

"What?" I sputter, my mouth falling open. "I'm not doing that."

She takes a step forward, like she means to intimidate me. "It's the right thing to do. And isn't that your thing?"

I shake my head, my eyes blurring with a sheen of tears. I hate that she's like this to me. And I hate that my body's response to extreme anger is tears. Like that's ever helped anyone.

She scoffs and leans back. "Ugh, don't start crying. That might've worked on Grandmother, but you know I'm immune to your antics."

I rear back and look at her. Really look at her. She's thin, too thin probably. Thanks to whatever fad diet my mother is shoving down her throat these days. Her hair looks duller than usual, and her ends aren't the same razor-sharp edge they usually are.

"They're not antics, and I'm not your enemy. I can't change Nana Jo's will and neither can you. These were her wishes, Lizzie."

"I don't have time for this. I have rehearsal tonight. You

know, for the world tour I currently stepped away from to come to this shit podunk town. You'll be hearing from my lawyers, Evangeline."

She didn't listen to a word I said. What else is new?

I watch her walk away, her red-soled heels clicking on the pavement. My heart pounds inside my chest, the anger and exasperation swelling into a wave that I can barely contain.

I'm not in a celebratory mood any longer, my sister successfully squashing that with her little temper tantrum. I never even got a chance to ask her what Nana Jo left her.

It's just as well. I bet Cora can find out without either of us having to talk to Lizzie though.

Tomorrow, I'll ask her. Tonight, all I want to do is go back home and dive back into my binge-watch of my new favorite MC show.

As I turn to walk away, I notice a man standing on the corner, staring at me intently. He's tall and broad-shouldered, with sandy blond hair and piercing blue eyes. Something about him sends a shiver down my spine.

I can feel his gaze on me, like a predator sizing up its prey. My instinct is to turn and walk away, but a part of me is just angry enough that I do something rash.

I turn around, and walk toward him. I don't make it more than three steps, before he pushes off the light post and briskly walks down the street, away from me.

33

SILAS

MY MIND IS heavy as I trudge up the steps to Ma's house. The smell of her making dinner smacks me in the face, and my mouth literally waters.

Damn near every window in her house is thrown open wide, the faux wooden blinds inside rattling as the wind whips through from the meadow behind it.

Two minutes ago, I was dreaming of an easy but delicious dinner. But one whiff of sage and rosemary grilled chicken, and I've forgotten all about pizza.

Now, all I'm thinking about is how I can convince my mother to let us join her for dinner without asking outright. It's this game we play sometimes, where she acts like we're doing her a favor by eating dinner together.

I reach for the screen door handle when her voice whips through the air and freezes my hand. "I'm out here."

I jerk my gaze to the left, where Ma sits in her favorite chair, reading a book.

"Oh, hey, Ma. Where's Hunter?" I take a few steps toward her, scanning the yard for the familiar dark mop of hair.

"He's inside with the nanny. They're making dinner," she says without lifting her eyes from her book.

I stop in my tracks and stare at her. "What do you mean the nanny is with Hunter? What nanny?"

She flips a page and rocks her chair slightly. "The one I hired."

I blow out a breath and drag a hand down my face, tipping my ball cap up a bit. "Ma. We talked about this, yeah? You can't just hire someone. I have to meet them first."

"You did." She still isn't looking at me, like my imminent freak-out isn't noteworthy enough to stop reading her romance book.

I feel my face scrunch up in confusion. "What? When?"

She looks at me finally. "You gave her a ride from the garage the other day."

I shake my head, my mouth pinching into a frown. "What? I didn't—" I stop myself mid-sentence, remembering exactly who was on the back of my bike that day. My muscles lock down, tension rolling down my back. "You hired her to nanny Hunter?"

Ma only nods, her eyes narrowing like she's unimpressed with my tone of voice. But I'm almost too far down the rabbit hole of shit to notice. Almost.

I narrow my gaze right back at her, scanning her face for any cracks in her armor. Does she know what happened between us?

Not that anything did happen. Not really. I took her out on my bike, then I took her home. That's it.

But I suddenly have an irrational fear that she does know how fucked up inside I was about the whole thing.

"*Why*?" I drag the word out, my jaw clenching tight enough to hurt.

"She's Josephine Carter's granddaughter." She says it so simply, like that explains everything.

I glance at the ceiling. "I figured as much when I took her

home. Which by the way, I never got a chance to thank you for that intentional miscommunication. I thought you were setting me up."

"I was."

"With a woman, I mean."

She nods, eyes still glued to her book. "I was."

I sigh and pinch the bridge of my nose. "No, Ma. Like for me to take her out or something."

She looks at me, her gaze sharp. "Do you want to take her out?"

I drop my hand to my side, annoyance swiftly rising to the surface and overshadowing my common sense. "What? No. Why on earth would I want to date her?"

Ma's expression doesn't change. "Because she's a beautiful woman."

I shift my weight to my other foot. "She's my nanny." It comes out sharper than I intended, but I'm not taking it back now. Then she'll really know something's up.

"She's still a beautiful woman who seemed to enjoy your company," she says.

"She's my *nanny*," I grumble through my clenched jaw.

She shrugs, a small smirk brightening her face. She looks back at her book. "Alright."

I start to feel uncomfortable, like I walked into a trap or something.

"What, Ma?"

She slides a bookmark in the open page and closes it, all while giving me *that look*. "Nothing, Silas. I'm just pleased that we finally agreed on someone."

I stare at her, dumbfounded for a second until I replay what I said to her. Twice. I knew she was setting me up.

"Why are you pushing so hard? I told you I can make it work while you recover."

"Because I'm having surgery in less than two weeks, Silas. And you've said no to every other person I brought you to watch Hunter. And despite the fact that you can make it work, you don't need to. That's so much extra stress that you don't need."

I fold my arms across my chest and try not to look like the sullen child who just got scolded by their mom. Then I try the one angle that never fails. "Didn't you say she was new to Rosewood? How do you know Hunter is safe with her? You don't even know anything about her."

She sighs and dips her chin once. It's the best concession I'll get from her on this. "Sure, but I've known of her for years. She's one of Josephine Carter's granddaughters. And Silas?" She pauses, waiting for me to swallow my immediate disagreement. "She's been here for two days now. She's good with him. And he adores her."

I cut a glare to the screen door, like I can magically see inside to the kitchen. "He loves everyone," I grunt out.

It's not entirely true. Hunter's a personable kid, and while he generally gets along with everyone, there have been a few people he never warmed up to.

She tsks. "Not like this, honey. Not like this. Evangeline brought over art supplies and they made a summer adventure mood board. I've never seen him sit still for that long before. Not unless he was watching one of my movies," she adds the last party dryly.

I guess I don't hide my distaste for Disney movies and musicals that well.

My chest tightens, my anxiety sparking as I think about the possibility of some stranger coming into my house to watch my son.

"Fine. But I'm going to run a background check on her tomorrow."

She smirks. "You insult me, son. Like I didn't run one the moment I offered her the job."

My own lips tilt up in the corners. "Of course you did. Two-week trial-run, then we'll see about the rest of the summer."

Ma chuckles. "Don't tell me that. Go tell her."

I adjust the brim of my ball cap, spinning it around to face the back as I exhale. It's fine. I'm just going in to talk to my son and his new . . . nanny. Evangeline.

The word feels weird on my tongue, the letters wrong. But her name feels more right than anything ever has.

It's gotta be because she represents help. Help that I need for my son. Yeah, that's definitely it.

And I'm just not going to think about the way she felt clinging to me on the back of my bike.

Or the way she laughed when I opened it up on the highway.

Or the way I fucked my hand in the shower that night to fantasies of her pouty pink lips stretched around my cock.

I'm not going to think about any of that. I'm going to keep it professional.

I straighten my shoulders and march through Ma's house, careful to not let the screen door slam behind me. I want to see if I can observe her with him for a few minutes.

People mostly show their truest selves when they don't think anyone is looking.

I turn the corner and stop just outside the kitchen and take in the scene.

Evangeline is sitting at the table with Hunter, a massive pad of paper spread out in front of them. They're both hunched over, their heads bent low, as they work on something together. Hunter holds a purple marker, his tongue poking out slightly in concentration as he carefully draws something. Evangeline is watching him with a soft, patient expression on her face.

My chest tightens as I watch them, something warm and

protective stirring in my gut. This is my son, and this girl is a stranger. But something about the way they're working together, so in sync, like they've known each other for years, makes me feel like I'm intruding on a personal moment. Which is fucking ridiculous, considering he's my kid.

But then Hunter looks up and sees me, his face lighting up with a huge grin. "Dad!" he exclaims, jumping up from his chair running to me.

I bend down and scoop him up, bringing him to me for a big bear hug. He's five now, and I'm not sure how many more years I'll get where he wants me to lift him up in big hug displays like this. So I try to take advantage of them when I can.

Evangeline stands, her cheeks going pink as she looks from Hunter to me. "Silas," she says, her voice soft and lips parted.

I tuck that expression away for later.

"Evangeline." I try to be polite, but it comes out more gruff than I intended.

I set Hunter down on his feet and he dashes back to the table, which I can see now is covered in various papers.

"Dad, come look at what me and Eve made today!" he says, waving me closer.

"I—I didn't know Hunter was your son," she says, clasping her hands behind her back. It only serves to push out her chest further. It doesn't matter if she's completely covered by a faded tee, I remember the way those perfect tits felt pressed against my back.

I arch a brow and stop a foot in front of her. "Is that going to be a problem for you?"

She arches her neck to hold my gaze. There's a spark of defiance there, and I find it all the more alluring.

"Is it going to be a problem for *you*?" she murmurs.

"Look, Dad," Hunter says, tugging on three fingers on my right hand.

I drag my gaze from her to focus on my boy. "What am I looking at, bud?"

Photos torn out of magazines, colorful pieces of paper, words written in marker and crayon, and shapes outlined in some kind of puffy, glittery paint.

"It's Hunter and Eve's Summer of Adventure!" he exclaims, raising his arms up high in the air. "We're going to find seashells on the beach and go to rummage sales and play kickball and bake cookies every day!" His volume increases with each word until he's nearly shouting with glee by the end.

I notice everything he said represented on the collage somehow.

"That sounds like fun, bud" I say, my throat tight.

"*I know*," he says, eyebrows wiggling. He's grinning so wide it takes up half his little face.

I curl my palm around his shoulder and pull him into my side for a hug. I look at Evangeline and murmur, "It sounds like a lot of fun."

In the span of minutes, I went from determined to find fault in her as a nanny to desperately hoping she's as good as she seems.

34

NOVA

WE PULL up to Ma's house, more than happy to help her with dinner. I always know she's lying when she says she made too much food but I don't care. It's a little game she likes to play with me, like I wouldn't spend time with her if she doesn't twist the truth like that.

And since we need to debrief Silas and he's here, we're all eating dinner at Ma's tonight.

Bane throws the truck into park, and I'm out the door in the next second. It's not like I'm eager to detail the shitstorm we witnessed. More like, I just need to get the fuck out of a car.

The urge to get on my bike and feel the wind whip around me is strong. But my urge to eat a real home-cooked meal and crash is stronger.

I'll rally for some texting with my girl though, that's for sure.

Silas stands on Ma's porch, arms crossed tightly and legs planted in a wide stance.

"We get it, bro, you're top dog. Relax, will ya?" I call out, scoffing at him.

He's always so rigid, so serious. I can only imagine how tense he's going to be after we fill him in.

He jerks his chin toward me. "Let's talk out here."

I climb the porch stairs two at a time. "What? Ma said dinner was ready."

"It is, but we're talking first. I don't want Hunter to overhear anything," Silas says, not budging from his stance in front of the screen door.

Just then, I hear Hunter's delighted squeal, coming from somewhere outside. Probably Ma's backyard, if I had to guess. That kid can turn a cardboard box and old tire into a game that keeps him on the go for hours.

I arch a brow and sidestep my brother, pulling open the screen door. "Sounds like he's outside. And I'm fucking starving. We've been detouring for far too long."

"What happened?" Silas asks, hot on my heels.

"We followed our old protocol, made sure we weren't followed before we came home," Bane says from behind me.

"I wondered what the hell happened. What did you find out?" Silas asks.

"We're fucked," I quip, following the delicious smell into the kitchen.

"Seems like Savage Souls and Hell Hounds are in bed together. We need allies, Silas. And we need them now," Bane says, his tone conveying the gravity of the situation we could be facing.

Silas exhales. "Fuck. Tell me exactly what happened."

I tune out Bane's play by play, distracted by the woman running around the backyard with Hunter. A woman with long dark hair, a perfect ass in jean shorts, and a smile that makes my chest ache.

I blink several times, trying to clear my vision. That can't be right, can it? I mean, what would she be doing here?

My head pounds from being awake for too many hours, and I've all but convinced myself that she's not really here. She's a figment of my subconscious because she's been on my mind constantly.

"They opened fire on a decades-old neutral zone? They might as well have pissed all over the covenant all the clubs made," Silas says.

"Aye, they were making a statement," Bane says, glancing out the patio French doors.

I know all the sayings about fighting fair. And while I agree with the sentiment on some moral level, all that shit goes out the window the moment I'm backed into a corner.

Because the only thing more dangerous than a man with nothing to lose, is a man who's protecting his world. That man will bend every rule, cross every line, and burn the fucking world down to protect the people he loves.

And I think I could love Evangeline Carter.

"What's she doing here?" I interrupt, indicating the woman outside with a jerk of my chin.

Silas moves to stand next to me, shoulder-to-shoulder. "That's my nanny."

I rear back and look at him. "What?"

Silas wiggles his shoulders a little, like he's settling into his shirt or something. "I said, that's my nanny."

My heart stops inside my chest, the cold, slimy feeling of dread crawling through my veins. Could this all have been a play to get to Silas? It wouldn't have been the first time a girl—or a bunny—used this tactic.

But fuck me, because I never cared about them the way I already care about her.

"Since when?" I'm proud of how even my voice is considering I feel like I'm in a bad mosh bit inside.

Silas shrugs, like the details don't matter. But that asshole isn't fooling me. He's always all about the details. "Since a couple days ago, I guess. Ma hired her." He twists to look at me. "Why? You know her?"

"Aye, I fucking know her. That's my girl."

"Nah," Silas says, shaking his head. His brows dip low over his eyes. "That's my nanny, man. You wouldn't know her."

I smirk at him, letting my thoughts of just how intimately I know her play all over my face.

"She can be both," Bane says. Silas and I both glare at him, but he's unfazed. "It's true. They're not mutually exclusive."

Something about his tone is off and I squint to take a closer look.

"And you? Do you want to attempt to lay claim on my nanny too?" Silas grumbles.

If I wasn't watching so closely, I would've missed it. Bane smirked, it was small and quick. But there's something else going on with him, outside of the obvious house stuff.

And he hasn't told Silas yet. Which is arguably the most interesting thing.

An idea flashed like someone turned on a light bulb. I rock forward on the balls of my feet, feeling a grin spread wide on my face.

"What are you so happy about?" Silas says, his lips pursed into a frown.

"Just realized that now I'm going to get so much more time with her. So this nanny thing at our house really works out well for me," I say around a chuckle.

"Are you forgetting you have a job?" Silas asks.

"Nah, I can do a lot from anywhere. Looks like I'm going to be remote a lot more, bro."

"I'm paying her to nanny Hunter not flirt with you," Silas snaps.

Evangeline chooses that moment to come inside, hollering over her shoulder, "Five minutes until dinner, Hunter."

She turns around and sees all three of us just inside the kitchen and jumps, her body jerking in shock.

"Jesus, you guys need bells or something. You scared the crap out of me," she says, pressing a hand to her heart and looking between the three of us. "Follow up: *what* are all of you doing here?"

"You know why I'm here," Silas says, staring at her.

She nods, holding Silas's stare. "Right." She tilts her head toward us, like she's asking him a silent question.

Jealousy spikes inside me. I want her gaze on me. It should be on me and not him, not when we've gone days with no contact.

I step toward her. "He's my brother."

Her attention shifts to me, and I have to fight the inclination to preen like some proud peacock who got the girl's attention.

"Huh. What a small world," she murmurs.

"Rosewood is small," Bane interjects.

Evangeline smiles at Bane, and I feel that same pang of jealousy twist inside me. I want her to only have eyes for me.

"Well, dinner is almost ready," she says, turning to head back into the kitchen. "Hunter helped make it, so I apologize in advance if it doesn't taste good. He got a little heavy handed with the cilantro."

"Aren't you staying?" Silas asks.

"Ah, no. But thank you. I have dinner plans with my cousin," she says, glancing at me to gauge my reaction. "I'll see you tomorrow morning."

Silas only grunts in response. Fucking typical.

She turns on the oven light and bends over to peer inside. "Hm, a few more minutes and it should be perfect. I'm going to say goodbye to Hunter."

"I'll walk you out," I say, stepping behind her as she walks outside.

I'm content to just be next to her right now, observing the way she talks to Hunter. She's good with him, really good.

I walk with her around to the front of the house after Hunter gets exactly six hugs from her before he lets her leave.

"Hey," she says, bumping her shoulder into mine. "I'm sorry if this is weird now. Me nannying your nephew."

I toss my arm across her shoulder. "Nah, it's not weird. I was just surprised to see you, that's all."

"Well, to be honest I wasn't sure if it was going to last—I'm still not. Silas seems very particular about things, and I'm not always the best with rigid structure, ya know?"

"I understand, and for what it's worth, I think you're excellent with him." I pull her in closer and brush a soft kiss across the crown of her head.

"I gotta go," she murmurs, but she doesn't step out from under my arm yet.

"See you soon, yeah? Clearing up some work stuff, otherwise I'd be by your place tonight."

Her hands wrap around me, her giggle against my chest soothing the earlier ache. "So confident. You can come by anytime, Nova."

She pulls back, and I skim my lips across the corner of her mouth before she lets go.

"You're spoiling me, ya know?"

"Remember what I said about that?" I press a kiss to her temple.

"I remember," she whispers.

"Good. I'm happy to remind you whenever you need it," I tell her, chuckling.

She pulls away and walks across the driveway to her car I

didn't notice before. I watch her walk away, my mind on a constant spin since we gleaned this information.

It's hard to make sense of the evil actions of asshole people.

Following them definitely gave us some general answers, but it opened up about fifty more.

There are too many variables, and I fucking hate all the unknown. I know we have to set a meeting with the sheriff, and I can only hope his replacement is on the same page right away. Or our lives are about to get a lot more complicated.

35

EVANGELINE

MY PHONE VIBRATES on the island next to me. I found a small filing cabinet in the formal family room, hidden inside a china cabinet. Just packed to the brim with papers.

So even though I'm tired after another fun day with Hunter, Nana Jo's house isn't going to organize itself.

I figure my progress will slow down considerably since I'll be busy most days with Hunter. But every little bit helps, so here I am, sipping a delicious iced chai and sorting through what amounts to be a lot of old appliance manuals, bank statements, insurance papers. At least so far.

My phone vibrates again, and I reach for it blindly. I swipe open my notifications, surprise tipping up the side of my mouth at the four text messages on my screen.

Nova: Are you home?

Nova: Because I am

Nova: At your home, I mean

Nova: Open the door, sweetheart

I sink my teeth into my bottom lip, dragging them across as I think of how I want to respond.

Nova: If you're playing hard to get, it's working

I laugh outright now, my fingers flying across the screen before I even realize it.

Me: I wasn't but I kind of want to now

Nova: let me in. I've missed you

Me: what if I'm not home?

Nova: if you're not home, then you're being robbed by some Taylor Swift fans. I can hear the music from outside.

I set my phone down and pad down the hallway to the front door, barely able to contain my grin. I open it, delighted to see Nova on my front porch. He looks like he stepped off of a magazine photoshoot.

Dressed in ripped jeans, a faded olive green tee, and his leather kutte. Several day-old scruff covers his jaw, hair messy like he spent the last few minutes running his fingers through it.

He's leaning against the side of the door frame with one palm, and he lifts his gaze at the sound of the door. One half of his mouth curls into a sly grin, his eyes practically twinkling with mirth.

He holds up a brown paper bag of something greasy, areas on the sides growing dark in a few spots.

"Hey, sweetheart. Gonna invite me in?"

I lean my shoulder against the doorframe on the inside of the house, folding my arms across my chest and crossing one ankle of the other. I tap the pad of my index finger against my bottom lip and pretend to think about it.

"Decisions, decisions."

His smile grows wider. "I learned my lesson about doughnuts, so this time I brought something better. French fries."

My stomach growls, betraying me so quickly at the idea of our favorite food.

I push off the frame and nudge the door open wider with my bare toe. "Well, why didn't you say that?"

"Lead with fries next time, got it." He steps into the house, closing the door behind him and flicking the lock.

"Oh, so there will be a next time?" I ask over my shoulder, walking toward the kitchen. This is still so new,

"Definitely. Sometimes I have to run some errands for work. It's not often, but it happens."

"That's some errand," I mutter as I pull some dipping sauces out of the fridge.

"Hey," he says, his fingers circling my wrist as I reach for the ketchup.

I startle, not realizing that he moved so quickly.

"If there's something you want to ask me, ask me, yeah? Because this thing between us is serious to me. I wasn't off fucking around on you or anything like that."

My shoulders sink. "I didn't mean it like that. I'm sorry."

He nods, his thumb brushing across the sensitive skin of my wrist in a gentle caress. "It's fine."

I glance away, resisting the urge to flee to the other side of the kitchen. I didn't think I was irritated about him just going dark for days so unexpectedly, and I'm *not.* Angry or irritated.

But it poked at one of my ever-present childhood wounds.

It's always felt like a cliché to me. Sad little girl who's wealthy parents don't hug her enough. I never wanted to play into that, but that doesn't mean it wasn't true.

My parents didn't hug me. Like ever. Thank god for Nana Jo.

And I guess I didn't realize how that might affect me in a relationship.

Ugh, I'm getting ahead of myself again. I don't really know *what* to call this thing between us, but there's a part of me that can't help but feel a little guilty.

Because I can't stop thinking about Bane, who I swear is my mystery man's long-lost doppelgänger.

And also that motorcycle ride with Silas. I mean, can you even blame me though?

I clear my throat and absently scan the contents of the fridge. "Besides, you're free to do . . . whatever, you know. We never put a label on it or anything."

His free hand cups my jaw and gently turns my face back to his. His expression is drawn tight, as serious as I've ever seen him. "Let me put a label on it for you then, baby. You're mine, yeah? I don't care what you call me. Your boyfriend, your man, your fucking husband. It's all the same to me, as long as you know I'm yours."

I blink, my throat dry at his unexpected declaration. My heart flutters inside my chest, like it sprouted delicate wings that it doesn't know how to use yet.

I open my mouth in an attempt to reply, but Nova leans in and swallows my words with his kiss. He doesn't deepen it, pulling back after a few moments. I can feel the heat blooming in my cheeks.

"That work for you?" he asks, his gaze fierce.

I nod, finally finding my voice. "Yes. Now kiss me."

Nova chuckles, low and rough. "Feeling bossy, are we?"

I push onto my tiptoes, my hand snaking up his chest to grip the fabric of his shirt, and press my lips to his. His lips curl into a smile against mine. It only lasts a second before he takes control of the kiss.

He tastes like moonlight and dark promises, and I'm lost to it.

He steps into me, and I shuffle back a step, the cool fridge at my back. It's the perfect contradiction to the heat coming off Nova. I let myself get lost in the tangle of our tongues and the way he angles my head to deepen our connection.

All too soon, he pulls away. He leans his forehead against mine and murmurs, "If I don't stop now, I'm going to forget I planned something for us and throw you over my shoulder and carry you upstairs instead."

My eyes are slow to open, the haze of lust thick around us. "If you're trying to dissuade me, it's not working."

He steps back, tugging me away from the fridge with his hand still holding onto my wrist. "You didn't happen to find a cooler in here the other day, did you?"

My brows fly to my hairline, my curiosity piqued. "Yeah, I found a couple of them. And a thermal one too." I glance at the bag of fries behind him on the counter.

"Tell me where it is, and I'll grab it."

I tilt my head to the side and look at him. Excitement swirls inside my belly, splashes of anticipation licking up my spine. "What are you up to? And do I need to change?"

He surveys me slowly, running the pad of his thumb over his lower lip. My skin burns as if he's touched me, and he seems to take forever until his gaze hits mine again.

"You're perfect, sweetheart," he rasps.

My heart flutters at his words, and I can't help but feel like I'm falling deeper and deeper into him. I watch as he strides across the kitchen, his body radiating confidence and power.

My gaze zeroes in on his ass, because god damn does that man wear the hell out of a pair of jeans. Honestly, I was joking when I thought there was something in the water in Rosewood. But the longer I'm here, the more I see, I'm not convinced it isn't true.

"Cooler, Evangeline?" There's amusement in his tone, and I glance up to find him looking over his shoulder at me.

Busted.

I grin and slip my hands into the pockets of my dress. It's a casual ocean blue strappy linen summer dress that falls mid-thigh.

"In the back hall. Gonna tell me where we're going yet?"

"Nope." He grins and disappears in the back hall, leaving me at the mercy of my curiosity and imagination.

I love a good surprise, and Nova has a way of making everything feel like an adventure.

36

EVANGELINE

FORTY MINUTES LATER, we're comfortably seated in the bed of Nova's truck at the drive-in theatre, aptly named The Drive-In.

Honestly, if I wasn't already falling for the man, this kind of romantic gesture would tip me over the edge.

A thin twin-sized air mattress, several plush blankets, a mini cooler that looks like that one character from Star Wars, and two of those reading pillows that have a backrest and arms all make up the perfect little space to watch a movie outdoors.

The last of the sun's rays smudge the horizon in golden oranges and bright pinks, and the air is finally starting to cool off.

We have a prime spot in the lot, not too close to the screen but dead center. He even has two little bluetooth speakers, already tuned in to the movie, on either side of us.

The volume is low, since the movie hasn't started yet. Commercials and movie trivia will continue to play for another ten minutes or so, until the previews start.

He's leaning against the back of the cab, cushioned by his olive-colored sherpa reading pillow, legs outstretched and crossed at the ankle. A beer in one hand, his gaze firmly on me as a smile flirts with the corners of his lips.

I've got my legs crossed, sort of perpendicular to him, just annihilating the French fries he brought. They're not hot anymore, but the aluminum foil and Nana Jo's old thermal cooler kept them warm enough.

It's honestly perfect.

"You ever been here before?" he asks.

I wipe my salty fingers on the corner of a napkin. "Yep. But not since I was a kid. I used to come with Cora and some of my other cousins."

"Ah, Coraline Carter, the cousin who hates me," he says, grinning. He doesn't look too broken up about it, even if I think he's exaggerating.

I roll my eyes. "She doesn't hate you. She doesn't even know you."

He smirks. "She's just being protective of you, and I get that. But she doesn't need to worry about me. I'm not going to hurt you, Evangeline."

To curb my instinct to kiss those sweet words off of his too-handsome face, I put away the rest of the snacks. I toss the dirty napkins in a little plastic garbage bag and pop the leftover food into the cooler at the end of the truck. Right next to a giant bucket of popcorn Nova insisted we get, despite the little picnic he packed.

The trivia music fades and the screen brightens with The Drive-In's general welcome message. The previews are going to start any second.

I settle in against my own pillow, close enough to feel the heat from Nova but still leaving a few inches of space between us.

"Remind me what movie this is again?" I murmur.

"It's an action movie. Something about the apocalypse, I

think. The guy who owns The Drive-In likes to play a lot of indie movies too."

I wiggle my butt and slide down a little, getting comfortable on the air mattress and pile of blankets beneath us. "Oh, I love a good action movie. I always wished they had more romance though, ya know? Like when the stakes are so high, that kind of instalove just makes sense."

I glance at him to find his gaze already fixed on me, dark and intense. I feel a blush creeping up my cheeks. He reaches over and tucks a strand of hair behind my ear, his easy touch sending shivers tumbling down my back.

The sound gets louder, breaking the spell he was weaving over me. I blink a few times as Nova leans forward and adjusts the volume on both speakers.

Then we settle in to watch the movie, the apocalyptic world unfolding on the big screen before us. The action scenes are intense, but I find myself more drawn to the chemistry between the lead female character and her male counterparts.

All three of them.

They're constantly saving each other, even when they're grumpy about sharing face time with the girl. I can't figure out if it's the actors' intrinsic chemistry with one another or if the actual story was written that way.

I get my answer ten minutes later, when all four main characters seek shelter together. They have one of those *oh my god, we might actually die* type of moments and that's the moment they give in to their desires.

The camera pans out to show the four of them tangled up in each other, their bodies writhing in pleasure. It's all done creatively with suggestive angles, shadows and the play of light obscuring the more explicit details.

But oh holy shit the sounds they're making are actually the most explicit part of it all.

A full-body flush rolls over me, and I shift a little bit, squeezing my thighs together tightly.

I'm no stranger to porn, and hell, I read some of the filthiest smut you could imagine. But I've *never* felt like this from a movie.

I chance a glance at Nova out of the corner of my eye. But he's not watching the screen anymore. His focus is entirely on me, his eyes dark with a lust that sends heat pooling between my legs.

There's this charged moment between us, the air actually fizzling with tangible lust. I can feel it crackling across my skin, and my heart races inside my chest.

We're having our own moment. We're not about to die like the people in the movie, but in some ways, I feel like if he doesn't touch me soon, I might actually combust.

Or say fuck it, and touch myself.

We're hidden under the cover of darkness and an illusion of privacy in the back of his truck. I'd bet Nana Jo's cowboy boots that most of the people in the surrounding cars are fucking around too.

I swipe my tongue across my bottom lip and shift to my knees and inch closer to him. My heart pounds so loudly in my ears, it nearly drowns out the moans and grunts coming from the speakers.

Shadows play across his face, highlighting the cut of his cheekbones and darkening his intense gaze.

My bare leg bumps against his thigh, and his hand wraps around it from behind, the tips of his fingers on my inner thigh.

It's the encouragement I needed.

I swing my leg over his lap and straddle his legs. I take my time sinking into his lap, relishing the way his eyes rake over me, his teeth sinking into his bottom lip, like he's physically holding himself back.

I appreciate the sentiment, but I don't want him to hold back. I want to feel his hands on me. And his mouth. And his cock.

Oh *god*, do I want to feel his cock.

I rock against him, just a tiny shift of my hips, my center pressed against his hardening cock. And I'm rewarded tenfold.

He groans, a low rumble of appreciation in the back of his throat. Both of his hands are on my thighs now, gripping tightly but not hindering any movement.

Every inch of my body is aware of him. From the way his gaze devours me to the slight flex of his fingers still clutching my thigh.

I've never felt so feminine, so in control.

It's *intoxicating*.

I exhale a quiet breath, my face so close to his that an inch of space separates our lips. My entire body aches for him, my core pulsing with a need that belongs wholly to him.

But I don't rush it.

I take my time, reveling in the feeling of the slow back and forth of my hips. I slide my hand up his chest, curling it around the back of his neck and sinking my fingers into the small hair there.

And that's all it takes for him to rid himself of whatever restraint he was practicing. His hands slide up my thighs, underneath my skirt, and don't stop until he's clasping my hips. His thumbs swipe slow strokes over my hip bones, and it's the only thing soft about him.

His lips crash against mine, his mouth anything but gentle as he devours me. It's more than a kiss—it's a claim.

A label I'm more than happy to give him.

The chemistry between us is electric, each touch and swipe of his tongue ramping up my swelling desire.

I break the kiss, and we both gasp for air. Nova's eyes are squeezed shut, brows wrinkled in concentration as his lips part with a slight pained expression. He applies pressure to his hold on my hips, stilling me.

"If you keep that up, I'm going to come in my pants like some punk kid," he says as he exhales.

I dip down and drag my lips across his jaw, scraping my teeth along his stubble until I reach his ear. "What if I want to make you come," I murmur.

He shivers hard enough that I feel him tremble beneath me. He pulls me back and I see his eyes are open now, the color totally eclipsed by the dark lust swirling in his gaze.

"You first," he promises, his voice low and husky.

I nod and he takes my mouth again. I expect him to slide my thong to the side or tease me over the thin cotton. But he doesn't do either of those things.

Instead he lifts me up and off of him. My hands fly to his shoulders as he guides me to walk backward on my knees a few steps.

He rips his mouth from mine, flashing me the most carnal grin I've ever seen on anyone. There's fervent need in every taut muscle and shadowed line of his face.

"Now turn around."

I do as I'm told, bringing my attention to the movie screen. Where another group scene is happening. Arousal soaks my thong and my cheeks heat. I'm not sure if it's from the movie, Nova's touch, or the thought of what's to come.

Probably all of it.

"That's my girl," he murmurs. "Eyes on the screen, yeah?"

I nod, determination competing with lust inside of me.

I hear fabric rustling, and my fingers tingle with anticipation. I spare exactly one worried thought that people can see what we're about to do. Even though I don't even know what we're doing. But I dismiss it as quickly as it comes.

As long as I keep my shirt on, the sides of the truck bed are tall enough to conceal pretty much everything.

With his hands on my thighs, he drags me down. I don't

know what I expected, but it certainly wasn't him tonguing the soaked triangle of cotton covering my pussy.

"Nova," I gasp, pushing off his face in surprise.

"Shh, sweetheart. I'm trying to eat." His reprimand is muffled, his words vibrating against my most sensitive area.

One hand wraps over the top of my thigh, pulling me back down against his face. He peels my thong to the side with his free hand, the stitching on the hem dragging across my clit with the perfect amount of pressure.

"Oh," I gasp, my back arching.

"Ready, baby?" he asks, his lips brushing against my pussy in the most obscene way.

I'm nodding enthusiastically, my eyes half-open with pleasure. I think I might come just from the idea of him eating me out.

Which seems insane, but the idea that anyone can see me—hear me—is amping everything up tenfold.

My chest heaves and I lean forward to brace my hands on my legs, right above my knees.

"That's it, just like that. Ride my face, baby."

His quiet praise strips away the last thread of hesitation, and I roll my hips against his mouth. He responds with a growl, like he was waiting for my green light. He drags his tongue through my folds, swirling it around my clit before he sucks it into his mouth.

I'm spinning out of control quickly, the sensations too intense, the pleasure too great. I moan, unable to hold back any longer, uncaring of who can hear me.

He pulls my thong out of the way further and slides his finger inside of me. At the same time, he lightly drags his teeth over my clit. It spears bright, hot sparks of pleasure through my body, and my hips start rolling over his face in earnest.

He slides another finger in, angling them just right and grazing that magical, almost mythical spot inside of me.

My eyes slam shut and my back stretches into a deeper arch, desperate to hold onto that feeling.

I shouldn't have worried though. Nova picks up on my response instantly. He keeps his fingers there, brushing them side to side as he holds me firmly against his mouth.

"Come for me, sweetheart, give it to me," he commands, his teeth nipping at my clit.

And then I'm flying high, obliterated into a million pieces of bliss and floating away in the atmosphere.

I don't care that I yelled his name in the middle of a drive-in theatre. Or that a guy I barely know just ate my pussy like it was his favorite meal. Or that my body feels like a spineless, misshapen puddle of lust.

All I can think about is how badly I want to do that again.

37

EVANGELINE

IT'S SATURDAY MORNING, and I have the day off from my new nanny position. Which is honestly still kind of wild to me. Cora didn't seem as enthused about it, but she'll come around.

It's actually pretty nice that I'm off today, considering I've made almost zero progress on Magnolia Lane since I started.

A knock startles me, and I push off the plush carpet in the living room and head to the front door. All the same piles of Nana Jo's things are still scattered around, so I have to weave around a box of figurines and hop over a pile of cross-stitch. I mentally add another task to my to-do list today: calling Aunt Hazel to come over and start going through everything.

I worry the inside of my cheek as I think about reaching out to Mom and offering the same thing to her. I don't even know if she'd come, but it feels like it's maybe the right thing to do.

If, you know, I don't take into account what Lizzie said the other day. Just the thought of having both of them and my dad in here freaks me out. I'd probably have to sage the place after.

The shape of a man is visible through the frosted panes of the front door window, and déjà vu slams into me. My heart skips a beat and I feel a little guilty for instantly hoping it's Bane on the other side of the door.

I'd be just as glad to see Nova too. But there's something about Bane that keeps pulling me in.

I pull open the door, and my face splits into a wide grin.

Bane's on my front porch in what I'm starting to assume is his signature style: Reaper kutte over a black tee and jeans. Hair a little disheveled, enough for me to imagine running my fingers through it.

And holding a tray of to-go iced coffees.

"I thought you could use some help, especially now that you're watching Hunter. I know firsthand how wild that boy can be."

I shake my head slowly, my grin not fading one bit. I pull the door open wider and gesture for him to come in. "He's not wild, he's just a five year old."

"Here," he says, bending down and picking up two boxes. "These are on your porch."

"What, no doughnuts this time?" I tease, taking the boxes from him.

"Oh, I got you, baby girl." His voice is low, but that nickname sends a shiver down my spine like he murmured it directly into my ear.

He has the kind of voice that you'd hear in audiobooks, captivating and low with some grit.

"One of those for me?" I ask, following behind him to the kitchen, and appreciating the hell out of those jeans of his.

"Dirty iced chai, just how you like it." He takes both coffees out of the tray and nudges one to me, placing a straw on top.

"I still can't believe you got it right. Out of all the coffee drink combinations in the world," I muse, adding the straw and taking a sip.

The first notes of warm vanilla and cardamom hit my tongue

and I audibly sigh. I swear a little bit of my soul leaves my body every time I taste the perfect dirty chai.

He grunts a little, and I flash him a sly grin. I hold out my cup to him, wiggling it back and forth enough to hear the ice shake. "Want to try it?"

"Nah, I'm good with mine. That's all you."

I tilt my head to the side and regard him. "You're too good to me. It's liable to give a girl ideas."

He watches me intently, his gaze heavy as it drags over my features. "I want you to have ideas. Lots and lots of ideas about me."

My cheeks flush, and I can't decide if it's my dirty mind that's going there or if he really meant it as an innuendo.

I clear my throat and reach for the scissors on the island.

"What's in the boxes?" he asks, brushing over the moment like it was never there.

"I'm not sure. I didn't order anything and I haven't even officially changed my address yet. It's probably something from my cousin."

I cut through the tape on the sides of each box and set the scissors to the side. Bane moves around the island to stand next to me, his curiosity as bright as mine.

I flip open the lid, and my brows crash together. "What is all this?"

It's full of seemingly random items. Stuff you might find in a keepsake box or a time capsule. Concert ticket stubs, letters, blurry Polaroid photos, old postcards, one of those miniature stuffed animals with the beans inside, a neon pink kids watch.

My heart pounds in my chest, and my mind scrambles to make sense of it all.

"Is this yours?" he murmurs, reaching a hand in the box and moving some things around.

A pressed flower, a cheap silver locket, a seashell, one of those stamped pennies.

I shake my head, confusion seeping over me like ice water, stark and brisk. "No, it must belong to someone else. Maybe they dropped it off by mistake."

I see him arch a brow out of the corner of my eye, but I can't peel my gaze from the contents of the box. There's something familiar about some of these things. Maybe it's familiar in the way of a shared childhood. I'm pretty sure I had one of those watches when I was younger.

"It's probably a coincidence, but let's look inside the other box. Maybe it'll tell us who it's for." My reasoning sounds weak, even to my own ears. But I'm invested, if a little freaked out.

I flip open the lid on the other box, but this one isn't full. In fact, it only has one piece of paper inside.

A vintage-looking postcard of the Welcome to Rosewood sign. Before Nana Jo and the committee changed it and painted it fresh every summer.

I flip it over, expecting a creepy message on the back like I'm unknowingly in some horror movie. But it's blank.

I don't know if I should be relieved or worried.

I hold up the postcard to Bane. "It's blank. Maybe it's some weird prank? Like you know, send the new Rosewood resident a box of random stuff?"

His mouth flattens into a frown and he plucks it from my fingers. "If there was such a thing, I think I'd know about it."

I roll my eyes playfully. "Of course. I forgot that the Reapers are in the know when it comes to this town."

He grins, his eyes sparkling a little as they look at me from over the back of the postcard. "Now you're getting it."

"Well, I guess I'll keep it for now, give whoever it was a chance to realize they dropped it off at the wrong house. If no one comes in a couple of days, I'll toss it."

"Hm," is all he says, focus still on the postcard.

"What are my chances of convincing you to help me do some more sorting?" I bat my eyelashes at him, holding in my smile.

It isn't until an hour later, when Bane is helping me sort through Grandpa's vinyl collection to make sure they all work that it comes to me.

Those boxes were never postmarked. Someone dropped them off at my door.

LATER THAT EVENING, after Bane's long gone, I collapse on the couch with my arm over my eyes. My phone vibrates on the cushion next to my head, and I blindly reach for it, swiping open my texts when I see a notification from Nova.

My heart squeezes inside my chest in the best way. Those almost girlish sort of giddy feelings spread like warm honey through my veins.

Nova: what are you wearing

Me: clothes

Nova: take them off

Adrenaline kicks in, potent and quick.

Me: are you trying to get me to send you nudes

Nova: if I said yes?

Me: I'm not sending you nudes

Nova: not even on my birthday?

I can just picture that dimple popping out and his broad, infectious grin.

Me: Is it your birthday?

Nova: it's my half birthday

Me: that doesn't count

Nova: tell that to Hunter. He says half birthdays are worthy of celebration

Me: Don't bring Hunter into naked conversations

Nova: so you are naked

I laugh, full-on, out-loud laugh like he's right next to me cracking jokes instead of sending me charming texts.

Fuck it. I'll play.

Me: I wasn't before but I am now

His reply is instant.

Nova: I'll be right there. Wait for me

My thumbs fly over my screen as I giggle.

Me: No, no. I was kidding. I'm not naked

Me: I mean, you can still come over

Nova: I'll be there in ten. And as much as I hate to say it, you need to be dressed

Me: Another movie?

Nova: There's a little thing happening at the clubhouse

Nova: And I want you with me

My mind conjures up the kinds of parties at the clubhouse on that show I can't stop watching, and my stomach dips.

Me: What kind of thing?

Nova: small, casual. Drinks and games and music.

I swipe my tongue across my bottom lip, excitement popping inside of me like a bubble machine.

Me: I'll meet you there

Nova: I'll be waiting

38

EVANGELINE

"I BARELY KNOW YOU." I keep my tone light. "Unless you count what your tongue feels like inside my pussy—"

He sputters, a mouthful of beer flying from his mouth.

I continue my thought, like I didn't get the exact reaction I wanted from him. "Then I guess I know you pretty well."

He arches a brow and drags the back of his hand across his mouth. "Oh, that always counts, sweetheart."

"Tell me something about you." I lean my back against the bar behind me. We're on the very end, close to the wall. Enough space around us where we don't have to yell to be heard over the music and conversation.

And there is a lot of music and conversation happening inside the Reapers clubhouse. It's cleaner than I expected it to be, but I bet it won't be tomorrow morning, after this little party ends.

Nova steps into my space and regards me with a smirk. "You want to have a meaningful conversation *here? Now?*"

My smile falls into a serious expression and I nod a few times, clasping my drink to my chest. "You're right. This is no place for those kinds of chats." I feel my mouth curl into a sly smile. "Let's play truth or dare instead."

He takes a swig of his beer, but I can see his smile behind the bottle. "Only if I get to go first."

I shake my head, my hair falling from its position tucked behind my ear. "No way. I came up with the idea. That means I definitely get to go first."

He laughs, a deep sound that warms something inside my chest. "Alright, go ahead then."

I purse my lips to keep them from stretching too wide. I'm entirely too giddy for this admittedly juvenile game. "Truth or dare?"

"Dare," he says quickly, excitement flashing in his eyes.

"I dare you to kiss me."

As far as dares go, it's a solid one. Or it would be if we hadn't already kissed before. But I have a strategy here. It's about the long game.

"If you wanted to kiss me, Evangeline, you didn't have to dare me. I'll kiss you any time."

He takes a step forward. "Any place." He slides his hand along the side of my neck, tipping my face toward his. "Any *where*," he murmurs against my lips.

I shiver at his innuendo, but he distracts me with his mouth against mine. His tongue flicks against the seam of my lips, coaxing them open easily. Our tongues meet in a slow, searching kiss. He pulls back too soon, and I already know my cheeks are flushed.

"My turn." He grins, still standing in front of me. "Truth or dare?"

"Dare," I murmur.

"I dare you." His lips tease mine, a whispered taunt meant only for my ears. "To get on the bar and dance with the bunnies."

My nose wrinkles at the use of the term bunnies, but I overlook it when he places his big palm on my hip in a possessive gesture.

I shift closer to him and rest my arm along his shoulder, toying with the hair at the back of his neck. I drag my mouth along the scruff of his jaw, stopping when I reach his ear. "If you're trying to call my bluff, you're going to be left wanting, Nova. I took dance for ten years back home. This is nothing."

His hands settle on my waist, the tips of his thumbs brushing against my ribs. "Well, get on up there, sweetheart. Make me eat my words, and then I'll eat your pretty pussy."

"Promises, promises." I smirk.

He hoists me up onto the bar, my breath trapped in my throat from the dirty picture he painted for me. I bet he even did it on purpose, that little sneak.

The music is loud, the speakers vibrating with some country song I've only heard a couple of times. I experience a moment of blinding panic, flashing white-hot across my vision.

This isn't me—dancing on top of bars, having more than two drinks, letting a guy whisper filthy words in my ear. But it's a fleeting thought, gone the second the two girls on either side of me link their arms with mine.

Maybe I hadn't done those things before, but that doesn't mean I couldn't have some fun now.

I laugh, the sound blending in with the music echoing off the walls, and fall in line with the dance the girls are doing. It's like a two-step hip-hop remix, and I pick up the steps easily. Shaking my hips, moving my arms, twirling the girl on my left around—I can't remember her name—our hair flying out behind us.

I feel lots of eyes on me, but I only care about his. I catch Nova's gaze and toss him a flirty little wink. His gaze darkens as he gives me a proper once-over as he takes a deep pull from his beer. Someone must have just handed that to him, because he didn't have a drink when he lifted me on here.

Whistles and catcalls pierce the silence the moment the song ends. I laugh, breathless and exhilarated. I feel light and almost giddy, like I can do anything right now.

I turn toward Nova and bend down until my ass hits my heels. I curl my hands around the edge of the bar, my lips tipping to a grin. I've surprised him, I know I have.

"Have you seen enough?" I tease, arching a brow.

His gaze is hot as it rakes over me. He sets his beer on the bar next to me and steps closer. From this angle, I'm a couple inches taller.

"I think I need a closer look," he says, his voice a low rumble.

My smile broadens and I move closer, my lips reaching out to meet his in a moment of instinctual desire. His hands slide to my ribs the moment his lips meet mine.

Little sparks of pleasure shoot through me, and I moan softly into his mouth. He deepens the kiss, his tongue sliding against mine in a heated tangle. I'm so focused on the way he feels, I barely realize he's pulling me off the bar.

My feet touch the ground, but he doesn't release me right away. One palm slides from my ribs, across my back, and into the hair at the nape of my neck.

His hand should feel domineering cupping the back of my neck like that, holding me exactly where he wants me.

But it doesn't .

It makes me feel bold, like he can handle anything I throw at him.

He breaks the kiss first, pulling back far enough to smile against my now-puffy lips. "You win, sweetheart. And I gotta say, I can't wait for you to collect."

A laugh tumbles out of me. The sound joyful and carefree. That's exactly how Nova makes me feel.

I like to tease him that he's too charming for his own good, and I still stand by it. But his unending self-assuredness is just part of him. And there's nothing about him I don't find attractive.

Plus, the man kisses me with a passion I thought was reserved for romance books and that famous war's end kiss.

We haven't known each other long, but it doesn't feel like that. It feels like we could coast through life together so, so easily.

Nothing in my life has ever felt so effortless before. I could get addicted to him.

"Neither can I." I push onto my tiptoes and plant a chaste kiss against his lips.

His hand settles right on the swell of my ass. It's a possessive move, a statement to everyone in here. Not that anyone has hit on me or anything like that. But I'd be lying if I didn't love the way it feels.

I lean in close and pitch my voice louder so he can hear me over the music. "I'm going to head to the bathroom quick."

"I'll go with you." His reply is instant.

I scoff and roll my eyes, not that he can see me. "It's literally across the room. I'll be fine. Stay here and talk to your friends." I pat his chest a couple of times, tilting my head to the Reapers standing in a loose semicircle on the other side of him.

He drags his hand across the small of my back, pressing his lips to my temple. "I'll watch you from here. That's my compromise."

I chuckle and pull away from him. "I'll be right back."

I'm still chuckling to myself as I weave around a long L-shaped couch packed full of people. I'm pretty sure there are some people close to fucking in the dimly-lit corner over there. I've never tried voyeurism before—well, outside of our little tryst at the drive-in.

But it's not the same as hooking up in the middle of a party like this. I'm not sure if I'd like it. But never say never and all that.

I'm busy thinking about hooking up with Nova while a certain Reaper watches and maybe joins in when a hand wraps around my bicep and pulls me into the hallway.

It's dark in here, the sconces along the walls casting a soft, almost orange glow. I trip over my feet, but his strong grip keeps me upright. For a second I think it's Nova, somehow reading my thoughts.

But then he backs me into the wall. And it's not Nova. Or even Bane.

It's Silas.

39

EVANGELINE

"WHAT'S WRONG? IS HUNTER OKAY?" It's the first thing out of my mouth. In my slightly inebriated state, it's the only reason I can come up with why he'd pull me out of there like that.

"Of course Hunter's okay," he says it like he's offended by the simple question. Like it's a dig against him.

"Okay." I look up at him, flattening my back against the wall behind me.

He's breathing heavily, leaning into me with a hand on either side of my head. He reminds me of one of those romantic heroes from a historical romance novel Nana Jo kept in her nightstand. All brooding and intense.

But this isn't a novel, and I'm not some swooning heroine.

Mostly.

"Then what's wrong?" My brows sink together and I scan what little of his body I can see, looking for obvious injuries. I can't imagine another reason he would be here, like this.

"What's wrong?" His voice is deceptively calm as he steps into me.

Our bodies are flush against one another from the waist down, and he's leaning his entire forearms on the wall.

My eyes lower the moment I feel his cock, thick and hard against my lower stomach. I don't really understand what the fuck is happening right now, but I'm not sure I need to.

Our bodies seem to know exactly what's going on. I arch into him on instinct, and he uses his hips to hold me still.

"What's wrong, Evangeline, is that I got ten different messages that my sweet little nanny was shaking her ass on top of my bar."

His breath wafts over my lips, and I recognize the scent of whiskey. I bet he drinks the really expensive stuff, in a fancy glass. Probably never overindulges. He's too responsible for such frivolities.

Except for tonight it seems.

I tilt my head back to catch his gaze. I can barely see it under the shadowed cover of his ball cap.

Wordlessly, I reach up and spin it around. There, now I can see his eyes. They're angry, molten hot and dark. He looks like a man possessed, and I absently wonder if I'm seeing a side to him that he never would've willingly shown me.

Strange how alcohol can do that. In some ways, it can be freeing. But it's all an illusion. Something to lay blame on if our true desires are met with ridicule and shame.

What does Silas desire, I wonder.

"And what's wrong with dancing?" I ask.

Let's see how far Silas St. James will bend. I want to push him a little, but not so much that he snaps.

He bends his knees and presses his hips into me, and oh holy fuck.

The hard planes of his body press against me, my breasts crushed against his chest. His hips shift subtly, pressing into the growing heat between my thighs. My breath hitches again, and I bite my lip as arousal pools between my thighs.

I can't stop myself from rocking into him. I bite down harder to curb the moan that's desperate to spill free.

"Now every motherfucker in here is going to picture you when they bend a bunny over the nearest surface," he growls.

It takes a second for his words to register, the lusty haze enveloping me completely. Confusion pierces my little bubble, and some of the fog seeps out.

"It's none of my business what anyone else does or thinks while they're doing it."

"They're *fucking*, Evangeline. If you can't say the word, then you don't get to be here and participate."

My face flushes with both anger and lust. It's a potent combination. "I'm not afraid to say the word fuck, Silas." I glance at his lips, plump like he's been biting them tonight. "In fact, maybe that's why I'm here: to fuck someone."

It's not a lie, but it's not exactly the truth either. I don't need to come to their clubhouse to fuck around. But I would be lying if I said I didn't fantasize about all the different ways and places Nova could make it up to me tonight.

His lips flatten into a straight line and I see his fists clench out of the corner of my eye.

"Is that right, hm?" He brushes a lock of hair behind my ear, his gaze following his hand. "Are you trying to destroy my club?"

Mutely, I shake my head.

"Just my family then, yeah? What a beautiful, poisonous butterfly you are, Evangeline Carter," he murmurs against my lips. "So beautiful. So tempting."

His left hand trails from the end of my hair down my side, over the curve of my hip, and settles against the outside of my thigh.

I get a flashback to the way he palmed my thigh when he

took me on the back of his bike. It's a sharp contrast to the way he softly drags his fingertips up toward my waist. I hyper-fixate on the sensation, goosebumps flowing freely down my leg.

I exhale a small sigh, though it comes out more like a groan. It should be illegal for something so innocent to feel so indecent.

But it's not just his fingertips caressing my skin. It's the way he crowds me against the wall and shatters any illusion of space between us. It's the way his cock barely rocks against my pussy, sending little shockwaves of pleasure zipping down my spine.

It's the way he makes me feel bold.

"Do I tempt you, Silas?"

He dips his head once. "I thought you were my temptation alone, but now I know."

I lift onto my toes, getting impossibly closer to him. I won't bridge that gap though. With any other man, I'd happily take charge. But not with Silas St. James.

No, he needs to be the one in control.

"You're wrong. About so many things," I tell him. From this close, all his features blend together and the only thing that stands out are his eyes.

They've darkened to the deepest blue, like a brewing storm over the lake.

It's the last thought I have before chaos erupts.

40

NOVA

RED DESCENDS my vision when I look for Evangeline and see my brother pinning her to the wall just inside the hallway. It's too loud in here, and I'm across the room, so I don't have a shot in hell at overhearing them.

But I don't really need to listen to know something isn't fucking right. I can't even see her anymore, he's blocking her out entirely.

And that just won't fucking do.

I hand my beer to whoever is standing next to me and march across the room. I wind around people and hop over a fallen chair. If anyone tries to talk to me, I miss it completely, my focus entirely on him.

I'm ten feet away, close enough to see he's got her completely pinned against the wall.

Five feet away, and I can see his hips are moving. Is he—is he *fucking* her?

Two feet away, and I see him lean down like he's going to kiss her.

And then I'm there, clamping a hand into his shoulder and wrenching him off of her in one violent movement.

He spins around, brows high with surprise and eyes narrowed. I wasn't expecting him to turn around swinging, but I guess I should have.

I dodge to the right, and his knuckles crash against the side of my jaw. Enough to send my teeth into the side of my cheek. Blood fills my mouth, and I turn to the side and spit it out on instinct.

I take it as an invitation and throw my own punch. I wasn't intending on getting into a fight tonight, but my brother and I have been scrapping since we were old enough to watch those wrestling shows with Dad and Uncle Walker.

He used to be bigger than me, but that was years ago. Now, we're evenly matched.

Blood spurts from his nose like a goddamn geyser. And tomorrow I might hate myself for it, but I feel a sick sort of satisfaction at the sight.

Mr. Calm-and-Collected looks unruly for once. I tongue my cheek and grin at him, hoping I look half as crazed as I feel.

It's then I noticed we've garnered the attention of nearly everyone in here. I feel their collective stares on us, and I roll my shoulders back under their weight.

The music still blares from the speakers, but the conversation has quieted down to low murmurs.

Fights aren't unheard of, but they're not commonplace either.

"Nova?" Her voice is hesitant, quiet even. Fuck knows how I heard it over the blood whooshing in my ears.

I glance up to find Evangeline's horrified eyes on me. Her terror takes the wind out of my sails faster than anything else could have.

The fight doesn't drain out of me, I'm not a fucking robot.

But it does cool enough for me to back-burner that shit and switch my focus to her.

I make it to her in three steps, my hands finding the sides of her face. "Fuck, I'm sorry, sweetheart. Are you alright?"

Her eyes are bloodshot. Wide and glassy. Like one sweep of those long lashes will send tears cascading down her cheeks. Just the thought of making her cry pierces my already bruised heart.

"Me? Are *you* okay?" Her hands land on my shoulders, fluttering around my face. "Oh my god, Nova. You just punched your *brother*!"

Her voice pitches high by the end, and like her voice alone conjured him, I feel him behind me.

"You and me, outside, right the fuck now. Before I forget that you're my brother," he snaps.

Her hands fist my tee. "What's happening? I don't understand! Why are you guys fighting!"

"It's nothing," I reassure her. The lie tastes like ash on the back of my tongue.

"No, it's not nothing," she counters. Some of the fire sparks back to life in her gaze, and that eases some of the tension in my shoulders.

"Outside, Nova," Silas barks from somewhere behind us.

I see Jagger hover just to my left. He may be a Reaper, but he was my fucking friend first. And loyalty means everything in a club, even a reformed one like ours.

"You good, man?" Jagger asks, keeping his voice low.

I don't take my gaze from Evangeline, my words for both of them. "Sometimes brothers fight. It doesn't happen often, but it does happen. Nothing to worry about."

Jagger nods. "Got your back, brother."

I glance at him over my shoulder. "Appreciate that. Do me a favor, yeah? Make sure my girl gets home safe."

"What?" she asks, pushing off the wall to stand up. "I'm not leaving yet. Not when I caused this mess."

I brush some of her hair away from her face. It's a little damp from her dancing, but she's still the most beautiful thing I've ever laid eyes on.

"It's not your fault, sweetheart. Just some club shit Silas and I need to work out between us. Jagger will make sure you get home safe."

She arches a brow and folds her arms across her chest, defiance painted across her face in bold strokes.

It backfires though. Because all it does is push her tits up. My gaze drops to those creamy swells and my cock automatically twitches in my pants.

Read the fuckin' room, bro. Now is not the time.

She glances away, nibbling her bottom lip. "You promise it's not about me? I don't like the idea of causing problems in your family."

I guide her chin to face me again. "You're never a problem, yeah?"

Her gaze bounces between my eyes, worry turning them down in the corners. "Maybe I should talk to Silas first—"

"He's fine. And he's not going to fire you, don't worry about it. Let me handle my brother."

"Alright," she says, almost begrudgingly.

I slide my hand to the back of her neck, using my thumb to tip her face up. "And sweetheart, let me in when I come by later, yeah?"

"Okay," she breathes.

I don't wait for her to finish her word, sealing my lips and swallowing anything else she has to say. The kiss is slow, soft. As if I'm trying to make up for the fact that I just punched my brother in front of her.

She leans into me, moaning in my mouth as our tongues

dance with one another. All too soon, I pull away. I regret it immediately, and I realize with stark clarity that I could spend the rest of my life kissing Evangeline Carter. Happily.

"Go home, sweetheart," I say, my voice gruff with need.

"Okay," she whispers, her eyes glassy for an entirely different reason than before.

I watch her walk away, my heart thundering in my chest. "Follow her, make sure she gets home safely."

Jagger steps out of the shadows to my left. "On it. You sure you'll be okay? I've never seen Prez like this before."

I nod, keeping my gaze on my girl until she turns the corner. "I'll be fine."

41

NOVA

SILAS IS WAITING OUTSIDE, calmly pacing the sidewalk kind of like a caged animal. He stops the moment I step into the parking lot.

"What the fuck, Nova?" he snaps.

I wiggle my fingers out, letting my hands hang loosely at my sides. "What the fuck is right, *Silas*."

I use his name intentionally. Right now, he's my brother, not my fucking president.

He takes a single step toward me, pointing his index finger toward me, eyes wide. "Stay away from her, Nova."

My mouth drops open and I stare at him. I never put too much stock in aliens and shit, but for the first time, I start to wonder if there's a bodysnatcher situation happening right now. I've never seen him act like this before.

"Are you fucking kidding me right now?" My voice is low, as even as I can make it with the incredulity coursing through my veins.

"That goes for all of you. Stay the fuck away from my nanny," Silas bellows, totally disregarding me.

Several of the guys back up with their hands in the air, palms facing him in the universal gesture for surrender.

But not me. I'm so fucking far from surrender it's laughable.

"Hey, no problem, Prez," one of the brothers shouts.

"It was all above board, Prez. We were just having a bit of fun," Gunnar chimes in, backing up a few steps.

"Alright, alright. Show's over, yeah? C'mon, boys, there are bunnies inside. Let's not keep 'em waiting, yeah?" Ace shouts. He flashes me a concerned glance, which I promptly ignore.

The parking lot clears out, leaving just me and my brother under the street lamps in our parking lot.

He spins to face me. "Stay the fuck away from her. I mean it, Asher."

I laugh. I can't help it. I tip my face toward the moonlight and let out my disbelief. I turn and look at him. "Are you fucking for real right now, man? You're going to try to scold me with my real name like you're Dad? Who the fuck do you think you are talking to me like that? Huh?"

Tension lights up my body like a fucking Christmas tree, and I worry I might be wrong. Everything isn't going to be fine.

"Who the fuck am I?" he yells, advancing toward me and tapping his chest. "I'm your motherfucking president, so you better fucking listen to my orders." His words are damn-near snarled, his index finger pointing toward me.

Two more steps and he'd be officially in my face. Guess he's not eager for another shot to his pretty boy face.

I arch a brow, feeling the cruel twist of my lips. "Oh, it's an order now, huh?"

He scowls, his jaw clenched. "Aye, it's a fucking order." He takes his hat off, runs his hands through his hair, and settles it over his head once more. All done in these fast, quick movements.

And I realize all at once what's happening. Shocked feels like an understatement, but now that my head's cooled, I can reflect on that little scene inside the clubhouse with perspective.

He wasn't forcing Evangeline, and she wasn't trying to get away.

My brother wants my girl, and it's tearing him up inside.

A release a low chuckle into the warm night air, the sound harsh even to me. "You're jealous, aren't you." It's not a question.

He bristles, his eyes narrowing. "I'm not fucking jealous. I'm you're fucking president, and I'm giving you an order."

I back up a few steps, forcing my smile into something closer to normal, and holding out my arms wide on either side of me. "Alright then. I guess I'm out."

His brows cave in and he plants his hands on his hips. Hands that were all over my girl ten minutes ago.

"What do you mean you're out? You can't leave *family*."

I don't say anything, just continue to walk backward toward my bike.

"You don't leave the Reapers, brother. You know that," he says, his voice low and full of warning.

It's wasted on me though. This isn't about the club, not really. And I'm tired of all the fucking secrets in this family. The rambling confessions of a man on his deathbed have haunted me for five years.

"Maybe not ten years ago, but this is the new chapter, *brother*. We're not even in the real game anymore. So all this"—I hold my arms out and spin in a little semicircle—"it's not even real."

"But she is?" he presses, his eyes narrowed.

"I don't know, man, why don't you tell me?" I challenge him.

He doesn't say anything then. He just looks at me with his hands on his hips and his ball cap low over his eyes.

"You're going to throw your family away for her? Me, Bane, Ma? *Hunter*?"

I stop. "Fuck you, man. Fuck you for making it a choice. Not everything is black and white."

"I lived in shades of gray for longer than you will ever know. So don't preach to me about choices."

I slide both of my hands through my hair and tug on the ends, puffing out a breath. "Why can't you just admit it, huh? Why can't you just say 'I'm sorry. I stepped in on your girl because I can't help myself and I'm fucking jealous.'"

He scoffs. "Are you drunk, man? I'm not fucking jealous," he seethes like the whole idea is preposterous. "I'm looking out for the best interests of my family. Hunter fucking loves her already. Are you going to be the one to break the news when she stops coming around because you fuck up? Huh?"

He could have punched me in the face again and it would have hurt less than this.

"Wow. Nice to know that's how you really think of me, brother."

His face loses some of that tension, his scowl still in place. He shifts from foot to foot. "You used to run through women like water, man. That shit's common knowledge."

I shrug. "Not for a long time, man. I'm a changed man and all that. It's irrelevant through, because me and Evangeline? We're fucking end game, bro."

He smirks but it's mean as hell. I already know he's going to run his mouth again.

"Yeah, totally looked like it when she was grinding against my cock inside the clubhouse."

My temper flares because yeah, that shit still feels weird. First Bane and now Silas?

"Are you *trying* to get punched, man? I'm doing my best, but I'm only fucking human. Stop pushing me," I warn.

He shrugs, looking smug as fuck. Like he dropped a little bomb on me I didn't know about. But I'm not a fucking idiot. I saw the way they both watch each other when the other isn't looking. It's the same way her and Bane danced around one another at Magnolia Lane.

"Just laying it out for you, so you know exactly who you're trying to walk away from your family for."

"Stop acting like you did something for my benefit. We both know exactly why you were all over her tonight." I sigh, suddenly tired of these circles we're going in. "We both know I'm not choosing her over you or anyone. Just like we both know you're not really ordering me to stop seeing my girlfriend. So we're at an impasse for the night."

He grunts, which I guess is as good of a response as any.

I walk backward, toward where I parked my bike. "So I'm going to call it a night. I have a gorgeous brunette expecting me. Don't wait up."

I flash him a wink just to be a dick. Silas hasn't stayed up for me since I was fifteen years old, but I bet my bike he's going to stay up waiting for me tonight. If only to see what time I come home.

Unfortunately, he's going to be tired as hell tomorrow, because I don't plan on coming home at all tonight.

42

EVANGELINE

I HEAR a thumping noise over the low hum of the water running. I turn off the tap and dry my face. That was fast. I didn't expect him so soon. But that must be a good thing, right?

I've been home for a few minutes. The first thing I did was march upstairs and take my makeup off.

Jagger waited until I got inside before he pulled out of the driveway, a kindness I find endearing. Actually, the fact that he even followed me home was kind, even if he did it as a favor to Nova.

Guilt swirls around in my gut like a maelstrom. I don't believe him for one second that I didn't cause . . . whatever that was.

Maybe it's conceited of me to think it was all me, but it definitely had something to do with me.

Also the fact that I was enjoying the way Silas felt between my legs. Yeah, that adds a dollop of shame onto my guilt storm.

Everything feels sweaty, and I'd love nothing more than to hop in the shower and wash tonight's events off. But another thump sounds from somewhere outside, so the shower will have to wait. Guess Nova's here already.

And it has to be Nova, because there's no way Silas would come running after me. Please, I can't imagine that man ever bent for anyone, let alone his nanny.

Which is all I'll ever be in his eyes. I don't even have the energy to unpack those feelings tonight.

And I don't know where the hell Bane was, but it wasn't at the clubhouse.

So, yeah, that leaves Nova pounding on my front door. I can't decide if I should be annoyed with myself for my instant relief. Or just revel in the fact that he's already here.

I won't deny there's something alluring about a man possessed with the need to help his woman. Or hell, maybe it's just me.

I swear my feminism takes flight half the time I'm around those St. James men.

I think we need to have a conversation tonight. One where I try to articulate that I have a growing attraction to his brother and his cousin. On top of my feelings for him.

And then maybe if all goes well, I can convince him to join me in the shower.

I meant what I said though. I don't want to cause problems for anyone. They're *family*.

And I haven't known Hunter very long, but he's easy to love. I would never make his life confusing or complicated.

Mostly, I just hate that Silas had a point. Kind of.

It's hard to remember what his point was when his lips were so close to mine. I could have sworn he was two seconds away from actually kissing me.

I hear another thump. This one sounds like it's coming from the living room. I'm pretty sure I locked the door, even though everyone repeatedly tells me I don't need to. It's a habit for me, and except for that one time with Bane, the front door remains locked even when I'm home.

I take my time dressing, figuring I'll make him sweat it out a little more. I wonder if he brought me French fries instead of flowers. I giggle at the image in my mind of him organizing an elaborate display of fries and dipping sauces on the island.

Dressed in an oversized tee that I found in a box of my old stuff and a pair of short shorts, I throw my hair up into a messy bun. The tee is so old, the graphic is mostly faded, but I think it's some nineties band. The collar is stretched out, so it's always slipping off my shoulder.

But it might be the softest tee I own, and right now, I could use a little comfort.

I skip down the stairs, thinking about Nova and French fries when the sound registers.

It's not knocking on my front door, or even Nova setting anything up in the kitchen.

Someone's rifling through the piles of Nana Jo's things in the living room.

I tiptoe closer, my heart lurching inside my chest. No, not someone. Three someones. Dressed in dark colors with hats or ski masks on. They're murmuring to one another, tossing everything they can get their hands on in big black garbage bags.

My hand flies to my back pocket, where I always keep my phone. But when I hit soft nylon, I remember I left it upstairs. I curse the fact that these shorts don't come with pockets as I proceed to have a five-second absolute panic meltdown.

I don't know who's in my house or how they got in here or if they're armed.

Bottom line: I need my phone.

I try to steady my breathing as I take a step back, going up the stairs. And I hope like hell they don't turn around and see me. I take another step back, staying on my tiptoes.

This stair creaks, and I freeze. It's quiet, soft enough that I don't think they hear it over their low murmuring. My heart is thundering in my ears, and a flush of fear rolls down my body.

Their conversation doesn't pause, so I'm in the clear. I make it another two stairs before I hit another creak. And I know I'm in trouble. It's loud, too loud to go unnoticed.

"Hey, did you hear that?" someone asks, their voice a little louder, like they're coming toward me.

I don't have time to think. I turn on the ball of my foot and sprint upstairs. I only make it two stairs before a hand clamps around my bicep.

"Where the fuck do you think you're going?" a low voice growls from right behind me.

I struggle against the grip, thrashing as much as I can to get free. My bare toes slip on the stairs, and I lose my balance. The person holding me grunts and swings me into the wall with such force that it stuns me still.

"What do we have here, huh?"

I peer up at the person in front of me. He's the tallest of the three people, leering over me while the other two hover by the front door.

"What's going on?" one of the other people ask.

"Found us a little bonus present," the tall guy in front of me says. He sounds entirely too joyful for the situation, and it makes something inside me curl up in fear.

"What do you want?" I flatten myself against the wall, trying to appear as small as possible. I creep further away, bracing myself to inch up another stair and get further away.

"Everything," he says.

43

EVANGELINE

"STOP MOVING," he commands.

Quicker than a snake, he lashes out, palms my head, and shoves it into the wall. Pain burst behind my eyelids.

"Fuck, man. C'mon. She's not part of the mission tonight," one of them says.

"You said there would be jewels and cash here. A shit ton of valuable shit," the tall guy shouts at one of his accomplices.

"There is," the shortest one grumbles, voice pitched low.

"Where?" the tall guy snaps.

The shortest one shifts from foot to foot, pointing a finger at me. "Ask her."

I blink several times, trying to get my vision to clear. I hit the wall hard, but I don't think I'm seriously hurt. I know I can't outrun them, not when they're boxing me in on the staircase like this.

"So much for the place being empty. We pulled you in and this is the thanks we get? A botched fucking job. The boss is gonna love this," the tall guy says, leering at the other two.

"Well, it looks like we're fucked then, eh? Best get on with it," the shorter guy says.

I try to swallow my whimper, my mind going straight to the worst scenario. "Please don't kill me."

The tall one grabs me by the top of my hair, and my hand flies to grab onto his wrist, like that's going to stop him. My fingers dig into the leather gloves he's wearing, and I have half a thought to sink my nails into his skin. They can extract DNA from underneath my fingernails. I've seen it on those crime shows.

But then he tugs, like he knew my attention drifting for a second. I arch up to try and lessen the strain. His face is less than a foot in front of mine, and backlit by the lamp from the hallway, he looks like some kind of demon sent from hell.

A black ski mask covers everything but his eyes. Dark pools of inky black greet me, his pupils blown so wide, I can't tell where they end. His gaze promises me pain, so much more pain.

I flinch, but it only pulls my hair harder.

"We're not going to kill you." He pauses and cocks his head to the side. "Well, at least not until after we get what we want."

"No cleanup," one of the two grunt behind him.

I can't see his face, but I just know he's grinning behind that fabric mask. I can feel the cruelty roll off of him in waves.

"You two, go get what we need from this floor. And you, answer our questions and I'll make it quick and relatively painless for you."

I lick my lips, my temples throbbing. "Okay."

He lets go of my hair and backhands me. It was so quick I didn't see it coming and didn't have time to brace for anything.

My head snaps to the side, and I can feel the sting radiating throughout my cheek. Tears prick at the corners of my eyes, but I refuse to let them fall. I won't give him the satisfaction.

"That was just for fun. Now we can get started," he says.

"Hurry up, man. I got a bad feeling," one of the accomplices mutters.

"Yeah, yeah." He reaches down and grabs two fistfuls of my shirt, pulling me off the stair. "Where the fuck is the jewelry, bitch?" He's in my face, shaking me with each shouted word.

I try to bring my hands up to my face when I feel something wet and warm by my hairline. "Wh-what?"

He elbows my hands away and lets go of my shirt. I hit the stairs with a thud, the edge jamming into the middle of my spine.

"I said, where's the fucking jewelry?" He backhands me before he finishes asking the question.

I hear yelling in the background, but my ears are ringing too loudly for me to make out any words. My head lolls to the side and I try to cup my cheek on instinct.

But I feel like I'm underwater. My arm feels heavier than it should be, and it takes too long to bring it to my face.

He bends down, so his face is right in front of mine. Terror scrambles my senses, and my hands and legs start trembling. I look at him with a sobering realization.

I might die tonight.

"I asked you a question, bitch," he growls.

He's close enough that I can smell his breath, even through the mask. My stomach churns at the sour, putrid stench, and I try not to gag.

Though maybe vomiting all over him would actually help. Might buy me enough time to scramble up the stairs and find a weapon.

"I don't have any jewelry," I tell him, trying to keep my voice steady. But it started trembling with the rest of my body, and now I can't seem to make it stop.

"Wrong answer," he snaps.

He reaches behind his back, and fear unlike anything I've ever felt before floods my veins. I scramble up the stairs in the strange crab-walk position I'm stuck in. I make it two stairs before there's a gun in my face.

An honest-to-god gun.

I've never even been this close to a gun before. Everything inside me slows down. I don't feel myself trembling or hear my ragged breathing. I don't see anything beyond the radius of this evil man in front of me, holding a gun to my head.

And then one sound filters in. It might be the best motherfucking sound I've ever heard.

A motorcycle.

I look at the man in front of me, and I grin.

"Fuck, someone's coming," one of them rushes out.

"Time to go, asshole. Leave the girl," the other one says.

The guy in front of me doesn't move though. "We didn't complete the mission. I'm not going back empty-handed."

"We're not. We got plenty of shit. Let's fucking go," one of them insists.

I still can't see anything beyond the man in front of me. I'm doing my best to block out the fact that I'm inches from certain death, but a cold sweat breaks out along the back of my neck. I'm trying my hardest just to hold on.

I've never passed out before, but if I had to guess, I imagine the black spots dancing at the edge of my vision are a good indicator.

He climbs one step, looming over me once more. "Just tell me where the fucking jewels are and this will all be over."

I shake my head, my vision swimming. "I don't have any."

He brings his hands to his head, resting his gun on top as he leans back. "Fuck," he yells, elongating the middle of the word, stretching it out into several syllables.

"Fuck this. If you want to go down because you don't know when to walk away, fine. But we're out of here," the talkative one says.

I don't hear the other one say anything, but I assume they leave too. Rustling and clanging rings out through the house as they make their big getaway.

The guy takes a step away from me, and I watch him with bated breath. Maybe he came to his senses and he's going to follow his buddies too. Maybe everything will be okay after all.

My hope incinerates in front of me when he quickly back-steps down the rest of the stairs. He presses his back to the wall next to the door, gun raised. He puts his index finger in front of his mouth, telling me to be quiet.

Fear seizes my chest, and I open my mouth and scream Nova's name.

I'll be damned if I sit by and do nothing as he hurts Nova.

He moves fast, bounding up the stairs in the time it takes me to blink.

"You fucking cunt," he yells, bringing the gun down on the side of my head.

Everything goes black.

44

BANE

SHE SCREAMED my cousin's name. But considering I just left him and Silas arguing in the parking lot, I know he's not here.

Which means she's in trouble.

My heart pitches up my throat as my mind spirals into the worst possible scenarios. Are the Savage Souls and Hell Hounds making plays already? It seems sloppy and random.

Unless they've been watching us. They would've seen her with all of us.

I kill the lights and open my saddlebag at the same time. Two seconds later, I'm creeping along the exterior wall of the house, my favorite gun raised and ready.

I haven't used it in a long time. And I was happy for it. But I've never been more fucking glad to have it on me than I am right now.

I have no idea what kind of situation I'm walking into, but if there's one good thing my ma always taught me, it's to prepare for the worst.

The front door is cracked open, but Evangeline is silent. I don't know if that's a good sign or a very bad one.

Fuck this. Time to get it over with.

I toe open the door, flicking my ankle to send the door flying into the wall behind it.

There, crouched over my girl's prone form, is a walking dead man.

I don't warn him or give him a chance to explain. I point my gun and pull the trigger.

He lets out a surprised grunt, clutching his chest and falling to the stairs next to her.

Well, that won't fucking do, will it.

I rush inside the house, acutely aware there could be more people lying in wait. I don't lower my gun as I take the stairs two at a time until I reach them.

I kneel down next to Evangeline, my heart throbbing inside my chest like someone reached in and squeezed the fuck out of it. I press my fingers against the side of her neck, sighing when I feel her pulse. Strong, steady.

A relieved breath escapes my lips, and I murmur a silent thanks to whoever the fuck listens.

I hate to leave her, but I have to clear the house first. I brush my lips across her forehead and go room to room in record time. I'm back by her side and pulling my phone out. I have to call this in.

And call in a cleanup crew. I glance at the asshole sprawled along the stairs. As much as I want to move him, it's better to leave him where he is. Then the crew knows exactly where they need to clean.

I hit his contact in my phone, put him on speaker, and set my phone by her head.

He answers on the first ring. "If you're going to lecture me, save it," Silas says.

"Meet me at St. Mary's hospital in fifteen minutes." My

words are clipped. I don't give a fuck about his squabble with Nova earlier.

"Who." The word cracks through the line like thunder.

"Evangeline."

He inhales sharply. "What happened?"

"I went to her house and caught someone robbing her. At gunpoint."

"Motherfuckers," he seethes.

I can feel his anger through the phone. It serves as kindling for my already explosive rage. I tamp it down. Again. And focus on her.

"I need cleanup."

"Fuck. No answers then I take it?"

"Nah, didn't have a choice. You know I wouldn't have put him to ground if I didn't have to." It wasn't like I was morally opposed to putting our enemies to ground. But we don't even know who this asshole is.

He could be some random guy for all we know.

Except nothing is ever random in Rosewood.

"I'll take care of it." He clears his throat. "Is she hurt?"

"Aye, she's fucking hurt. Knocked her around, I think. I'm taking her to St. Mary's to get checked out."

"I'll meet you there. Did you tell Nova?"

"You were my first call."

"I'll call him. He'll likely be there soon," he warns.

"Well, he'll have to turn his ass around then." I end the call and tuck my phone back into my pocket.

I scan her face, noting blood coating one side of her face, along her hairline. I trail the tips of my fingers along her left eyebrow.

"Evangeline?" I murmur. Her eyelashes flutter at the sound of my voice. "C'mon, baby girl. Open those pretty eyes for me."

She blinks several times before finally focusing on me. "Bane," she breathes. "You're here."

"Wouldn't be anywhere else."

She smiles, it's thin and it doesn't light up her eyes, but I'll take it. She pushes to sit up, reaching out to grasp my bicep. I slide my arm underneath her back, hesitant to move her until I know what happened. But if she's able to move on her own, there must not be anything major broken. Not externally at least.

"You really are my knight in shining armor." Her voice is soft with awe.

I let my gaze bounce around her face, memorizing every little detail. "Only for you, baby girl."

Her breath hitches at the nickname like it always does. And then I do something I've been thinking about for eight long years.

I brush my lips across hers and whisper, "I've missed you, Evangeline. I've spent the last eight years dreaming of the way you taste."

Her mouth parts and she exhales my name, like it's a prayer. "Lincoln."

45

SILAS

"EVANGELINE'S on her way to the hospital."

Ma gasps. "Oh my god! Where are you? What happened?"

"Looks like an armed break-in, but I don't know," I mutter, looking around the parking lot. "I'm heading there now. Bring Hunter and meet me there." It's not a question.

She hesitates, and I know she's worried it's a trap. She's not alone in that fear. The thought has crossed my mind too.

It feels entirely too coincidental that I completely lose my shit in a semi-public setting and within an hour, Evangeline gets assaulted and robbed.

"Are you sure that's a good idea? And what about the boys?"

My nerves are shot, and I'm trying to remain level-headed about all of it, shoving my personal feelings aside to look at things from an outside perspective.

But I fucking can't.

Every time I try to be objective about it, the thought of someone busting in there and hurting her pushes all rational thought aside. I need Bane to walk through everything with me, make sure I get all the facts.

I rub my thumb and forefinger over my brows. There's so much tension bunching my brows up, I worry it'll never leave me. "I can't concentrate if I'm worried they're going to come for Hunter."

"He's safe with me, and we're at your house, safely within the compound," she reminds me.

She's not unkind about it, more matter-of-fact. She's probably not even that fazed by all of this, she's been in worse situations with the Reapers and Dad's shit over the years.

But that was before Hunter. Having a grandbaby both softened my ma and made her more protective. I know she would jump in front of a bullet to save my boy, but I don't want her to have to make that choice.

"I know. The boys are going with me to the hospital though. I just need Hunter close. "

She's quiet a moment. "Alright, I'll get us packed up and we'll meet you there." She ends the call without saying goodbye.

I blow out a breath, some anxiety lessening knowing it's one less thing I have to worry about.

I hit my brother's contact and listen to it ring and ring and ring. That asshole isn't going to answer, I know it. I hate the idea of leaving him this kind of message on a voicemail, but his stubbornness is making it difficult.

"What," he answers on the last ring.

"Where are you?"

The wind is loud on his end. He must be driving still. "You know where I am. What's this about?"

I sigh. "Turn around and head to St. Mary's. There's been a situation and Evangeline's there."

"What," he explodes.

"She's fine, okay? Bane is with her. He said she's alright, but she's getting checked out as a precaution. And Nova, don't make me regret telling you this now. You better drive fucking safe."

He ends the call without another word, no doubt his attention shifted to getting to the hospital.

Which is exactly what I'm about to do too. I rush to my bike and tear out of the compound with regrets nipping at my heels. Evangeline is under my protection. She's my fucking employee, so an attack on her is an attack on me.

And no one fucks with the Reapers and lives to tell the tale.

"NAME?"

"Eva," I grunt. "Uh Evangeline Carter."

The receptionist takes entirely too long, tapping at least ninety-seven keys on her noisy as fuck keyboard.

"Okay, got her. She was taken back."

Nova shoulders his way next to me, planting his palm on the desk in front of us. "How is she? Is she okay?"

I got here a few minutes before him, but I waited in the parking lot. I knew he'd come in hot, and I didn't want him to do something rash in the heat of the moment.

And yeah, maybe I was trying to keep myself in check too.

The receptionist taps some more on her keyboard, her gaze never straying from her computer screen. "I'm sorry, but I can't discuss patient information like that."

He leans forward, his jaw clenching. "I'm not asking for her medical information. I just want to know if she's okay. Alive, breathing."

I feel something tug my pinkie finger and look down to see the wide dark brown eyes I love more than life itself.

"Hey, bud." I curve my hand over his shoulder, tucking him in close to my side.

He leans into me and wraps his arms around me as best he

can. "Is Eve okay? Nan said she wasn't feeling good, so she had to go to the doctor."

I glance behind me and see Ma. She stops behind Hunter, the skin around her eyes tight with tension. "How is she?"

I jerk my chin toward the woman behind the desk. The one who's still ignoring Nova. "We just got here, and so far, they haven't told us shit."

"They wouldn't even let me go back with her, and I'm the one who brought her here," Bane damn near snarls.

The receptionist sighs. "I'm sorry, sir, but I can't release—"

Bane slams his hand down on the desk, startling the receptionist enough to garner her attention. "I'm her motherfucking husband. So why don't you tell me where the fuck my wife is."

The receptionist's mouth drops open, and I'd honestly find a little humor in it if I wasn't side-eying the fuck out of my cousin.

"Oh, well, why didn't you say that from the beginning," she stammers. "That changes everything."

"Yeah, well, I'm her husband too," Nova snaps, leaning back on his heels and folding his arms across his chest.

"Wh-what?" the receptionist pauses, her hands hovering over the keyboard.

"Aye, me too. So why don't you tell us where our woman is, yeah?"

Her mouth snaps closed and her gaze narrows on the three of us. "Lying about your familial relationship is one way to get escorted out of St. Mary's, gentlemen."

Ma shifts forward a step, her hand resting in the middle of my back. "Honey, why don't you save yourself the headache and tell my boys where she is, yeah?"

"And who are you, *honey*? Her wife?" The receptionist arches a brow, sarcasm thick and lips flattened into an unimpressed smirk. It's such a sharp contrast to her genuine shock literally thirty seconds ago.

Ma reads the challenge and steps to it. "Nah, sugar, I'm their mama." She jerks her head to the left, toward us. "So I guess that makes me *her* mama too."

"Well, she's *my* nanny!" Hunter crows, pushing entirely too much possession into four little words.

The receptionist leans over the desk separating her from us and glances at Hunter.

I keep my gaze on her when I smooth my fingers over his shoulder, offering him some comfort. "That's right, bud, she sure is. We have to be patient with people, right? Sometimes they don't realize who we are."

There's a beat of silence. The receptionist lets her gaze crawl over us before she zeroes in on me. It feels annoying in the way that a mosquito is constantly buzzing around your face.

Nothing like the way Evangeline's gaze feels on me. And that comparison is enough to have my hackles rising higher. Again. I grit my teeth, prepared to lean into this role that's been handed to me. A role that I never knew if I really wanted it or if I thought I did because it was all I ever knew. It was a position in this community that afforded my father a lot of perks while he wore the patch.

I've never flaunted my patch, never played that game. Never found the need to. But maybe my penchant for peace is mistaken as weakness. Maybe it's time I remedy that, starting with the woman in my way.

There are only a handful of people in this world I'd fully embrace the patch for, and four of them are standing next to me.

And they care about her being back there, hurting. Alone.

So now I fucking care about it.

And this woman is standing in my way. She's an obstacle that needs to be removed, and I'm not going to waste any more time playing this stupid game.

Hunter's hair brushes against my forearm as he tilts his head to look at me. "Who are we, Dad?"

I stare at the receptionist, my patience long since shredded. "We're the motherfucking Reapers."

"Jar," Hunter murmurs.

The receptionist's eyes widen, and I can see the fear tightening her features.

"Good. Our reputation precedes us." I lean in, resting my elbow on the desk. "Now tell us where she is."

46

NOVA

"AND YOU MUST BE the family that has Nancy all flustered," a cheery nurse says as she bustles in the waiting room, holding a clipboard. She leans toward Ma and offers her a conspiratorial wink. "Don't worry, Nancy is always a bit prickly. Follow me, and I'll bring you back to her."

"Thanks," Silas grunts.

Bane glares at the receptionist as we leave the waiting room, but she's not even paying attention to us. Already back to typing on her computer.

I stay silent, doing my best to shut everything from earlier out. Stuff that shit up in a cabinet and forget about it. Not that I would bring it up now.

I said everything I had to say to him, and even if I wanted to rehash it, I wouldn't do it with Hunter glued to Silas's side.

Worry wrinkles my brow as I wonder what he must make of all of this. I have to believe that if Evangeline were in real bad shape, Bane would have warned Silas the moment he saw Hunter and Ma walk through the door.

He's a tough kid though, resilient as hell. He's a St. James after all.

We follow the nurse down the corridor, and I rub a hand over my heart absentmindedly. It aches like a sore muscle days after a heavy lift.

Fear and I are old friends, but I've never felt the pinch of it like I did when Silas called. The way my heart seized when he said Bane was taking her to the hospital, I thought I was going to lay my bike down.

Déjà vu punches me in the gut, stealing my breath as memories superimpose themselves over my vision.

I walked down this same exact hallway when Dad was here. He was shot, high as fuck on the cocktail of pain meds and recreational drugs he already had in his system, and spouting shit I didn't understand.

We were used to the benders he went on after a good run, but this was something different. It was like he was recalling details of someone else's life, talking about other children and different jobs.

I blink, and I can still hear the sounds of his labored breathing, the way the machines beeped in time with his heart.

And now, here I am again. Walking down this same damn hallway, but instead of my father, it's Evangeline.

"How is she?" Bane asks. He skirts around me to walk next to the nurse.

For once, I'm grateful for his need to gather information. Not only do I want to know the answer, but his arm brushed against mine, snapping me out of that déjà vu spiral. I haven't thought about that night in years.

"Well, that's what we're going to find out," the nurse says, flashing him a bright smile.

"Why hasn't she been treated yet?" I hear the sharpness in my voice, but I don't temper it.

The nurse glances over her shoulder and me, her smile growing tight. "Well, in case you're unfamiliar with how emergency rooms work, they're triaged."

My jaw clenches with her thinly veiled sarcasm. "We know how emergency rooms work."

The nurse stops in her tracks and turns to face us. "I understand you're worried about your loved one, but there are other patients here who also need medical attention. We do our best to prioritize those who require more immediate attention. Plus, we're short-staffed."

Ma steps forward, her voice low and steady. "We're not asking you to neglect other patients. We just want to know how our girl is."

The nurse gestures to the room behind us. "Well, let's go find out, shall we? Normally, we don't allow this many people back here, but I'm making an exception for you all."

I spin around, my arm reaching for the door handle before she finishes talking. I feel like I'm crawling out of my skin. Guilt wraps around my lungs like barbed wire, shredding the soft tissue with every moment I don't have eyes on her.

"Sweetheart?" I call out, stepping into the room. My skin feels tight, buzzing like a hundred fireflies are dancing around.

"Nova." My name sounds like a prayer on her lips, and I feel a rush of relief wash over me.

She's sitting up in the hospital bed, her face pale and drawn, but her eyes are bright. My feet carry me to her without a second thought. I sink my hands on either side of her neck, my thumbs stroking the soft skin under her jawline.

I search her face, cataloging each bruise, swollen, tender bit of skin. Every scrap of evidence of the violence she endured.

"I'm going to kill whoever did this to you, baby," I murmur, leaning down to press my forehead against hers. "That's my promise to you."

"When did this happen?" Ma murmurs sharply. I hear some grunts behind me too, but I ignore them, giving my girl all my focus.

"You scared the shit out of me," I say, my voice cracking.

"Out of all of us," Bane says.

"I'm sorry," she says, pitching her voice to carry to the rest of the room.

I shake my head a little, rolling my forehead along hers. "Don't apologize. It's me who should be apologizing. I should've been there."

Her hands run up and down my arms, soothing me. "It's alright. I'm fine."

"You don't look fine," I grumble.

"Well, I am." She laughs, the sound low and amused. She pulls back and glances behind me. "Thanks to Lincoln."

I file away the use of his real name, something he doesn't usually allow most people. It's not important right now, though. What's important is the fact that he was there for her.

I turn my head to look at him, and he meets my gaze evenly. There's no hostility there, at least not toward me. There's a shared rage between us, an understanding.

"Thank you," I say, my voice rough.

He smirks. "I didn't do it for you."

I match his smirk with my own. "Aye, I know. But I'm thankful all the same."

47

SILAS

HUNTER TUGS ON MY HAND, and I'm ashamed to admit it takes longer than it should to peel my attention from her.

From her and *them*.

"Yeah, bud?"

He doesn't say anything, just tilts his head toward her and widens his eyes comically big.

"Let's give her a few minutes, yeah? There's not a lot of space right now."

Of course, she heard me. And of course she chooses this moment to challenge me.

"I'm alright, Hunter. You can come on over if you want," she says, waving her hand and patting the space next to her. "But I'm kind of dirty and sweaty, so come closer at your own risk." She flashes him a wink.

Hunter lets go of my hand immediately and practically bounds over to her. He doesn't get on the bed though, which is good. There's only like three inches of space on that small as hell little stretcher bed thing.

"I live with my dad, remember? He gets so sweaty after lifting weights in the garage that sometimes it looks like he just got out of a pool," Hunter tells her seriously.

Evangeline rolls her lips inward, staving off the laughter I see twinkling in her eyes. "Ah, well then you're probably pretty used to it, huh?"

Hunter lifts a shoulder and trails his fingers down the metal part of the bed frame. "Yeah. But Eve, are you hurt real bad? Nan said you go to the hospital when you get *really* hurt, not just when I scrape my knee."

Her face smooths out, a tender sort of affection replacing her amusement. She reaches over and runs her fingers through the top of his hair softly. "Yes, your Nan is right. But sometimes you have to come here because you need to see a doctor quick. But I'll be fine, okay? Don't you worry."

He nods slowly, like he's weighing her words. "And you'll be okay for all our plans this summer? We made *a lot* of them the other day."

She laughs, and something in my gut clenches tight. She smooths the hair down she ruffled with her fingers, squeezing his shoulders.

"Of course. I wouldn't miss our summer adventures." She lifts her face to look around the room. "I'm fine, really. All of this is unnecessary," Evangeline says, waving her free hand around to encompass the small room we're all stuffed into. The other hand grabs for an ice pack next to her.

"Well, now, we can't send you home just yet. You came in with a pretty serious knock to your noggin. So we gotta check you out. Alright?" The nurse sidles up next to the bed, cutting off Hunter from Evangeline. Her pen is poised over her clipboard, her gaze focused on whatever paper she has there, so she misses the sharp glare Evangeline sends her.

But I don't. I don't miss her displeasure at being separated from Hunter like that. Evangeline leans around the nurse, catching Hunter's gaze. She sends him a warm smile, and I see his little shoulders straighten.

"Come on back here by me, bud."

Evangeline's gaze finds mine across the room, eyes wide like I startled her. She looks small sitting on top of the bed. Delicate. I nod imperceptibly.

Hunter stands close to me, crossing his arms over his chest and watching Evangeline and the nurse intently.

"Alright," Evangeline says with a dip of her chin. "Whatever we have to do so I can leave."

The nurse pivots on the ball of her black sneaker, popping her hip to the side, and stares at the five of us creating a barricade around Evangeline's bed. "Family, I understand you're worried. But rest assured, we're going to get her fixed up and on her way as soon as possible. To do that, we need a little privacy."

I shift my legs, planting my booted feet wide on the floor. "Nah, we're not leaving her alone."

"Yeah, 'sides, Dad can't fix Eve if he's not in the same room as her," Hunter says, his tone conveying exactly how ridiculous he thinks us leaving is. It's then I notice he's mirrored my body language. His little arms folded across his chest, his superhero pajamas on display. One eyebrow arched high on his little forehead.

"Well, I don't know what your daddy does, but I'm a nurse, and I'm real good at my job. Alright, honey?" She switches her gaze from Hunter to the rest of us. "So I'm going to need you all to back up a step, give us a little breathing room."

No one moves, not even Hunter.

The nurse huffs, focusing her glare on Bane, like she can reason with him. "Do I need to call security?"

He tips his chin up and stares at her. "We're not leaving her, so do what you need to."

Always the fucking diplomat. I suppose it's okay though. She wouldn't want to hear what comes out of my mouth right now. The tight grip on my control has slipped, and not even I can predict what I will do if people keep fucking pushing me tonight.

"It's fine, they can stay. I'm a little sore, but I'm alright," Evangeline says.

Her voice doesn't have the same exuberance I've come to expect, and the difference sets my teeth on edge. I shift toward her, my shins bumping the side of the bed. Her gaze snaps to mine, and her eyes go all soft. I don't even know how to unpack that look.

"You heard her, start the exam," I snap, glaring at the nurse.

The nurse sighs, like she's over my shit already. Like I fucking care about her beyond her capability to make sure my girl is okay.

Fuck. She's not *my girl*. She's my nanny— I mean Hunter's nanny. And as her boss, I have a moral obligation to make sure she's okay.

That's it.

What happened at the clubhouse was just that. Me looking out for my employee.

"Okay," the nurse says, clapping her hands together once. "Let's get started with some basic questions. Our database system crashed about ten minutes before you got here, and we're down a laptop tonight anyway, so I'm going old school."

She perches against the side of the bed, edging Nova out of the way. "Why don't you tell me what happened?"

I step in front of Hunter, blocking his view and resisting the urge to cover his ears. "Hey, bud, why don't you ask Nan if she brought your tablet. You can check out those chairs and watch something." I tip my chin toward the other side of the room, where two blue chairs are tucked into the corner.

"Here, honey, I thought you might need this," Ma says,

handing Hunter his green tablet and guiding him toward the chairs.

I tune back into the conversation to see Nova step forward, his arms crossed tightly over his chest. "Did she lose too much blood?"

"What? She needs blood?" Alarm bells go off in my head.

The nurse doesn't pause her exam, carefully parting Evangeline's hair. I watch her face, clocking the moment the nurse prods a tender spot by her wince.

"No. Head wounds are notoriously dramatic. They like to make sure everyone knows they're there. But I learned to never say never in this job," she answers Nova, but she doesn't pull her focus from Evangeline's wound.

"So, Evangeline, you're a universal donor," she says in a singsong voice. She glances over her shoulder, sweeping her gaze over us. "Do we have other O negs in here? You're all family, right? Mom, what about you?"

"Aye, we're family." I nudge Ma, a soft tap of my elbow.

She startles, pulling her gaze from Hunter, who's happily watching something on his tablet to the nurse. "Uh, AB positive."

The nurse cocks her head to the side, pausing to look at Ma. "O neg can't have an AB pos parent."

Ma shifts her weight to her other foot and fiddles with the small cross charm at the end of her gold necklace. "Oh, then AB negative, I guess. It's been a long night."

The nurse hums and shakes her head, not unkindly. More matter of fact, like she's on hour six of a ten-hour shift. "Nah, an AB parent can't have an O neg kid at all—positive or negative."

This nurse is weighing on my last thread of patience. I step forward, my eyes narrowed at the nurse. "Does she even need this? If not, let's stop playing guessing games with our blood types and move on."

"I don't think so, no. It's just a tiny gash, one that's easily fixed by a few stitches or the skin glue."

"I'm O negative, too. If she needs it, I mean," Nova says, pushing the pointless topic still. He moves to stand by Evangeline's free hand.

"You're her husband, right? How fortunate for you both," the nurse says, stepping back and pulling off her gloves.

"Fortunate how?"

"Well, you're universal donors, so you can give to anyone, but you can only receive O negative. It's not the rarest blood type, but it's the pickiest."

"Lucky them," I grumble under my breath. Bane sends me a sharp glare, but I pretend not to see it. Just like I'm pretending not to feel jealous over something ridiculous as not being able to give her blood if she needs it.

She's not a fucking vampire, for fuck's sake.

I scrub my hands down my face, applying a little pressure on my palms and dragging them over my tense muscles.

"Glue's fine. Then no shaving, right?" Evangeline asks.

"You don't want a mohawk, Eve?" Hunter asks, his eyes bright. Okay, so I guess the tablet's not distracting enough.

The smile she sends my boy takes me out at the knees.

"That would be pretty cool. But I think I'll leave the mohawk styles to you. You've got the head shape for it," Evangeline teases him.

Hunter's little chest puffs out and he smooths his hand over his head. "I do have a nice-shaped head, don't I, Dad?"

My lip twitches. "Yeah, bud, you do."

I clear my throat and look over my shoulder, meeting Ma's gaze. "Hey, bud, why don't you take Nan and buy her a coffee in the cafeteria down the hall?"

He arches a brow, the expression so similar to mine, it feels like a vise around my heart. "What about Eve? Are you going to protect her from the bad guys?"

I ruffle his hair and work to soften my expression. "Of course I will, bud. Just like this guy does." I flick my gaze to the character on his shirt.

His mouth purses to the side, like he's really thinking about it. A moment later, he nods. "Alright. Can I get something too?"

I reach into my pocket and pull out a twenty dollar bill. "Something healthy, yeah? It's already past your bedtime."

"Bedtime, schmedtime. Batman fights crime only at night, Dad." He hops off the chair and takes the money with one hand, scooting around me and grabbing Ma's hand with the other. "C'mon, Nan, Dad said you need a coffee."

"Thank you," I murmur to her. She's distracted though, Hunter telling her about his latest superhero adventures, I'm sure.

I watch them leave for a moment, sure that they'll be safe down the hall for the next ten minutes. I tune back into the quiet conversation between Evangeline and the nurse.

Tension radiates from Nova and Bane like waves in the ocean during high tide. It raises the hair on my arms, and my senses rise to the shift. I'm on alert, half-expecting someone to charge the room we're in.

Not that they'd make it very far between the three of us. Too many years spent living in flight or fight situations. My body is already on high alert. Now it's my mind that plays catch-up.

48

BANE

"ALRIGHT, JUST FOLLOW THE LIGHT, OKAY?" The nurse pulls a pen light from her pocket, clicks it on, and shines it in Evangeline's eyes.

Silas catches my gaze and jerks his chin to the other side of the room. I nod once, understanding the silent communication. I tap Nova on the shoulder and move to the other side of the room. It's not what I would consider a big space, but it gives us the illusion of privacy. Silas, Nova, and I stand shoulder to shoulder in a loose semicircle, all of our eyes trained on Evangeline. The tension in the room is palpable, and I can feel it thrumming through my veins.

Actually, I think it's been buzzing since the moment I pulled into her driveway. I know from experience that I can withstand so much more.

I haven't had to in years, but some things are like muscle memory. And tempering anxiety is one of them.

I watch the nurse check her vitals, murmuring something too low for me to hear. Evangeline just shakes her head, her gaze flitting back to bounce between the three of us.

We're making her nervous, I realize.

"What's going on?" I ask Silas, making sure to keep my voice low.

"Tell me what happened," he says.

I glance around the room, looking for any obvious cameras. I think there's a rule surrounding surveillance inside a hospital room like this, but I don't know for sure. "Before I do, did you send someone to take care of the problem?"

Nova's gaze snaps to me. "What problem?"

"I needed a cleanup." I stare at him, letting him read between the lines.

Nova shifts to face me, tension rolling off of him in droves. "How many?"

"One."

He nods, his shoulders losing some of their tension. "Did they say anything?"

I shake my head and grimace. "I didn't give him a chance."

"Tell us what happened," Silas demands, his gaze flicking around the room. "As much as you can in here."

I clear my throat and try to recap everything without letting myself visualize it. Once was more than enough. "I saw her leave and when the two of you were still in the parking lot ten minutes later, I dipped out to check on her."

"I sent Jagger to make sure she got home safe," Nova interjects.

"Yeah, he did. I passed him coming back," I say, nodding.

Silas narrows his gaze on me. "Why were you going to her house anyway?"

I match his look with one of my own. "I just told you why. To check on her."

"Then what happened?" Nova rushes out, anxiety bleeding from his voice.

I've wanted Evangeline Carter for the better part of eight

years. I warned her once that if she gave me a taste, I wouldn't be able to let her go.

I wasn't exaggerating.

I searched for her for weeks when I woke up alone on that beach. I started thinking she was some kind of faerie, a mythical creature I dreamed up after one too many drinks.

But she was real.

And fate brought her back to me. Now that she's finally within my reach again, I will *never* let her go.

Only fate fucked me because he set her in Nova's path too. And I don't know what the fuck that means for any of us now.

He's my brother in all the ways that matter, and I don't want to cause him harm. But I'm not going to lie either.

I drag my hand across the back of my neck, glancing at my shoes. I lift my head and look at my cousin. "When I got there, she was screaming for you."

His mouth falls open and his eyebrows fold inward. "Fuck me," he grunts, shaking his head and swallowing thickly.

"Then I walked in, saw him standing over her with a gun in her face. I pulled the trigger before I realized what I'd done. It was unavoidable."

"Did you recognize him?" Silas presses, stepping closer to me.

"Nah," I say, shaking my head. "I didn't have time to search him though. I brought her here right away."

Nova looks shaken, the skin around his eyes tight. "Did she say anything?"

I shake my head. "Just that there were three of them, came to rob her. I didn't press her though, figured getting her out before she realized what I'd done was more important. The cleanup crew will let us know anything noteworthy."

Silas pulls his phone out of his pocket and glances at the screen. "Aye, I have to meet them in two hours."

"I'll go," Nova says, shoving his hands into his pockets.

"What?" Silas tilts his head to the side.

Nova shrugs. "I'll go meet the cleaners, get the report."

Something doesn't seem right here. I watch him carefully, a knot of suspicion growing in my gut.

"I'll go with you," I offer.

"Nah, you should stay with her, and Silas has to take Hunter home. That leaves me."

Silas studies Nova for a beat, his gaze heavy. "You sure?"

He nods, determination thick in his eyes. "Yeah. I want to know who it was."

Silas nods and tucks his phone back into his pocket. "Alright, but be careful. There's a storm coming tonight, and I don't love the idea of you being out there alone. We don't know if this was a coordinated attack. Or if they're watching us. Or who the fuck is behind it." He grits the last part out between clenched teeth.

A chill rolls down my spine, but I keep that shit to myself. I've never been superstitious before and I'm not about to start now.

"Aye, I'll be fine," Nova says with a decisive nod. He turns toward me, his eyes softening. "You stay with her, yeah? Make sure she's safe."

"You know I will," I tell him.

"Good news, family. She mostly likely has a mild concussion, but nothing seems broken. We'll run a few tests just to make sure. I'll go get that started and hopefully we can get her out of here before the storm hits," the nurse says, pitching her voice louder before she leaves.

Nova beelines for Evangeline, and I watch the two of them embrace. I've never seen Nova like this with anyone before, and I can't decide if I should be worried or not.

Silas claps me on the back. "I'm going to go rescue Ma from Hunter in the cafeteria. Keep me posted, yeah?"

I watch Silas approach the other side of Evangeline's bed. He leans down and murmurs something in her ear, and she nods several times. Nova brushes a kiss across her forehead, and I watch the two of them leave.

The knot in my gut grows tighter. Something isn't right.

WELCOME TO ROSEWOOD

IT'S YOUR FAVORITE NEIGHBOR, ***and I'm back with the juiciest gossip in town. And let me tell you, things are heating up faster than the heat lighting streaking across the sky.***

Word on the street is the St. James brothers are feuding. It seems the once tight-knit trio is now at odds. Could our unnamed woman be at the center of this scandal?

But that's not all, dear reader. The youngest Reaper was spotted tearing through the streets tonight like the devil himself was on his heels.

Doesn't he know there's a storm brewing. If he needs shelter, I know plenty of willing tributes.

Until next time,
—Rose

49

NOVA

LIGHTNING STREAKS across the horizon and ten seconds later, thunder rumbles. The air hums with the static electricity, just waiting for the perfect moment to combust.

If I believed in god, I would say he's mocking me. This storm feels like an allegory, a symbol of the rage warring inside of me.

I've been turning over this information for the last two hours, taking it apart and putting it back together in a million ways.

And still, the end result is always the same.

This revelation is too heavy, too fucked-up. It can't be true.

I won't allow it to be true.

I pound my fist on the door, ignoring my phone vibrating in my pocket.

"I'm coming, Jesus," she shouts from inside the house.

I brace both of my hands on the doorframe, letting my head hang as I focus on my breathing. The door swings open, but I don't lift my head. I don't think I even can. This two-ton secret is an albatross around my neck.

Her bejeweled black flip flops come into view. She called them her house shoes, said they were more comfortable than slippers. "Asher. Why the hell are you beating my door down at this time of night? And why didn't you just walk in like usual?"

I lift my head and look at her. And whatever my expression is, hers draws up tight with fear.

She sucks in a sharp breath. "What happened?"

My gaze flies around her face, cataloging her features and mentally mapping them to mine.

"Ma." My voice comes out a croak, my tongue thick in my mouth.

She steps forward, the soft light from her living room spilling into the foyer and casting her in a yellow glow.

"What happened? Hunter or Evangeline? Your brother?"

I shake my head, swallowing down the scoff at the word. But I can't force any more words past my lips.

"Tell me who it is. Whatever it is, we can fix it," she says, pitching her voice low. She reaches out toward me, like she's going to grasp my shoulder and pull me into a hug like she has thousands of times.

I push off the doorframe and jerk back a step, out of her reach. The move doesn't go unnoticed, and she narrows her eyes on me.

"Tell me. I can handle it, whatever it is." There's a tremble in her voice, but I can't find it in me to soothe her.

I exhale and look to the sky for a moment. "Tell me who my mother is."

"What?" she chokes out the word.

I focus back on her, finding my well of calm in the midst of the chaos. "Tell me who my mother—"

Her brows crash together as she looks at me. "I heard what you said, but I don't know why you're asking me that. I am your mother."

My head is already shaking before she finishes talking. "My biological mother."

Her mouth parts and I watch her scramble for lies, excuses, and half-truths. It's what my life has been based on.

Her chin wobbles a little bit, but her lips remain shut.

I spin around and look out into the sky. It's too cloudy for stars to shine, so it looks unnaturally dark. Foreboding and ominous. Just like the truth lurking in the shadows.

"I thought he was high, you know?"

"Who?" she murmurs from behind me.

"I didn't think much about it then. I thought he was high or drunk when he told me. Probably both."

And I haven't thought about that night for years. But going back to the hospital tonight brought it all back. The questions and tests and surgeries.

If I think hard enough, I can recall the way he looked like he was in physical pain as he told me the story of a man who fell in love with another woman.

"He told me about an affair he had," I say, my voice almost toneless as I watch lightning streak across the sky.

Eight seconds later, thunder rumbles. It's getting closer. Won't be long now.

"Your father wasn't perfect. I know that," she says.

I look over my shoulder and tell her, "When I was laying in that hospital bed, fresh out of surgery to remove the bullet I took for him, he told me he chose the wrong woman. That the woman he loved had hair so dark, it was like looking into the sky. Waxed on about how smart and wealthy she was."

I regret it the moment the words leave my mouth. She flinches, her face crumpling like she felt my words as a physical blow.

Fuck, maybe she did. I don't feel lighter for having said them though. If anything, I feel like they're weighing me down further.

"He told me he was going to leave you and she was supposed

to leave her husband. They were going to make one big blended family. But then, she went back to her husband."

I hear the scuffle of her flip flop on the floor as she shuffles closer to me. Her palm rests in the center of my back, her heat grounding me in a way.

"It's important to me that you know that I always loved you. From the moment I knew you were coming into this world, you were my boy. You may be biologically only Ray's, but I loved you like you were my own blood. And I'll never apologize for that."

I turn around, desperate to see her face. "Who was she?"

She looks absolutely gutted, but her mouth pinches with resolve.

"Your father had an affair with a married woman. Someone who used to be a friend of mine," she says, shaking her head. "She came to me when she found out she was pregnant, and still to this day, I'm not sure why. But we were best friends once, and by that point, I'd had three miscarriages after Silas."

Tears pool in her eyes, and I don't know who they're for. Her, me, both of us.

My life feels like it's slipping through my fingers like sand.

"All I'd ever dreamed of was being a mother, and my body had betrayed me in the ultimate way, worse than any of your father's affairs. And then, when I'd given up hope of expanding our family, she shows up. Claims she's pregnant with Ray's baby. She didn't want the child, but she thought I might. It was bold of her to come to me. I'll give her that. But five days later, I got a call from the hospital that you were born." She pauses, drawing in a shuddering breath. "And all I kept thinking was *this is my miracle*."

I stare at her, my mind reeling with the weight of her words. I came over here with the intent to demand answers, but there was a small part of me that hoped she'd laugh me off and tell me I was full of shit.

But this feels more like a punch to the kidney.

"Who was she?" I ask a third time, my voice rising with every word.

She shakes her head, her lips trembling. "She's not around here anymore."

Desperation claws against my ribcage as thunder rumbles only a few seconds after lightning flashes across the sky. The storm's crescendo is coming, and I'm afraid of the aftermath.

Nausea churns in my gut. Too many coincidences are piling up. My mind races, piecing together the fragments that suddenly make sense.

We share the same rare blood type.

The familiar, recognizable long dark hair.

She's smart as hell, with a wealthy family.

She grew up here, roughly the same age as Ma.

Sweat breaks out along my brow, and I exhale sharply. I look at my mother, my chest tight with anxiety. I physically can't keep the words inside any longer, and they burst from me in a desperate plea.

"Please tell me it's not true. Tell me Virginia Carter isn't my mother."

To be continued . . .
in Shadowed Obsession
Preorder it here

bestie,
I know that last line was a little wild,
but I'm asking you to please trust me.
Not everything is as it seems in Rosewood.

AUTHOR'S NOTE

Dear reader, thank you so much for picking up Moonlit Temptation!

I sincerely hope you enjoy the first book in this brand-new world I created! I've been aching for a romance with these tropes and characters, so I hope I did the beginning of their story justice.

As always, my DMs are open when you hit that cliff at the end!

Happy reading!

xoxo—pen

A NOTE FROM PEN

When I sat down to start plotting Rosewood, I knew Nana Jo was going to be a big part of Evangeline's story. And I knew that she was already gone when we meet our heroine.

See, Nana Jo is largely inspired by my own grandma. We had a close bond, and even though she's been gone for several years now, I still miss her like crazy. Some days more than others, sparked by the most random events.

And then while I was writing this book, we lost Grandpa Black.

Suddenly and tragically.

Many of you might remember the funny stories I'd tell about Grandpa Black and the moments he chose to tell me what chapter he was on. Usually at a family dinner. It usually went something like: "Can you pass me the potatoes? Say, Penelope, I'm on chapter twenty-five, by the way."

And then I would blush, murmur a thanks, and be distracted for the rest of dinner until I could sneak away and check what chapter he was on. I'm not kidding when I tell you, it was almost always a spicy scene.

Grandpa Black was funny like that. I like to think he skipped over the especially spicy scenes, though. Or maybe he got a kick out of them.

The grief Evangeline feels (and will continue to experience) is inspired by my own. I tried to shape this overwhelming feeling, articulate it, and then bleed it onto the pages of this book.

So thank you for reading, I hope you enjoyed it.

ACKNOWLEDGMENTS

There are so, so many wonderful people in my life who continue to support me and lift me up every single day. And for that, I'm forever grateful.

Special shoutout to my absolutely amazing assistants, two women I feel luck to call friends. Jen & Erica, I couldn't have done it without you! And your endless patience when I routinely send five-minute voice memos to very simple questions.

To my beta besties: Tracey, Elaine, and Dorothy. Thank you for your continued and unwavering support. I'm so grateful for you all!

To all my author besties, y'all are the real MVPs. I can't wait to squeeze you at our next joint signing!

Big, big thanks to Mr Black for continuing to nurture my passenger princess life every time I claimed my muse needed a dirty chai latte from my absolute favorite coffee shop—which is 50 minutes round trip!

And thank you to my tiny humans for always being constant forces of light in my life. My son, who routinely asks me about my characters. And my daughter, who likes to keep track of my word counts. You'll never read this, but I love you both so, so much.

And to my readers: thank you for standing by me while I clawed my way out of burnout the first half of the year. I hope the St. James men help make up for that. I'm forever awed by your continued love and support for me and these stories.

ALSO BY PENELOPE BLACK

THE BROTHERHOOD SERIES

Wolf

Rush

Sully

THE FIVE FAMILIES SERIES

Gilded Princess

Twisted Queen

Vicious Reign

Fractured Dynasty

STANDALONES

When It Ends:

A Dark Apocalyptic Romance

In A Little While

THE KING SISTERS WORLD

The Wren

The Wild

ROSEWOOD

Moonlit Temptation

Shadowed Obsession

Printed in Great Britain
by Amazon

47671117R00199